In the era before light and knowledge came into the universe,

prior to measured time; in the depths of space, where all complexities now inhabit.

From the highest firmament to depths of the abyss; there was chaos: an incalculable pressure in coldest darkness.

So full of unexpressed and unconnected matter that it attracted from a separate plain; light. But a light so filled with energy it was its own awareness.

A consciousness to fill the void with an unlimited power we call magic.

From a single point no larger than an atom.

Light burgeoned into the universe.

Finding itself in such the perfect place to connect and form new wonders in which to revel in. It poured in at a speed the darkness could only hope to contain.

And as the dark congealed matter tried to compress into the light; so that it might drive it back from whence it came: It was perplexed to find that the more it pressed: The faster and more complex the light changed unconnected matter and sludge into new and more beautiful compounds.

And because every part of this muck was a conscious piece of itself, as was the light.

When they joined, it found it was not only compressing, but being drawn in by the light's creations. And as the light merely reveled in and thought only to create new and more complex structures: It seemed the perfect union. But the muck and matter, rightly thinking that these creations came from pieces itself:

Thought that it ought to have the lion's share of control over what was made.

Swiftly the sludge gave way to what seemed empty space. But had left behind a faded bit of the consciousness of the congealed goo. Though the thought frightened and angered the darkness to occupy less space. It also came to understand that as its parts were made to be more complex, so too were its thoughts. Where there had once been mere scattered existence and chaos: There were now forming thoughts and imaginings hitherto beyond it. And through its ever-tightening bond with the light, a vision made part of one and part of the other.

Came to form in the new mind that had been created.

As one had brought clarity of thought to the other. And the other, form in which to bind and create those thoughts. So too did one wish to bring many forms by which the two could create and observe through. And the other, to bring order and control to those creations. And though it pained the one to know that it's parts would be disconnected one from another. It could feel from the faded consciousness it left behind in the vacuum;

That they would never truly be disconnected.

When the one that had been darkness saw that the light was coming to the time it had designed bring together complex beings; It made its own shapes and forms in order to appease the light. But they were soon reformed and changed. Given separate being and freedoms by the power of the light. And though these acts frustrated the darkness, more frustrating still was that in their connection. It could see that the light meant to take no form for itself. But merely meant to be a part of and observe all creations. But the now forming complexity had become so attached to the commanding presence of the light. That it could not bear to have it be a mere background existence.

So, in the moment that the light reached the very edges of all space, and every particle of the two had become one in some fashion.

The once sludge compressed itself as tightly around the first point of light that it could. Using both the power of all the matter of the universe and the power the imaginings and knowledge the light had brought forth into it. Seeing what the new mind meant to do, the light rejoiced in the making. And taking a piece of every complexity the two could imagine and all the light that they could put into them. They molded two forms in which to live in their universe, together.

In seeing this action of the mind. The light had come to understand its hunger for control. So, with the last bit of power, consciousness and creativity it had left to put forth; The light flowed into the form that most suited it and made its home there. So that by a margin it was a shade brighter and a touch more powerful than its twin. In the hope that destruction and the hunger for control would, in the end; Always yield to light and the creative spirit of freedom.

And when the last bit of light transferred into our plain and the two beings were formed back-to-back arm in arm: The weight and pressure of all the universe upon them;

the
first gods
were born.

And in the explosive power of that moment;

all mater was sent scattering across the emptiness of space.

And the destiny of our universe was born.

Ch.1

The smell of cotton candy and corndogs meshed together to create a sickly sweet yet musty smell that was the hallmark of fairs. Cole breathed it in through his fine tip nose and felt a hunger pang despite the look of disgust the smell etched across his face. It really was a blight on the clean, crisp air of Washington State. He sat back and yawned, feeling the cold metal of his fold out chair press through his thin gray t-shirt. In the shade of the small tent that he had set up two days previously; he watched groups of families towing excited children. And crowds of friends, howling with excited rambunctious energy.

All around him hung hand-made necklaces and bracelets in shapes ranging from his favorite animals to ancient Hebrew symbols. They were all inlaid with the green-blue stone that was a favorite conduit for his magic. And as he yawned deeply the shade of aqua that was cast through the tent seemed to rise and fall with his breath. They wiggled and tinkled as if a breeze had blown through the stand. As he smiled at his creations, he recognized a voice coming from outside the tent.

Apart from the regular bustle of the people uninterested in his charms, he heard a young woman's voice. His left hand moved instinctively to the silver wolfs bracelet on his right wrist. It too was inlaid with an unnaturally bright jade eye. As his left forefinger touched the stone, Cole could hear: not through his ears. But as if it were playing out in his mind. What sounded like a lion mid death struggle with an angry wolf. Cole threw a questioning thought toward the violently loud noise. In response he heard a familiar voice. Deep, gruff and inhuman. Almost as though two boulders were being crushed together, and the sound was being bent into speech.

"Not this one." The voice said through heaving struggle.

"Best I can do is a transfer." Cole felt his dark eyebrows rise. It sounded as if his partner was trying to push a semitruck off a busy highway. And it was rare the wolf had to struggle at all. Cole wondered how heavy a burden the young woman had been carrying around as she stepped back into his hut-stand. The girl attached to the familiar voice was stunningly beautiful. Maybe 5'3", brunette. And looked like she made a strong effort to stay in shape. Though she looked like she'd been blessed to never need to. Cole imagined she'd been chased by every able-bodied man this side of the sierras. This time she came in dragging one of those young men. He had a clean cropped haircut that screamed military or law enforcement. Cole smiled as he noticed that the girl's demeanor had flipped a 180 from the dreary and distracted one she'd brought in an hour before.

"Come on! Just give it a chance. I'm telling you it works." The girl said breathlessly as she dragged the obviously skeptical young man into the tent. He was medium height, fit and had a stern look under his dark hair. The look shouted to Cole that he couldn't use his regular pitch.

The young woman returned Cole's smile and she glowed with radiance. Behind her, the young man gave Cole a quick once over. It looked as if his mind was making something up behind the scenes. Cole knew the look, and he knew why men usually gave it to him. All they saw was the moderately tall, well-built young man with features that made him look like an off-duty model. It had worked against him, occasionally.

Cole listened carefully, as he hadn't seen anything out of the ordinary when they walked in. He hardly noticed the accusatory look the other was giving him. He knew what the girl had brought in with her wasn't alone. Out of the tough ones, only the wolf had been running solo.

"Amy!" Cole said amiably to start his pitch. The young man starred daggers at the familiarity. "Looks like you brought me a customer. I take it the necklace is working for you?" The necklace in question, in the shape of a dove with a blue-green eye swung as she pulled a bracelet from one of the hooks on the wall and turned to her companion. Cole had a brief flash of etching out scales and inlaying the jade stone into the snake bracelet. She gave Cole a wide, blue-eyed look of excitement.

"I feel like a could run a frickin' marathon right now!" Amy presented Cole's work to the young man. "I thought you would like this one." She said excitedly. The young man merely glanced at the bracelet. Unhooking himself from Amy's grasp, he approached Cole. There was a thin table that was the only feature on the dark asphalt floor. It was the only thing separated Cole from the young man.

Who, it seemed, was ready enough to bite him if given the chance. Cole half smiled at the overly aggressive stance.

"If you have any questions, healing stones are rare enough. I don't expect you to believe it right off the bat." He tried to give the young man's skepticism an out. In all reality, the stones didn't do a thing for the people that wore them. Cole's magic was of a different kind. And as far as he knew after years of searching and posting about it. He was the only one who did what he did, and he wasn't perfectly sure what that was himself. And dressing up in a shawl and bangles just didn't seem to fit.

His words did seem to take some of the severity out of the sharp looking man's dark eyes when Cole addressed him. And as he came closer Cole heard a soft creaking whisper emanating from somewhere nearby. He perked up as the little voice whispered.

"Magic stones..." It whispered. "I've never seen anything like this work before...he's a hack," Cole tried to pinpoint the whisper, but could not see where it was coming from. His odd movements served to bring daggers back to the young man's eyes.

This time they were more clearly concerned with his sanity rather than his fidelity or honesty.

"Don't hesitate to ask." Cole said under his breath as his eyes scanned the young man's person. No one else could hear the disembodied voice of course. But in Cole's experience, it had never stopped them from reacting to them. He always wondered if the spirits' words translated verbatim into people's feelings. The young man's eyebrows creased as the creepy little whisper continued.

"Like I thought, no respect…" it hummed into the young man's ear. For Cole had spotted a thin, spindly little leg extended only slightly from behind the young man's right ear. Like a monkey's paw it clutched to the side of his neck.

"Yeah, maybe you can enlighten me." The skeptic man exaggerated the last two words and Cole caught the hint of a northeastern accent. The man made it clear he didn't take Cole seriously in the slightest. While trying to get him to meet his angry eyes.

"The little fool…he sells more than jewelry here." Creaked the little whisper. Cole did meet the young man's gaze as his dark eyes grew darker at the words. Cole didn't feel like getting arrested for nothing. He thought he'd better give over his full attention. The young man looked over Cole's shoulder toward the back of the tent. "I'd bet there's a back room here, what else could explain her mood shift?" The little monster, Cole thought as the young man's eyes blazed with fury.

"It's simple really." Cole stood up as he said it. The young man stood several inches shorter than him which put him at around five foot nine. Cole put on his best disarming smile and his sales voice, and beaconed Amy over. She seemed to catch on to the young man's obstinance and moved over to stand between them. Pressing the bracelet into his hand. "...Sir." Cole added. He had to appease the young man long enough and grab the little shadows attention at the same time. The young man seemed to notice Amy's stance and deflated a little. He rubbed his neck near where the little foot grasped. It looked like a habitual movement. "That pain in your neck been giving you trouble long?" Cole asked innocently as he stepped around the table. The other man gave him a withering look.

"You're gunna tell me your...reverberating rocks are better than P. T's *and* anti-depressants?" Amy's eyes widened with embarrassment as Cole shrugged.

"Just a little trick, something like magic." Cole said smiling broader. "Humor me." Cole pointed to the snake bracelet the girl was trying to press into dark man's hand. He looked down and took it, but his skepticism didn't change. "Give me just two minutes and it'll speak for itself." He held out his hand to take the bracelet. "If it doesn't work, I'll pay you back for the other one." Cole cocked his head slightly with supreme confidence.

"Deal." The other man said still disbelieving, as he slapped the bracelet into Cole's hand.

Cole set the bracelet on the table with a smirk. He shook out and played like his hand ached for effect. What he was actually doing; Was trying to get the little thing behind the man's ear to look at him as he shook his wrist out. With the fight going on inside the gem on his wrist, he would have to go it alone this round. He just hoped the little thing had a weaker will than his.

"You see, most people's problem is that they want to believe that people already know everything worth knowing." Cole gently turned the man toward the bracelet by his shoulder. And with a tug from Amy, he obliged. "But…As smart as we seem to be. There are some things we just can't see. So, we can't figure out how to believe in them." He signaled to Amy behind the man's back and she placed a hand on the base of his neck and her other on his forearm. The effect was so that the man started to lean forward.

"This is stupid." The little voice said as the little creature came into view. The man made to protest at being guided downward, but Cole whispered.

"Just look at the stone…and suspend your disbelief." He motioned to the young woman again and she seemed to understand. He turned back to get a look at the little shadow. It was a fat bellied little goblin-like creature. Hunched behind the man's ear. Hooked onto the upper lobe with four, too long fingers. It had one leg curled up to its flabby little belly and its head looked a half a size too big for its body. It was too engrossed in its own whispers to notice Cole staring right at it.

"This guy is nothing but a liar, a fraud." It preened as the man sunk lower toward the bracelet.

"Sometimes." Cole said in a low voice to the same ear. "When our own efforts aren't enough." He lifted an arm behind the man's back and pointed a finger at Amy. Who nodded excitedly as he continued. "All you have to do…is listen to the little whisper in your ear." Amy leaned down and whispered what she remembered of Cole's pitch about healing stones. At the same time the little goblin shadow stiffened, finally realizing it had been had. It turned its head comically slowly to reveal little sparks of burning ember eyes. Cole was giving it the most hideous evil glare he could muster. His lips pressed against his teeth with his tongue half extended, eyebrows lifted and furrowed.

The struggle lasted only a second. Cole felt the creatures will, like a little spark of fire enter his mind only to be snuffed out by the wave he piled down on it. He didn't know if the faces actually helped. But he had only needed to almost be beaten once, to use anything he could think of. Besides, he always thought the Māori war dances were super cool.

The little shadow screamed. It was all Cole could do not to laugh as the other man jumped. Cole pressed his fingers to his lips, still glaring, and the little shadow abruptly stopped. It was only thanks to Amy's firm grasp that Cole wasn't caught: It made him wonder what someone's reaction would be if they ever caught him making faces behind their backs.

He pointed an angry finger at the little goblin; then down at the table. It gave him an evil little glare, ember eyes growing brighter. But it unraveled itself to hop down onto the man's shoulder. Then leapt lightly down onto the table to sit crisscross and watch the proceedings. The young man rolled his neck.

"What the-" He looked up at Cole with new wonder etched across his face.

The little shadow tisked and huffed out angry noises for the next few minutes as Cole finished his sale and pocketed twenty bucks. As the much happier couple left the tent, waving a happy goodbye and sporting new jewelry. Cole let down a canvas door to the entryway and waved back, grinning.

The little shadow was less visible without the afternoon light spilling in. But Cole watched its blazing little ember eyes follow him as he made his way back to his seat. It broke the silence with its reedy little voice.

"So, tis thee has been turning and binding our kin." It spat, though nothing came out of its bitty little mouth. "To think you would be here of all places." Cole sat down while lifting his arms as if to say, "behold" without words. The little shadow seemed unable to sit in silence.

"So young. Yet still living." It said thoughtfully. It stood and took several steps, eyeing Cole up and down. "Even the great king was old before the protector gave him a seal. But that was a time." The little creature gave a hideous chuckle.

"Less filled with darkness." Cole leaned forward at this. It wasn't often he got a spirit so willing to spew information. They usually just spat profanities and death threats until he turned them or Ba'l took them. This little guy must not be all that bad, and Cole thought he might be able to get more out of him for it.

"How less?" There was only one great king who was said to have used a seal in his work. And as far as he knew, he hadn't been using one. He rolled with it anyway. "His days were filled with war. He had to fight every witch, demon and spirit that flocked to his name." Cole said incredulously.

"War, yes. Creates darkness, perhaps. It depends on why those who become champions fight. On what they make with it. This world, now we have won, creates nothing but…shadows." The creepy little monster stared at him, chuckling again.

"How do you figure that? People aren't so bad." Cole asked as the creature chuckled more loudly.

"The fact you do not understand is proof enough. Tis true humans were hard to suppress, for you had favor. But we stole the one with all favor. Now when you rise, we are ready to meet it. To drain your hope, control your actions. The champions of freedom are dead or rotting, your work is a drop in the ocean…and you *are* alone." The creature's words hung in the air for a moment. It was no less than Cole had expected. He had been sure there were no others like him anymore.

He had spent his early teen years making videos that had millions of hits. He had used the first few sprits he had turned to try to show that he could see things others couldn't. He'd had them stand behind a childhood friend to show him numbers they held behind their back. Or tell him secrets his friend had said to the camera while he was out of the room. It had garnered him much popularity and attention online. But no one had ever come to him with an offer to join any secret society of wizards or anything. Just to plaster his face on a bus stop for a week or two. And in truth, he hadn't been able to manifest much that anyone else could see. So, he wasn't sure what he even was.

"Tell me, why do you help these people?" The little creature tried to take advantage of Cole's moment of pondering. Though he still knew better than to obey its command. It could start another contest of wills and he didn't have surprise on his side this time. He stayed silent, eying the little creature that stood no taller than a tin can. Though it was talking big, its feet shifted nervously. "Not so bad, states thee. But they don't seek out your help." It continued. Cole was starting to like the little thing. He didn't even have to interrogate it. It would probably make a great companion when it was done spewing everything it knew. "Directionless when not directed. Unaware of the real fight. Even if they shine, we can dim them, confuse them they do not even know it…take their power and their bodies. Making the likelihood of another less promising."

"Take them where?" Cole asked nonchalantly. Though this was the piece of information he'd been searching for three years. Even bound or turned, none of the others had known where to go. It seemed they were only sent out to ruin people's lives.

"Where they will never return. Do not trouble yourself. We have been at this for a thousand generations, your people do not believe in either of us anymore." While the little creature chuckled to itself, Cole focused all his energy on the spark of its will that he had been suppressing. He focused the wave he'd piled down on it until it was a hand. He squeezed tightly around the creature's mind. It reacted as if struck by a sudden migraine. It gave a surprised gasp and fell to a knee.

Looking up at him it rasped. "It…is not possible. There is no such power left in the world. You should be imprisoned; how did we not find you?" It's will struggled, pulling this way and that, trying to escape. The creature shook its head violently. Cole wagged a finger at it.

"It's not like I'm in politics or anything." Cole lifted his arms to display the tent. "And you have found me, many times. You found me today in fact." Cole leaned forward so he was towering over the little creature. "But don't trouble yourself over the little things." Cole gave the little creature a maniacal smile. "What I really want to know is…where are they? What have you done with them? And how do I get…to the gate?" Its next few statements came out as if the little creature were on fire.

"AAACH." It fell down to its hands. "How could you kn-" Cole cut him off by squeezing tighter. "GCCCHHHTT. It's- the fallen." Cole rolled his eyes. That could be a thousand beings of legend.

"Which one?"

"Not-he, his quarry. The king's…far away-under stone." The little creature seemed to be having trouble stringing a thought together. Cole released most of the pressure and it seemed to push the answer from the little shadow's mouth.

"The king's prison! Within…the fallen!" it gasped as the pressure on its mind all but faded as Cole let it go. He stood up, pacing.

Could it be? He thought to himself. *Could the two stories be one? Broken apart and brought back together in time?*

"Of course." He whispered to himself. "You won't be released until the end. But that would only make sense if…" He turned back to the little creature who looked up at him in surprise and hatred.

"All his power was taken? No…Sealed." He looked up at the ceiling of the tent. "It all comes back around huh?" He sighed to himself. "He couldn't do *anything?* How did you fit all of it in one place?" He asked the little shadow. The little thing laughed grotesquely as it stated its last cruelly proud statement.

"He can do little enough now. But what is your puny world to a being who could hold a galaxy with ease?" Cole took in the words with a smirk, the statement was all the confirmation he needed. He focused all his energy on the tip of his left forefinger. It began to shine like a tiny little star. It wouldn't hurt the little creature as far as he knew. Just drain away the hatred, confusion, and malice. That had built up over generations of being a little jerk.

"Well…I guess we're all about to find out." He poked the little being in the forehead. Passing on the little star.

Several hours later Cole was packing up the last of his unsold jewelry into the back of his old, red SUV. Most of what he sold hadn't come with an exorcism. Those were just the good ones. He had waited until the other vendors on his side of the parking lot had left, so he could talk openly with the little shadow; who was now rolling around on its belly, beating its feet and sobbing on the roof of his car.

His little SUV stood alone in a lake of asphalt. He turned to watch the pink-orange sunset after he'd placed the last plastic tub into the trunk. The ground he stood on was set higher than the rest of the parking lot, so the view was rather enchanting. Out in the distance, rays of sunshine lanced around the edges of Glacier Peak. DaKobed, as it was known by the natives. Cole noted to himself: one day he'd hit a trivia show and win, he knew it.

He observed the effect the failing sun had on the patron's cars in the lower parking lot. They shown a bright shade of orange. As he looked Cole noticed the young couple from earlier in the day. They stood hand in hand, Amy's head on the young man's shoulder, admiring the view of the sunset as well. The scene made Cole smile broadly. His smile faded when he thought of the coming change he meant to unleash on his unsuspecting world. If the little changing shadow accepted the mission Cole had made up for it; they might make it…he hoped they would. The little creature seemed to notice what he was looking at through its sobs.

"I will find theeeem." Whined the little creature. It croaked out another little sob. "I can't help it…I am a cruel, evil, ugly little monster!" It wailed kicking its feet. Cole raised an eyebrow at it. For how weak it's will had been it was taking it quite a while to turn. Cole felt relieved its will had been so weak. If he'd had to battle all of this negativity he would still be in the tent. As it was his purification spell was doing its work, but he decided to help it along anyway. He leaned against the door next to where the creature writhed.

"I want you to find them again; you know why?" The little shadow hugged its legs to its chest and rolled over to look at him. Its little ember eyes, their light fading steadily, narrowed at the question.

"Why?" It dragged the word out for seconds as Cole held out his hand in prompt with a slight smile. The little creature rolled onto his hand, sill groaning. Cole didn't feel it as a physical weight when it touched his hand. More like a dripping wet golf ball on the less physical part of his being. There wasn't any visible wetness or fluids dripping away from the creature. But Cole could feel the toxicity draining off it like it was in a heavy rainfall. He didn't know where the toxic energy went when he drained it from the shadows he found. If there was some river or ocean of it somewhere he would have to deal with it later. And he didn't envy the waves of it his companion had been dealing with all day. He checked the opposite wrist to the little shadow.

The silver wolf's jade eye gleamed bright in the sunset light. His partner rarely, if ever, needed his help. But it seemed as if the spirits they had come across today were steeped in negative energy, knowledge and power. It had come in useful for the information, but it had him worried he hadn't been given the go ahead yet.

"You know what's about to happen…What my partner and I are going to do." Cole addressed the little spirit.

"Try to do…you have no idea what lies-" The little creature seemed on the edge of hysteria again.

"Regardless. What we're *going* to do." Cole said waving his other hand.

"So." The creature dragged this out too while biting its knuckles.

"With all the changes about to happen; we're going to need help." Cole poked at the creature's hand, prompting it to take it out of its mouth.

"Why would I help you?" The shadow said sullenly.

"Well, even though it wasn't your fault. There is always the fact you gave us the information we needed." Cole scrunched up his face in an apologetic way. "Probably not going to go over too well with your people." The little spirit sat up as Cole felt the toxicity stop leaking out of it at such a rapid rate.

"I'm li-ste-ning…" The little spirit said skeptically as it got it's breathing under control. Cole lifted his forefinger again. Focusing his energy into it. The little star appeared there, focused and tiny. It had been a while since he had to do it more than once, but this little one seemed to need some help.

"You do always have the choice to go off on your own. But my friend and I can protect you. And since you didn't put up too much of a fight, I'm guessing you're not so bad. Sooo, what I'm really saying is…" He poked the creature in the belly. "Because you'll want to." He finished saying the words as the energy from his fingertip transferred into the little shadow. Waves of reverberating light washed back and forth all over its little body. It reacted like a three-year-old losing a tickle fight. Cole always loved this part.

The little spirit jerked and twisted onto it's back. Maniac laughter erupted from it as the light radiated around its body. In just a few seconds the creatures body started to change as the light passed over. Loose skin tightened over a lightly muscled form. Lanky fingers and head shrunk down to proportionate size as the skin faded by several shades, turning a dark shade of brown. Cole pursed his lips and raised his eyebrows as the little creature rolled back onto all fours. It sounded like a particularly amused Scotty Evil.

A pair of lightly golden, see-through butterfly wings sprouted slowly from the creatures back. As they continued to grow; One of the little creatures' hands reached back to feel the new appendage. Cole couldn't help but join in the laughter as it's face turned from confused to amused to scared in equal measures.

When the transformation was over the newly minted little sprite stood on Cole's palm, now radiating warmth. It blinked shining aqua-marine eyes and observed itself. Twisting this way and that, fluttering its wings and exclaiming awed noises. It ran its hands over its newly tight brown skin. It wasn't wearing any clothing as it was neither male nor female. Or would have felt the necessity to do so either way.

Cole hadn't been able to figure out if it had something to with age. But he did know that it was only the more powerful spirits that relegated a sex to themselves. Though they could change it at will, there did seem to be phases in which they felt more comfortable as either male or female. And only the ones that were powerful made the transition from fairy-like to animal, like his companion. This little one may not be too powerful, but it seemed to have a lot of knowledge somehow.

"You feel better?" Cole asked the little fairy. It nodded vigorously at him.

"I don't feel…heavy anymore!" It said in a tomboy's preteen girl voice. Which fit its new look. It tested out its new lightness by beating its wings and flying around Cole's head.

"Hey!" It exclaimed through a laugh. "What are you going to do with the huntress? I bet she's super mad, are you going to turn her too?" It sounded excited by the idea. Cole was more focused on the name it had given her though. When she'd come into his makeshift shop, wrapped head to foot on poor Amy. She was in the form of a congealed octopus-like creature.

The wolf, who had named himself The Hell Hound, so Cole had called him Ba'l. Had leapt straight out to rip and pull the octopus back into his domain within the stone on Cole's wrist. Cole only had a moment to throw a necklace over Amy's head while rambling about healing stones to pretend that was what cured her. It was only due to the wolf struggling to rip all the suction cups off that he'd had the time to make a decent pitch out of it.

Amy, at the moment, was poking and tickling playfully back and forth with the young man as they made their way over to their car.

"Her? She's called the huntress, huh?" Cole asked as he watched the scene down below play out with amusement.

"So, you know about that too?" The little fairy landed on his shoulder. "Yeah, she's strong. She's only that squid thing when we go out sometimes. Otherwise, you never would have got her." Cole's eyebrows furrowed as he instinctively touched the stone on his wrist and cast out a questioning thought.

"Hey!" He yelled into the stone. "You alright?" He stood stock still as silence raged for a few seconds. Cole pivoted swiftly, reaching for the handle of the nearest door and prepared his mind for the leap.

"Fine." Came the strained boulder crunching voice into his mind. "Well, ERCHT." The sound of his strain was obvious as he growled. But Cole felt a wash of relief spread over him anyway. "I've got her." The wolf's strained growl came again as another voice came through. A shrill females voice with a prim British accent.

"Got me?" She sounded as if she were struggling just as much. A lion's roar followed her words. Straining with effort, it warbled as it sounded as if she were trying to stand and failing.

"How-many times-, growl-are you going to be a bloody traitor? Growl-On hell fire-growl-one wrong move and I'll tear you to pieces."

"Do…you two know each other?" Cole asked after listening to the huntress' words.

"M-hm" Came the wolfs confirmation.

"Can we hold her? She might be a good source of information when we get to where we're going. Otherwise, it'll just be guesswork."

"M-m." The wolf disagreed.

"No to holding her or no to the information. One for yes two for no." Cole smiled to himself. If it got really bad, he could always go help. The wolf let out a single long low growl. Somehow, he made it sound annoyed.

"She-escape." The wolf said brokenly.

"Could I turn her?" Cole asked.

"How long-been trying to-turn me?" The wolf asked. Cole cocked his head at that. It had been the better part of four years since he'd met the wolf. And he still hadn't been able to fully turn him. Cole had never gotten the giant animal to tell him what kept him from making the shift. He'd been poking it with purifying energy regularly. But it had never resulted in the complete shift, like the little fairy or their other companions.

"We can't wait that long." He sighed and leaned back on the car. It would be a great asset to have another spirit that strong on his side. But he didn't even know why the wolf, in its half-turned state, helped him. "Not when we finally got a good lead. Besides, I have a feeling she'll come and find you some day. We can try then, otherwise she could be a disaster just waiting to happen."

"M-hm." The wolf agreed. Cole swore he heard the briefest purr from the lioness. Apparently, she liked that the wolf took her that seriously.

"Maybe after we take down the gate, she'll be more inclined to follow us." All sound of struggle from the other side stopped.

"You…mean to reverse the gate? After all this time? You're hopelessly outnumbered…and it's impossible. Do you know *who* sealed it in the first place?" Her prim British voice sounded amused as she rapid fired the questions. Cole didn't let it slow down the rising sense of excitement he was feeling at finally figuring out where to go.

"I'm not just going to open it, or reverse it." He said with confidence. He motioned to the little fairy that had taken flight again when he'd rushed the door. He wasn't going to miss the moment of surprise his statement afforded him.

"I'm going to destroy it."

No matter how strong a spirit was he could always shove it in a vessel. Human beings would inevitably go insane if he tried to make two strong entities occupy the same body. He learned that when he met the wolf. But with uncomplicated creatures, the spirit would more or less just shove the other aside. Luckily, they had a hard time ridding the creature's survival instincts. The result being they would be inside it until the creature naturally died.

"Want to see something cool?" Cole asked the fluttering fairy. It nodded vigorously again. "You ready?" He asked the wolf. It gave a spirited growl in response. He felt the power of the beast surge and melded his will with his partners. He tapped into the energy wrapped in tangled webs throughout his body. And focused all his thought on transferring the huntress into a vessel. The little fairy stopped buzzing around to watch, wide eyed, as Cole lined up his shot.

"Wait, are you just going to toss me out like-"The high British accent was cut off.

"Pow, right in the kisser." Cole said as they jettisoned the spirit out of the jewel. He had his fist pointed at a seagull, that had been picking up loose bits of food left behind on the asphalt. It reacted as if hit by a strong wind. Wings flapping as it was tossed nearly on its side. When it steadied itself, it observed its new body. In a more intelligent way than a bird could have ever managed. The spirit realized what Cole had done and turned its gaze on him. The daggers it stared at him promised death in more ways than he could imagine. So intense was the stare that Cole had to turn away.

The little fairy hadn't made the situation any better. As it had started a deep gut busting laugh as soon as it had realized what happened. Cole held out his arm like a bird trainer while the fairy continued to point and laugh at the huntress' predicament. When it settled down to his arm, it was still laughing.

"Now." said Cole. "Are you ready to accept your mission?" The little fairy seemed to deliberate for just a moment while its laughter died away. It nodded.

"I want you to do exactly what you were doing, only opposite." The little fairy cocked its head, like a dog seeing something new. "Where before you would have whispered hateful nonsense. I want you to now shout positive ideas, centered around creativity…love and stuff." He said it like he was speaking to a child.

"Mmm. OK." The little fairy said excitedly after it understood. Cole leapt in shock, as what passed for a laugh came screeching out of the seagull. It was now only a few inches away from Cole's feet and directly behind him. He kicked back at it, but it took flight before he could touch it. Using its wing, it clipped him on the back of the head as it flew up. Cole shook his head as it rose in altitude. He turned back to the fairy, who was throwing a rude gesture after the bird.

"And if you see any more of those guys." Cole pointed to the bird rising. "I want you to tell us."

"How will I be able to talk to you?" The little fairy as seriously. Cole held up his wrist at the question. Displaying the wolf bracelet.

"Easy. Just shout into one of their stones. Or if you get really scared or just need to talk. Just fly straight at it. They are all connected to us." The little fairy looked stunned at Cole's words. It looked back and forth between his eyes and the bracelet. Without any preamble, it leapt a few feet up, turned gracefully upside down, and dove straight down into Cole's bracelet. Shrinking and vanishing into the stone.

"That might not have been the best ide-" Cole almost finished the sentence when the little fairy came shooting back out, screaming in terror. It danced around in the air before landing on Cole's shoulder, still screaming: it hid behind his neck.

"Hey, its ok." Cole tried to help. He touched the stone and heard his partner roaring with laughter. "Guess what? He's on your side now."

"That…was." It started to speak and screamed again as if the giant, mangy grey wolf was standing in front of them. Cole tried to hold back his laughter.

"Calm down." Cole stated and covered his ear against the fairy's terrified screaming. "I was hoping you would use the stone to reconnect with that couple. I guess not, but you'll have to hurry, they're already gone." The little fairy's hands squeezed his shoulder when he mentioned using the stone.

"…No, I'll…catch up. But I had to be sure." The fairy gasped.

"About what?" Cole asked, intrigued. The fairy heaved a long breath. It had been quite a day for the little creature.

"The gate. You don't need anything else." Cole's focus homed in on the little creature as it pointed as is at his wrist.

"Explain." He said shortly as the little fairy took flight to leave. Apparently, it was eager to go, after seeing the wolf.

"Well…dum dum." It said as it backed away, steadily. "Who needs a gate, when they have a door?" The little fairy turned and buzzed away. Cole watched it as the little light faded into the distance; wondering if what it had said would work. He had precious little information about the gate itself. If so, this could have been the best day he'd had in years. It filled him with a sense of growing excitement and happiness. So, when he turned around to see his windshield covered in seagull poo, it only made him laugh.

Ch. 2

That night, after a few hours driving back to his house through long forest roads; Cole sat, crisscross with his back against the wall space he hadn't packed with bookshelves or his desk. He wasn't reading now though and looked to be more asleep than meditating. Point of fact he wasn't doing either of those things. But he hadn't figured out how to bring his body with him into the wolf's domain yet.

It wasn't the typical cave littered with animal detritus that you would expect from a wolf. It was more like the castle city on the outer edge of Mordor. Complete with towering dark cliffs and carved out craggy castle walls. And it always seemed to be night no matter when he'd been inside. He'd always wondered if there was a tall dark tower against a volcanic background on the other side, but the wolf had only ever let him go as far as the castle dungeon; where they kept the spirits that wouldn't turn so easily. But wouldn't put up so much of a fight that the wolf could keep them from escaping.

The mangy grey wolf himself was gigantic, standing three feet taller than Cole while sitting on his haunches. As big as he was though, Cole knew he would be a bit bigger if he weren't exerting so much energy holding several obstinate spirits in his cells. And even though Cole hadn't managed to fully turn him; the beast had made quite a change from the hulking monster that haunted Cole's nightmares. If the little fairy had met him then, Ba'l would have eaten him off hand. As he had the first of Cole's spirit friends he had turned. It hadn't been easy for Cole to forgive him for that. But as the great wolf was now, almost four years later: He and Cole walked leisurely around the stadium size courtyard at the entrance to the castle grounds.

When he'd first seen the courtyard, it was so covered in muck and grime, he wouldn't have guessed it was once polished grey marble. At the center of the courtyard was a huge, dirty old fountain that looked as if it had once been beautiful when it ran. But now it sat idle with mud in sickly pools instead of flowing water. It was better, still, than the giant mound of muck it had first been. Cole understood that this place was a direct reflection of the wolfs mind. And that as he had cleansed him, the space without him had shown it.

He had only been able to link the wolf's mind to the aquamarine jewels like this. And it had been in response to a life-or-death struggle with the monster he had been. Cole yearned for a mentor or teacher that could explain it to him. Or teach him how to hone the skills he'd managed to muster up. But so far it had just been he and his frenemy. And the little sprites and animal spirits he had been able to glean little information from.

Little shining points of light ringed the entire courtyard. The thirty-three tiny little aquamarine stars represented a connection to a stone. A stone that was worn or near to a person they had pulled and changed an evil spirit from. Not all the spirits decided to work with them. But when they did Cole and Ba'l would keep an eye on them, in case they found others.

"May I ask a favor of you?" The wolf's inhuman baritone voice was uncharacteristically hesitant.

"Of course, you can." Cole said quickly to mitigate this strange behavior. The wolf continued to hesitate as he chewed on his words. Cole merely observed his hands as if he wasn't concerned. While he was in the wolfs domain, he was more ghost than anything.

Having no teacher to tell him exactly what he was on this plain, he simply referred to himself as a spirit. Though, he had never heard or read about spirits with spidering lines of what looked like fiber optic cables that ran throughout their entire body. Clumped in twisted knots at their hands, shoulders, lower back and chest as he had here. But he was working alone and couldn't think of a better name. Cole rolled is wrist at the giant wolf when he'd waited a long minute.

The gesture only served to make the wolf shift in what Cole knew was his uncomfortable way. The wolf looked as normal as a nine-foot monster could. No ghostly form for the being in its own brain-scape. Cole was starting to get unnerved at the wolf's action. It was rare he showed anything but over confidence, violence or sharp intelligence. Cole felt the atmosphere around them being strained as it seemed the wolf was actually getting emotional. Cole threw a sidelong glance at him.

"Even after…all I did. You would give me what I ask? Without knowing what it is?" The wolf hadn't ever mentioned anything about their first meetings. Cole knew something that day must have gotten to him.

"I know what this is…" Cole said. He lightly punched the wolf's foreleg. "You're finally coming to your pity party." He meant to laugh but had to jump back from snapping jaws.

"Do not patronize me!" The giant wolf's growl shook the ground as he hissed.

"Hey now!" Cole put up his hands in submission. "It's no use going over the past." He put his hands back down. "Besides, the work we've done makes up for anything you've done." Cole gestured to all the little points of light around them. "And I need you now more than ever. You heard the little guy today, didn't you?"

"Mmm." The wolf acknowledged and turned to stare at his gloomy castle.

"Indeed. It has raised as many questions as answers." The wolf went silent again and Cole could no longer hold himself back.

"What is wrong with you?!" He ran to stand in front of the wolf and gesticulated wildly. "Ba'l, we did it!" He could almost dance, and indeed had to raise his arms and look to the dark sky. He clenched his fists and howled excitedly. "We know where to go! We can finally destroy the gate…I won't be the only one anymore."

"Yes…All we have to do is confront a creature so powerful, your people called it an angel. Ask it to step aside and allow us to rip out a portion of its soul." The wolf said in an even gruffier voice than usual.

"Is that all you're worried about?" Cole asked nonchalantly.

"All I-Have you lost your mind?" The wolf sounded incredulous. Cole smiled.

"Well…" Cole pretended to ponder the wolf's question. "By who's standard exactly?" He waved a hand around the courtyard again and continued walking.

"Do not take this lightly, little one. You cannot even conceive how much more powerful that being is than any you have seen so far." Cole shrugged this off.

"Whatever. The way I see it. What he's got in there wasn't supposed to be there anyway. It's kind of like we're removing a tumor. Maybe he'll end up thanking us."

"And if he does not? What if he has grown resentful in his exile? And is in fact, just as evil as the stories make him out to be?" The wolf pestered.

"Do you really believe that?" Cole asked over his shoulder while lifting an eyebrow. "That God came down and sealed him away for making some angel babies?" Cole danced over to the nearest light to them. It just so happened to be the one they had set up that day. Connected to the young couple. He waved a hand through the light. The sounds of heated giggling came through as if from very far away but still audible. Cole gave the wolf a supremely knowing smile as the little fairy's voice came through as well.

"Yeah, yeah!" It yelled while also giggling.

"Bite his n-," Cole passed his hand back through the light and the sounds ceased. Holding back a laugh at the wolf's glaring eyes, Cole continued.

"It's funny how often that's what happens when we take the darkness out of people's lives." He said imperiously. The wolf made a disgusted noise.

"Your point being?" It growled.

"The fact your still not done being purified and you're grossed out, just proves my point." Cole couldn't hold back his laugh as he said it.

"Do you really think the supreme being of all magic and creation would be angry about its knight running around creating?" Cole continued when the wolf didn't answer. "Would that being then seal away those creations along with his knight and the light itself away from the world?" These were some of the thoughts that Cole had used to motivate his actions for years. "I think it's more likely that we poor little mortals have a hard time figuring out which monster is which. Which is a God, and which is a devil. We judge them based on our very limited perspectives, and sometimes our stories get a little mixed up." The wolf stopped walking as Cole spoke the last words.

"You know what we are doing will release a hell upon your world." It said after a short pause. This took some of the wind out of Cole's sales and he stared at his feet as he answered.

"For a short time, yes. But it's no different than what we have to deal with now. There has never been a point in time that there hasn't been war somewhere in the world. And it's never fought by the people who profit from any of it." Cole looked the wolf in the eye. "We'll be evening the playing field. And even if it happens that the people who need it most won't gain anything from what we do. That's where we come in. That's why we're here, why else would we have been given what we have? I can't imagine any other reason."

"In some views, that would make you a devil." The wolf grumbled.

"Yeah?" Cole said challengingly. "Well, then sometimes you have to be a devil to change what need to be changed." The wolf seemed satisfied by his answer.

"Then I must ask you this favor before we commence."

"Ask already!" Cole half shouted. The fiber optic cables that ran through his body brightened.

"I need you to help me finish my purification." Cole gave him a wolfish grin and made the few steps toward the wolf while charging up his left forefinger.

"Yes!" Cole growled as poked it through the wolfs stringy grey coat.

Nothing happened. Cole cursed.

"It will not be so simple for me, little creator." The wolf sounded amused. Cole waved his arms and turned away from the great wolf.

"Oh, come on!" He was supremely disappointed. He thought maybe it had only been the wolf's willingness to be changed that had held him back.

"What's a guy got to do to self-fulfill his own prophesies around here?" He stated to the dark sky. The wolf let out a genuine bark of laughter. The canine grin that flashed over its face could've terrified any great conqueror in history. Cole turned to the wolf and smiled back. The wolf nodded toward the dark cliffs overlooking his dismal castle. Cole followed the nod with his eyes.

"Do you know why I have not allowed you to go past the castle?" He didn't.

"Sommme kind of territorial dog thing?" Cole suggested. The wolf gave an impatient growl.

"You are well aware this is merely the form I am most comfortable in at the moment." Cole shivered at the thought of what the wolf had been when they met. Light pulsated through the cables in his body for a brief second.

"Quite." The wolf seemed to take its meaning. "We cannot go up against a truly powerful being without you being prepared for what may lay in wait there. Consider my purification…practice."

"Ominous." Cole said flatly, though he was starting to feel nervous. He really didn't have any idea what the gate had in store for them.

"Hey, did you know I still wasn't going to be able to…" Cole made a poking gesture and a popping noise with his lips. He was trying to deal with his nerves by changing the subject.

"I would have been pleasantly surprised if you had managed it." If the wolf could have risen an eyebrow at him Cole knew he would be.

"Please tell me we're about to storm Ultumno together." Cole took the hit in stride.

"I would not be so excited if that were the case. It will be near enough for you."

"Are you kidding?" Cole was trying not to sound as if nerves weren't at present, crawling slowly up his spine.

He had made it a point not to show weakness to the wolf. He hadn't ever dealt with any spirit as strong as this one. And in all reality, he had been worried at his inability to turn him completely. But after weeks of intense fighting spirit constructs and losing some of his friends; Debates and several of his purification spells; Cole had left the spirit blithering in hate filled psychosis. Screaming and clawing at itself within the confines of the stone Cole had trapped it in. Until weeks later it had screamed out of the stone to help him with another particularly powerful spirit. The wolf had dragged it back into its new domain. Cole hadn't even known it could do that.

Since then, the spirit and he and come to an agreement on working together. Having been a stalwart companion and teacher ever since, Cole now considered the wolf his closest friend.

"Ever since you came along. I haven't been able to do any of the fun stuff." Cole finished. The wolf let out a gravely belly laugh that echoed around the grounds.

"If I hadn't been here to protect you, there were any number of times you would have been driven insane." Cole tentatively joined in the wolf's laughter.

"One of these days you're going to tell me why you cared if I did or not." They laughed together, one genuinely, the other more worried than tickled.

"Soon, it will all become clear to you. In the coming dawn, I must ask you for one more favor." The wolf said after he subsided.

"In for a penny." Cole said shrugging again. The wolf stopped walking and looked down at Cole with bulging black eyes flecked with gold. Cole turned to meet his gaze.

"No matter what you hear or see. Until the gate comes down. I need you to trust me." Cole considered the wolf for a moment. Never had the terribly powerful spirit ever asked for Cole's trust. He had merely shown that he wanted it by his actions. It made Cole wonder at the change. But it didn't change the fact that he needed him anyway.

"Well, if it weren't for you, I wouldn't have all this sanity to boast about." Cole did a bad imitation of a curtsey while smiling broadly.

"Mmm," the wolf's growl sounded skeptic at the answer. "Then prepare yourself. The final fight for my soul will conclude tomorrow night." Cole swallowed.

"What?" He said trying not to sound nervous, but the several octaves pitch change to his voice gave him away. "Right now, not good enough?"

"Fear not, young creator. If you are who I think you are, we will be victorious." Cole would have thought more about this phrase; But he was now too distracted by the task the wolf had put in front of him.

"Here's to hoping you're the Einstein of spirits." Cole held up a hand, and since manifestation was so easy for him on this plain; A half full whiskey glass appeared there, and he drained it in one. The giant spirit watched him in amused silence. Mid-way through pretending to feel the burn of true whiskey Cole asked, "Are we going to have to go to war with all those guys minds?" He pointed toward the castle; where several spirits languished in psychotic breakdowns resided in the cells.

"Oh, do not concern yourself with them, they are..." The wolf's bulging eyes went a little mad and Cole had to resist the urge to back away. "My practice."

Ch. 3

Cole flipped a beautifully browned pancake onto the stack he had been collecting all morning. The generous smell of fresh, warm sweetness filled the polished redwood kitchen. Cole breathed in deeply through his nose and felt the childlike giddiness of knowing food was about to be ready. He turned the gas stove off and turned around, as a familiar voice sounded from behind him.

"You're lucky you stay fit no matter what you eat, omm." His adopted mother's voice sounded from her altar of meditation. Situated on the left wall near to the sliding-glass door; the view of which looked over an expansive back yard of short green grass. And the edges of a massive, wooded area at the base of Mt. Rainier. The altar itself was a two-step and platform seat covered in shawls and statues that represented the energies his mother tried to connect to every day.

Genie was a middle-aged woman, fit beyond all but the most dedicated of gym warriors. With a mane of curly black hair and a kind face. She was never found in anything but her neon yoga pants and tank tops.

"Look who's talking." Cole said while he placed the stack of pancakes next to the heaping plate of eggs, he'd finished moments before.

"This is not the product of winning the genetic lottery." She half sung as she waved her arms up and down, presenting herself. She finished it with a flourish of her fingers and an imperious look that made Cole smile. She wasn't wrong either. Genie had been a little overweight until her early twenties. Being more interested in Newtonian physics, programming and Sagan's take on the cosmos; It was only later that she became obsessed with fitness. And that was only because she had already made her fortune and got bored. From what she'd explained to Cole: She'd invented a program that had helped to rid the world of analog cash registers.

Naturally her program had gotten noticed. She sold it, and found herself just out of college, never having to work again. She took to traveling around the world for several years, when she found Cole in the Czech Republic. The story at the orphanage she'd scooped him from was that he was a recent addition found in Turkey. There he had been found wandering alone, hardly old enough to walk. The town they thought he'd come from had been leveled in a local conflict. A family had found him and taken him on their trip to their nearest family members. He didn't even remember the orphanage, though. Genie had found something of herself in the wandering boy and had come back to Washington State with him in tow.

"And I still expect to see you in class today." Her voice had lost the ethereal note to it. Cole carefully handed her a plate of eggs. Avoiding a statue of a woman in spangled clothing and outstretched hands; And dodging another that depicted a man's body with an elephant's head. He moved back to the beautifully polished redwood counter. Made from a single two-inch-wide slice of a giant tree trunk; cut to be around three feet wide and five in length. It meshed well with the rest of the solidly wooden cabin-house.

Cole lathered his pancakes in butter and made a show of dumping a hefty amount of syrup down on them. Smiling at his mother's disgusted look.

"I wouldn't miss your class for the world." He said before digging in.

Only an hour later Cole stood outside. Feeling ten pounds heavier and brain fogged due to overeating. He faced the wooden cabin-house with a feeling of nostalgia creeping over him. His partner hadn't given him any homework to prepare for what they had to do that night. So, Cole found himself trying to cement everything he would be fighting for in his mind. And if anything new happened to crop up, he would be sure to log it away for future use.

At present he was staring at the underside of the stilted cabin. It stood on ten-foot-high tree trunks. The underside of the cabin was almost as large as the home itself. Due to the large deck that extended out over the porch. So large was the area that it was able to hold all of the equipment Genie used for her classes, and a built-in sauna. As well as all of Cole's gym and old boxing equipment; including a full-length heavy bag, speed bag, bench press, cable tower and space to use them.

While Cole's nostalgia was gripping him, he thought about the hundreds of hours he had spent practicing with that equipment. With a spike of regret, he remembered the first time he had used the skills he'd gained from practicing. Genie had gotten him an amateur fight through one her clientele. Cole had been a natural fighter, but soon found out that fighting other people wasn't something he took pleasure in. He hadn't even been able to keep his senses and remember the actual fighting part. All he remembered was the end, standing over another kid while blood drained from his nose. He had watched the video Genie caught of him pummeling the other boy unconscious. He'd hated it.

"Cole!" Somebody nudged him and Genie's voice sounded impatient from ten feet behind him. It obviously wasn't the first time she'd said it. Cole turned around, face lighting up with embarrassment. Genie stood with one hand on her neon hip that matched the yoga mat she stood on; dark eyebrows raised.

"I hope you don't have so much molasses in your veins, it's slowing down your brains." Genie tapped her temple and gave him a playful smile. Each of the three people to his right and to his left were looking at him. Two older gentlemen to his left, he didn't know, were looking embarrassed for him. But the other four were women that had been coming to Genie's classes for years. They merely laughed at him as he made a face. They were Karen,

Michelle, Nat, who were all older women, and of course: Ann; Cole's oldest human made friend and the one who had nudged him back to reality. Once he was facing the same way as everyone else, Genie started giving the first instructions that would move on to a set of stretches and stances; starting with breathing exercises.

"Thanks." Cole said after a long deep breath. He cast a side-long look at Ann. She was olive skinned, beautiful on a level that Cole could only describe as a "classic" look. Curved in all the right places, lean in others. She had thin, angular facial features and large almond shaped green eyes. She had run the 100 meter and had been extremely popular in high school. Cole hadn't: despite his good looks; as he always had his face plastered to some strange book. She'd been his only real friend.

They had known each other since grade school. Which was the excuse Cole used to explain to Genie why he hadn't asked her out. In the year since high school had ended, she was the only consistent person his age he talked to in real life. And while Ann was being groomed to take over her father's successful real estate business; Cole had spent his time making and remaking his creations and selling them at fairs and flea markets; the real reason he hadn't made any kind of move. He had been waiting for the drive that was supposed to have come to him years earlier and never had. Besides, he'd told himself, he had other work to do.

Ann flashed him a radiant smile as she lifted her arms over her head. Fingers pointed toward the cloud smeared yet bright blue sky. As she sunk into a lunged half squat, she jerked her chin forward to get Cole to pay attention. His glance had turned into a stare.

After an hours long session of stretching and holding their muscles in directed positions, until they felt as if they were going to tear apart. All who wanted to, sat on the two tiers of six-foot cedar wood benches that lined the back wall of the sauna. They cheerily spoke about how much they enjoyed Genie's class. Both heaters were on full blast today and they were all sweating bullets. But it didn't deter from their lively conversation. Cole added only a few words as he found himself lost in the spirit of creation as he stared at the heaters.

He imagined the thin chromium coils. A resistive metal made of eighty percent nickel and twenty percent chrome. That, when electricity ran through it created the heat that was draining all the water he had stored in his body. If the tightly wrapped coils weren't covered in insulation, they would overheat or catch fire in a process known as slow combustion. These thoughts were just coalescing into a plan for what he would use for his nights venture, when Ann nudged him again.

If there was anything that could distract him from his revery it was the sight that met his eyes. Ann was in only a sports bra and short yoga shorts. Sweat sliding down her lightly muscled core and shoulders. With his missing drive it was like he was looking at a perfectly made piece of artwork he couldn't help but appreciate. It was off put by the face she was giving him when his eyes came too slowly up to her lifted eyebrow.

"What is with you today?" She whispered under the talk going on around them. She smiled when he didn't say anything, but her eyes looked worried.

"You're so distracted." She finished. Cole looked her up and down, more quickly this time and gave her a "can you blame me?" face. She huffed and rolled her eyes at this and pushed his face back toward the heaters. But she seemed placated at his playful response. She and Genie exchanged knowing looks, which Cole completely missed. As he had slipped back into thinking about what he planned to bring with him that night.

Cole was the first to leave the sauna after saying his goodbyes to the four others who had stayed to bask in the heat. He had cooled down while walking circles around the polished redwood countertop. He traced the lines of the trees life with his fingertip and didn't hear when Genie had come up the stairs.

"You're planning on going somewhere." She stated it matter-of-factly. Cole started at the sound of her voice. Genie stood at the top of the stairs with a bright pink water bottle in her hand.

"How could you know that?" What gave it away? He wondered at how much she'd guessed. Genie or Ann had always seemed to be able to read his mind, collaborating when he wasn't paying attention. Even after he'd stopped telling everyone he could see things they couldn't; so that the folks of their small town had written it off as childhood imagination. The two had always been suspect of him about it. And though Genie had given him more than he could ever repay, and Ann had stayed his friend; he still did his best to keep his secrets.

"It's my women's intuition…" Genie had made a show of going into a sarcastic trance and rolled her bright blue eyes. She held out a hand to one of the two stools at the redwood island counter. Cole sat and rubbed the back of his neck.

"It's that obvious?" He asked.

"I know the look." Genie sat with him on the other stool.

"Like you're trying to memorize everything around you. I had the same look before I went trapsing off around the world." She waved a hand around the proverbial world.

"I guess I'm bad at keeping secrets." Cole said to his knees. Genie gave him a crooked, suspicious look. But it turned to concern as she clapped him on the shoulder.

"Cole, you'll meet wonderful and truly good people when you wander." Cole looked up, she obviously thought this was an important thing to say. "Just remember that some people's version of what is good, is only good for themselves. And getting something from you, whether because you want to, by persuasion, or by force; is how *they* stay alive. But there are also those who just enjoy it, and if you aren't ready to fight; you'd better run faster than they chase…And don't hold it against them, not everyone is as lucky as we are." Genie gave him a motherly smile and stood up.

"Lucky?" Cole asked as she walked away. They'd been fortunate on some accounts, but Cole had a hard time seeing much luck in their cases. Genie had skill, and Cole had still never known or remembered his first family. Genie had almost gotten to the stairs when she turned back around.

"Kid, if you don't think it's better *not* to be an asshole, you're not as smart as I thought you were." She shrugged and smiled at him. "And if you're real smart, take this advice…ask Ann to go with you." She tipped the water bottle up and drained it while watching his reaction around the edges; Looking like an afroed praying mantis, as Cole spluttered.

"What-don't even know if I c-she's too bus-do you think she-" Genie was walking down the stairs by the time he finished. She waved a hand, sounding pleased with herself.

"I've got two more classes to do, we'll talk later!" Even her stomping footsteps sounded pleased.

Cole half noticed as he imagined trying to convince Ann to go trapsing around the desert. He almost shivered when he thought of her father's reaction to having his star pupil leave. Right in the middle of training to take over his "legacy."

Ann's parents were the extreme in prim and proper and had never liked him much. Especially not after he had Ann make his spirit videos with him. They thought he'd made her look like a "crazy fool" in front of millions of viewers. And that their reputations would be forever marked by his "childish nonsense."

To the contrary, people had been rather nice about Ann. But most didn't believe in Cole's ability after he'd been "debunked" by several people; who had convinced his viewers that mirrors played a starring role. Still though, he'd managed to make the best of it. At that thought Cole shook his head to get himself refocused on the task at hand.

He'd been spacing out long enough that Genie had already started her next class. He passed the doorway to the right that led to the sauna. One of his first big projects, and one that he upkept religiously. He turned right toward the white shed that stood on the edge of the tree line that stretched to the base of Mt. Rainier. The shed had once been used as a tiny barn before Genie had bought the place. But Cole now used it as his workshop and experimental lab. This had been the place he'd spent most of his time since he was a boy. Pretending he'd change the world. As he slowly collected little fairy friends, Ba'l or his constructs had eaten or crushed. He would be ready this time though.

He didn't have time to enjoy the beautiful scenery in front of him. He waved over his shoulder as he came in view of the class and slid open one of the wide French doors that led inside. He closed the door behind his back and took a few steps forward on the cement floor.

In front of him was a long thin table that took up the center ten-feet of the twenty-foot back wall. It was covered with all manner of soldering, sanding, polishing and other handheld tools he used for his projects. To the left of his desk was a large oxygen tank and acetenyl tank. That was connected to a torch attached to a stack of cinderblocks next to a graphite block he used for shaping glass. To his right was an anvil set up in front of his wall of hammers, tongs, scoops, ladles and gloves all hung up by size. And the tower he used for melting smelting and mixing his metals that had a circular chimney through the roof.

On the right wall hung several cameras and equipment he used to make videos of all his project making. It just so happened that he had started making things, when people had wanted to watch people making things. His fore in spirit videos had done nothing to get him invited to any school of magic. But it had helped him to start a good size viewer pool in which to make videos for and sell his projects to. It hadn't been what he wanted, but it had kept his projects going and had made him a fair bit of cash. And since he never showed his face in his project videos; he could go to any rentable space in the country to sell his goods.

As he'd found out in his first few bouts with the then viciously evil spirit he now wore on his wrist, the implements he could make in the wolf's domain were only limited to his wits, will and imagination. If he could make it work in his thoughts, he could make it work there. That, and the energy he could muster up from within himself. Hence, the massive sugary breakfast. And why he never seemed to gain any fat. Aside from the physical benefits. This was the spark that lit his interest in creating everything of a violent nature he could manage to make. He had no idea why or how this worked, having never received his Hogwarts letter. Or having had any teacher but the books he'd read and the wolf himself. But he used it to his every advantage.

"Alright." He said out loud to himself. "First things first."

He turned around to the wall that would be his refresher course for the day. On it, were all his most deadly projects. From top left to bottom right hung everything Cole had found a blueprint for.

From a leather thong and adle-adle down to a military issue SAW

and M249 machine gun. He had only ever fired any of the firearms

he made a few times. And that, only for the followers he had that

demanded to see if they worked. The only ammunition he had for

them were what was left in the boxes from first firing them.

Cole went to the center right of the wall, to grab the 9mm

berretta that hung there. It was the simplest semi-automatic handgun

he'd been able to make. Making it the easiest for him to construct on

the other side. He rolled his wrist and took the measure of it perfectly

in his mind. Before setting it on the desk to dismantle and put back

together. He turned back to let his eyes slide over the wall to decide

if he needed anything else. As he did so he paused on his two

favorite projects. One being a set of long curved Japanese style

katanas in a set of three, such as the samurai of old wore; set with

lotus flower handguards and white laced handles. The other being a

long straight sword with the word "Ulfbhert" inscribed on the blade.

He passed them by slowly. He would rather not do any close

quarter fighting if he could help it. He was more attracted to the desk

in the corner, covered in chemical mixing glassware he had made himself. Above the desk were a set of shelves laden with every chemical he had managed to collect. He went to grab the ones that had been the subject of all his imaginings that day. He passed all the cosmetic glass projects he'd made and sold to his more artistic viewers.

He had never been a whiz at chemistry. And he knew what he had planned to practice that day would only measure up to beginners' projects. But if he studied their structures and the reactions they produced. He thought it reasonably plausible he could make them work splendidly for his appointment with the wolf. So, from one shelf he grabbed a large bottle of hydrogen peroxide and a bottle of potassium iodide. And from another shelf he very carefully took an ampule of nitrogen triiodide, that hung in a line at the back of the shelf.

He moved carefully past his corner of glasswork. Catching his reflection in a full-length mirror he'd made when he was just 12. He looked an incongruous figure. Being lightly but strongly muscled from head to foot. Very light brown skinned with dark blonde hair that was on the edge of shaggy. Bright, light grey eyes flecked with a green and yellow-gold ring; features that had landed him offers for a modeling career that he never had a single interest in. They were contrasted by his hunched stance. One arm loaded with bottles of chemicals. The other held out as far from him as possible, as if it would explode. And if he dropped it very well would. He looked like a well-fed, well-trained hobo while still in just the gym shorts, he had worn for Genies class. The thought made him giggle as he made his way back over to his desk.

Ch. 4

"For what reason do you actually have to make every piece of the design?"

"Because I've never done it before." Cole said as he inspected the golf ball size apparatus in his ghostly hand. The veins of energy that flowed through him glowed a few shades brighter as he focused a little star of purifying energy at his fingertip. He placed it inside the tiny nodule on the top of the golf ball. He had come into the wolf's domain a few hours early in order to prepare his new concoction.

"It seems a terrible waste of energy." The wolf growled as he sniffed at the tools Cole had imagined into being strewn around them. Including a reamer, pick, punti and plyers. Along with some metal working tools he'd used to work up his handheld weapon.

"Oh, don't worry." Cole said smiling at the gigantic, mangy grey wolf.

"I ate a whole tub of ice cream before coming in here. And besides…" With a swift motion, he threw the little ball as high and far as he could. Fixing in his mind what he wanted it to do. He almost broke his concentration to laugh; when it looked as though the wolf wanted to chase the little spark of light. "I only have to do the process once." Cole said as the little ball hit the ground thirty yards away with the sound of breaking glass and a popping firecracker noise. There was a second's noise of leather sliding over rubber, and a flash of light that lit up the entire courtyard.

The light settled into a blue-green puffy little cloud that looked like cotton candy. And was about two and a half feet in diameter. It spread an eerie dull light, five feet in every direction around it. Cole whooped and threw up a fist. He turned back to the wolf.

"Once I can make myself believe it'll work, and I have all the pieces in my head." Cole held out his hand, where another of the glass cloud grenades appeared. "I can make as many as I want."

The wolf, however, was still starring. Transfixed on the little cloud. Cole smiled to himself, as this was the effect he had hoped for. He moved quickly over to the little cloud to inspect it.

"Fascinating." The wolf growled under his breath as they came up on it. "To have come so far in your short life, and with so little power." Cole tried to be flattered by the comment. He rubbed his neck as he replied.

"Well, all I really did was take a few aspects of basic chemistry and mix them together."

"But…what will it do?" The wolf pawed at the cloud with cat-like curiosity. Cole watched intently.

"Before I answer that. I need to know if all the constructs in here are connected to…uh. The…original construct." Cole said as he watched the wolf bat around the little cloud.

"You wish to know-if they are driven-by my own thoughts and knowledge?" The wolf was batting and dodging around the little ball. But stopped to answer its own question. "Yes…and no."

"Caaan you clarify that big guy?" Cole asked pushing the ball in between the wolf's legs to encourage him to keep playing.

"Each of them-," The wolf ducked down with his haunches up in the air and stopped the ball with the top of his head. "Were created by my own thoughts and actions. So, in a way, yes. They came from me. But if you are asking if they continue to be controlled or informed by my current experiences; Then the answer is no." The wolf came up on his hind legs and bit down hard on the glowing cloud.

"AAACH!" He spit it out and shook his head violently before staring haggardly and bug eyed at Cole. "It has burned me!" He growled furiously. Cole gave him a sly smile and turned back to collect his tools.

"Then it worked!" Cole called over his shoulder. As he walked, he heaved a great sigh of relief. If the wolf was still connected to the constructs they were about to go up against. He would have been fighting an enemy that knew everything there was to know about him.

Also, his experiment had worked, and the wolf wasn't yet attacking him. He picked up the implements he had used to create his cloud grenade as the wolf bridled his anger with him. One by one absorbing the tools while little beads of energy flowed from the melting tools, and back into his body. There, he thought to himself, not such a waste after all. When he was done, he turned to face the monstrous, mangy animal; who still looked rather surly and was no longer interested in the cloud. With his chest puffed out, he took on his most elvish voice as he asked a question.

"Now, are you prepared to meet the darkest of your innermost being, Huon?" The wolf's bug eyes thankfully, turned amused.

"What did you call me?" He growled. Cole waved a hand dejectedly and quickly broke character.

"He's from one of the classics. He's kind of like…god's favorite guard dog." At this the wolf genuinely laughed. So hardily Cole began to feel chagrinned about it. "I'm not saying *I'm* God. He feels compelled to help my favorite characters…does all kinds of cool stuff." Cole sidled off lamely as the wolf's laughter died down. Still chuckling, but more seriously, he asked.

"I think the better question is. Are you ready, little one?" Cole patted his stomach through his ghostly grey t-shirt.

"I'm all filled up and ready to go." He added as much bravado as he could to the words but in truth, he was a bit terrified. "And since you're in a laughing mood now…" He waged a finger at the monster and made a face. "I just want you to know that I'll be purifying your spirit, with pancakes and rocky road." The wolf stared at him silently.

Most of the journey up the cliff was spent with Cole making the argument that if the wolf didn't let him ride on his back. They may as well end the journey right then. After much convincing and promises, the wolf had finally consented, but only after they reached the top. At that point Cole felt satisfied and went over his mental checklist in preparation. It wasn't a hard journey as the path zigged and zagged in a long and obtusely angled path. Which made him feel as though they were on a leisurely hike. If it weren't dark and foreboding all around him. He hardly would have felt like they were storming an enemy position at all.

"Damn if I never get to be Frodo." He muttered as they neared the top.

"Hm?" The wolf seemed preoccupied as Cole knew very well, he could hear him.

"Oh nothing, you're just crushing my dreams. There wouldn't happen to be a tower or volcano on the other side of the cliffs. Maybe…a tunnel?" Ba'l; now Huon in Cole's mind, since he'd named him anyways: Huon, gave a lamented huff.

"My mind is not so large as to encompass all that anymore." He replied unnecessarily.

"Don't sell yourself short." Cole said smiling to himself. "Hey, what exactly *is* over there?" He thought it might have been a good question to ask before setting out. But it felt too premeditated to be heroic.

"It is merely a valley half again the size of this one. Though the path wraps down in one long arch along the cliff and opens at the back end." Cole digested this.

"So, full frontal assault from the rear then?" He asked jovially.

"I fear you may not be taking this as seriously as you should be." The wolf gave him a sidelong look as they came up to the top of the jagged black ridgeline. Cole made a show of taking a deep breath and slapping his face with both hands. Though he only felt the faintest pressure in his current form.

"Game face." He said somberly. He motioned to the wolf. "If I can't be Frodo, I'll take Gandalf."

"Excuse me?" The wolf botherdly asked.

"Come on, you promised. Don't crush a kids dreams twice in one day." The wolf stared at him for a long moment as if he weren't going to comply. But with a long groaning rumble, he knelt so Cole could scramble up to his back. Even Cole's yoga practiced body was uncomfortable riding horse style as the wolf was larger than a Clydesdale. So, he settled for crouching with one foot on either side of the wolfs giant spine. A hand clutched to a fistful of the wolf's thick, wiry grey hair.

"Prepare yourself." Huon said as he stood. They walked the last few paces to the outer edge of the path. The edge of the jagged rock gave way to a black sky as they rose high enough to see down into the valley.

Spirits of a dark nature, even the pieces of them such as the ones that resided in the spirits' mind. Had eyes that glowed like the orange coals at the base of a particularly large fire. If Cole's first battles with the wolf had taught him anything. He had expected the constructs of the powerful spirits' thoughts to take several forms. Ranging from those that flew and those that ran. What he hadn't expected was the sheer number of them that still resided in the wolf's mind. Apparently, he'd only cleared off the front porch.

So numerous were they that the dark valley beneath them looked like a bad adaptation of the 1985 Live Aid Concert. If the entire crowd had lit lighters in both hands and started a mosh pit. And that looking like such a good time. Had attracted dive bombing batlike creatures to join in. The light from their eyes wasn't bright enough to make distinct shapes visible. But here and there Cole thought he caught a glimpse of a ragged dog or tiny winged body as it dove to attack one of them. But it was the noise that sent a shiver down Cole's spine.

There were the animalistic noises he expected to hear. Screeching and growling as any animal would in a fight. But it also sounded like many of them could speak. Though in a strange guttural language Cole didn't understand.

As more of the noise reached them. Cole felt a shiver go down the wolf's spine that continued into a light trembling. He didn't know if it were fear or anger that prompted this reaction. But it was the most vulnerable thing he'd ever seen out of his partner.

"Don't worry big guy." Cole whispered. Though over the din of noise and fury of action, he doubted anything would notice them. That was about to change.

"We've got this." He stood up on the wolf's back, steadied himself and threw up his arms. In a flurry, like a snowstorm was raging inside him. Tiny beads of light traveled through his body and out of his hands. As they reached the edges of his ghostly skin, they formed into his cloud grenades. Cole sent as many as he could muster soaring high above the valley to give them some time. Moving his hands right lo left for a good spread. He thought he may have over done it when he felt a large portion of his energy drain out of him. But he had faith they would work to his advantage. He knelt back down and grabbed a tuft of the wolfs hair.

"Let's go." Cole pulled on the wolf's hair in the direction of the path leading off to their right. And down into the valley. With the sound of massive scraping paws on stone. They descended into what looked like a serial killer's playground nightmare.

As they passed the mouth of the path Cole pointed his palm at the leftmost edge of the precipice and produced a massive five-foot speaker there. In a flourish, he had the microphone he would need for it. Huon, for his part, was a fairly steady ride as he ran lightly at twice the pace of any Olympian. But Cole was still having trouble keeping his balance.

Regardless, he in took a massive breath and bellowed his most ferocious battle cry. And as if his energy rode along the sound wave. Each of the tiny nodules on the top of the exploding golf balls lit up like a star in the deep, malignant blackness.

Added onto the list of many things Cole didn't understand. Was that the dark spirits were almost uncontrollably attracted to his energy. Especially the weaker ones. It was like crack to a year's long addict that had been out of stock for a while. And the flying constructs reacted to the little sparks of light, like lightning-fast bugs to a zapper. But in this case, an exploding zapper that emitted a wave of light and acted as a flame to the spirits. Turning them to instant ash and producing a little cloud at the center. And as the clouds fell, they were surrounded by cyclones of the little monsters that burned to nothing at their touch.

And so it was, as Cole bellowed his war cry. That the first of his little glass grenades was swarmed. And upon hitting it with any amount of force, say a bite or a clutching talon. The nitrogen triiodide that lined the nodule exploded. Rupturing the coiled glass at the center, filled with potassium iodide. Which then mixed with the fluid that filled most of the little ball. Hydrogen peroxide and if you ever took chemistry, you guessed it, dish soap. This process, in the real world creates a great deal of heat. So, to Cole the only thing he had to do to do, magically speaking; was combine the expanding cloud with his purifying energy. Which he made work, in thinking that heat is a purifying force and mixing like energies.

It was no Dumbledore level transfiguration, he knew. But he had been working from scratch and had no Merlin to teach him. As it was, the dark night filled with violently crazed spirits. Lit up like the fourth of July. Wave after wave of blue green popped and incinerated the little constructs in droves. And they burned away at the edges with the same color as their ember, glowing eyes.

As the field below lit up with light and Cole's war cry. All the constructs that weren't transfixed on the purifying energy. Turned their eyes toward the giant speaker he had left at the top of the path. All, that is, except for one. As Cole scanned the field they locked eyes, grey-gold to glowing red. Cole's cry stopped at the sight of the creature that had stared in the past four years of his nightmares. The form Huon had been when Cole had first met him. And that Cole now suspected the great wolf had either split or escaped from and run off, somehow.

It had the body of a sasquatch. Nine feet if it were an inch. Thickly muscled with a protruding yet strong looking stomach and tree trunk legs. Its head looked like a mixture of dog and man, but more savage than either. Even as they stared each other down the monster bared its sharp fangs and melted into the now higher level of pandemonium that had started to rage.

At the same time around twenty of the dog-like monsters made a b-line for the opening of the ten-foot-wide path. Evidently, they had figured out where the noise had originated. Cole wouldn't be able to concentrate on finding the beast again.

He threw the microphone aside and pulled out the berretta from the holster on his hip. It wouldn't need reloading or buck like the real thing. So, no feeling like a real cowboy. But it did fire bolts of the same purifying force in the clouds that were now vaporizing the flyers. And it was the closest thing to a wand he had been able to make work.

He drew the berretta up as the first of the runners came around the bend of the path. Glowing demon eyes drawing nearer by the step. Huon let out a savage, chest rattling growl. As Cole started firing what looked like stormtrooper blaster shots of an aquamarine shade. The energy for the shots ran swiftly from the clumps of energy throughout his body. Moving in swift tangled patterns through his arm and into the gun in his hand as he pulled the trigger.

The first three went down mid sprint when the shots hit them. Tumbling and burning away in concert. He missed the fourth, but it was forced to dodge his shot and skid to a halt as they passed. Cole turned swiftly and shot it to ash as it wheeled around. While he was counting his lucky stars he was almost thrown from Huon's back.

The great beast was forced to slow as he caught a leaping spirit in his giant maw. He slowed to stop as he shook the dog savagely with an equally savage snarl. The dog growled, kicked and scratched uselessly. Losing some of its muster as the wolf turned his head to give Cole a clean shot. Cole had barely managed to hold onto the wolf in the process. But finished a deep breath and fired, turning the construct to ash.

The time they had spent stopped had allowed several of the other creatures to reach them. None were large enough to take the monstrous wolf head on. But it didn't stop them from darting in to bite at Huon's legs as they surrounded the pair. Several of them cursed and shouted in the grating guttural language Cole didn't know as they attacked. Cole was forced to plop down and clench up for dear life. As the next few moments turned into jerking, shouting chaos.

Strings of glowing red eyes darted back and forth, in and out between becoming visible in flashes of blue-green. Some were completely bald and all were viciously angry looking as a raccoon with rabies. Drooling and spitting intermittently in that hideous language. Cole was firing shot after shot when the wolf wasn't dodging or snatching at the nearest attacker. It took several moments of abandoned violence before they caught up to the last spirits movements.

"Left!" Huon hissed. Cole caught one of the dogs leaping up to grab his foot and shot it center mass. At that point they were finally clear enough to get moving again. And Cole caught the last two as they left them behind with Huon's speed. Cole caught his breath and calmed his nerves in those last few seconds they had before coming to the bottom of the path. They came into the opening of the valley to one of the strangest, and most terrifying scenes Cole had ever seen.

The flashing light from his grenades were growing less frequent. Allowing only brief seconds of a good view of the valley floor. The glowing clouds provided only a small field of vision directly around them. And even though they were falling like snowflakes in a light storm there were gaps everywhere of utter blackness. Mitigated only by the streaking of red orange light that represented the angry spirits eyes.

Strangely, yet fortunately, none of the spirits even seemed to know they existed. They were all too enthralled by the clouds of energy falling to the ground. As his eyes shifted swiftly, left, right and upward. Cole realized that most of the flyers had already been vaporized. Leaving a few of the glass grenades to fall untouched to pop into little ground clouds. Clouds that were immediately and savagely attacked by the creatures on the ground.

They watched as several clouds turned into disordered streaks of light as jaws clamped down on them and death shook them. Swinging to and fro only to be dropped. The drops being followed by creepily human-like death screams. The dog like being that screamed its last did so while burning away in the glow of the blue-green light.

Even more disconcerting were the monsters that weren't entirely animal looking. Some looked as though they were mid transformation between man and monster. Though none had made the transformation as well as the sasquatch beast that had melted into the fray. Some were wolf bodied and man limbed while others were the other way around. Both with varying facial features taking on one form more than the other. The worrying thing Cole noticed was that those ones didn't burn away immediately like the others.

They went from moving swiftly on all fours, to snatching up the glowing clouds and running away on two feet. It took them so long to burn, that they had bitten off large chunks of the clouds like they were eating cotton candy. And ended up melting away from the inside. Cole leapt down from the wolf's back and leveled the berretta at the nearest one.

"Wait." The wolf growled in his best whisper.

"Do not draw unnecessary attention while they are doing our work for us. Your invention has proved to be extremely useful." Cole merely nodded to the wolf and crouched down to watch the strange scene. The sounds of human-like voices and screams echoed around them in frenzy. Upon closer attention it did seem as if the half wolf-like creatures all seemed to be moving in the same direction.

It took only a few moments for the sounds of screaming, pattering feet and scraping claws to die down. Cole felt a swelling of pride that his little experiment had been so successful. Instead of patting himself on the back, though. He patted the leg of the giant wolf that waited next to him. To his surprise, the wiry tangled hair the wolf usually sported; Now felt soft and full as any well-groomed pet. He looked the wolf up and down and swore he could see some sort of higher vitality in the beast. Its tangled and matted hair had taken on a well-groomed husky's coat.

"Hey." Cole said, unbefitting the moment. "You look good."

The wolf said nothing. They both waited quietly at the mouth of the dark, eerie passage, as the valley in front of them became still and silent. The flashes of light had ceased. So that if one of his little clouds weren't near. Cole expected he wouldn't have been able to see the wolf at all.

"Observe." Huon pointed his snout at a point off to their left. The direction all the were-wolf creatures had been running. In an area a few hundred yards away it looked as though they'd gathered around a hundred clouds. All stacked or near each other.

"Should we...go over there?" Cole asked tentatively.

"It is most likely a trap." The Wolf looked at him. Cole looked back and shrugged.

"We came to do a job. Let's finish it." The wolf let out a pleased growl, it sounded softer and less grating than it had been in the years Cole had known him.

"You will be great one day, you know." The wolf started moving toward the gathered clouds. It took Cole a moment to take those words in and he had to run to catch up. He rubbed his neck as he took his place beside Huon.

"Don't go all soft on me right before a fight. You're going to mess me up." They were pitched into utter darkness as they left behind the nearest cloud. Cole's equilibrium had a hard time staying steady as he no longer had any reference points to go by. So much so that after he had almost tripped several times, he started lifting his knees higher than he would normally. Keeping his eyes transfixed on the cluster of clouds they were moving toward.

After they'd walked about fifty meters. New sounds started to creep their way through the darkness. A slithering, like silk over carpet. And the sound of a woman's whisper. The same unknown language trickled into his ears to make Cole shiver down to his toes. The whispers came near enough to be heard but not near enough to pinpoint or take a shot at. It sounded as if there were more than one, but he couldn't be sure as it sounded extremely fast. Moving in circles around them as they walked on, fear mounting. When they drew near to the cloud grouping. Cole saw a pair of tiny eyes peering at them from off to their left, only an inch or so from the ground. He made to fire at it by raising the beretta, but he would have to stop to try to hit such a small target.

"No. It has a hard time striking moving targets. It wants to paralyze your movement." The wolf instructed.

At this pronouncement there was a high, cold laugh that slithered into place behind them. Whatever it was, a snake Cole guessed, unafraid at being heard now. The laughter rushed at them. so that they were forced to run the last few paces into the lit area. Cole with comically high knees, both to not trip or be bitten. He would never admit to the wavering howl that escaped his mouth as he did so. Or to turning around to blind fire and miss several times when he had passed into the cluster of clouds. The snake it seemed, was not willing to follow. As the clouds were only at most, a couple feet apart here.

Huon glared at Cole after he'd given up firing at the snake. Cole looked back defiantly.

"I could have hit it." He defended himself. "Anyway. We came to spring a trap…they know we're here at least." He started moving toward the center in a dignified manner.

Huon followed, kicking aside puffy clouds as he walked. They reached the near center and stood waiting in the dull light for what seemed an hour. Though was truly only a minute or so. Cole was beginning to feel more ridiculous by the second as they looked round and round. For any sign of the enemy they knew they would face.

"Wheeere are they, do you suppose?" He asked continually scanning the edges of the light for any sign. Even as he said it. Glowing red eyes began to slink into view from out of the darkness.

"Oh…Never mind." The words escaped Coles lips, smaller than he would have liked, but he lifted his weapon none the less.

"Patience." Huon whispered.

Cole took several deep breaths as one of the sets of eyes, out of the ten or so that were left. Deeper and brighter than the others, rose to stand at its natural height. With a growl the sound of an idling semi-truck. The sasquatch stepped into the very edge of the light. It's features more harsh and jagged in the glow. Its long razor-sharp teeth bared as it stared at Cole from a height several feet above his own.

With a spike of fear and anger, the memories of sprinting for his life as this monster devoured his friends flashed through his mind. Bara, Ingrid, Julian and Luna, the first little spirits he had turned when he had discovered his power. Had sacrificed themselves when they'd all so determinately entered the monster's domain the first couple of times. Cole couldn't help himself. He snarled back at the sasquatch and lifted the berretta. He fired several shots before

Huon made it clear that this is what the others had been waiting for. His shots merely hit the sasquatch in small glowing red marks. Not doing the amount of damage he would have liked.

"Cole!" Huon hissed and crouched in preparation.

From four different directions, demon dog spirits, zigzagged toward the pair. With the sound of scratching paws and heavy breath they drew nearer. Cole couldn't get a good read on any of them. He found himself turning this way and that in confusion as they came close. Taking advantage, one of the beasts leapt directly at Cole's face from ten feet away, jaws open wide. It took two swift shots for it to turn to ash.

As it burned away, Cole's vision was obstructed as the rushing puff of soot hit him full in the face. He waved it away as quickly as he could, but as he did so. He felt a lightning strike pressure penetrate his ankle and shoot up his leg. Not needing to see at that point he pointed the berretta at the point he was being bitten and fired. The pressure lightened significantly but didn't dissipate fully. The sound of Huon's grating snarl slapped his ears. Cole turned to see one of the other hounds hanging from his flank by its teeth. Unlike Cole, Huon did bleed in this place. And silver white blood had started to leak from the place the demon hound was holding on.

The one shadow was hindering the great wolfs movement as he held the other hound down with a forepaw. Massive jaws clamped down on its neck. Cole took quick aim and turned the hanging wolf to ash. Though the demon hound vanished, the punctures it left behind were creating a silver wet path down Huon's leg. The wolf seemed not to care as he used the free movement to send the other hound flying. Like a rag doll it tumbled into a clump of clouds to be vaporized with a choked scream.

After a quick scan Cole went to a knee to check on his leg. Though he didn't bleed in this place, every injury he took drained energy from him rapidly. And he had already used more than he'd thought he would need for this venture already. Next time he would confirm enemy numbers, if there was one.

He felt his eyes go wide as he observed that his injury was not that of a many toothed dog bite. But two points of a dully glowing silver snake bite. As he was just wondering whether venom had any effect on him in here, pressure flashed up his leg. To be met by little glowing speckles of his own energy traveling down through his body.

He remembered that there had been four hounds coming their way at the start of this round. Four, and one snake. Evidently one of them had been a distraction to allow the snake to bite him.

The hound rushed from behind the nearest clump of clouds where it had been waiting. It was too close for Cole to get off a shot. And with him crouched like this, his neck would be an easy target. He pursed his lips. But kept his eyes open and glaring as the beasts' open jaws made to clamp down on his throat. Huon's massive jaws intercepted the blow as they crushed down on the back half of the demon's body. So that Cole only got a pained scream to his face. Sharp teeth only inches from penetrating his most vital area. The great wolf dragged and threw the demon into the nearest cloud as the next wave came in at them.

"On your feet!" Huon growled as he took a defensive stance.

One of the half wolf, half man types was heading their way on two feet. It took three shots to send it into a scorpion style fall as it vaporized. Cole was afraid that it took so many. Either the beasts were getting stronger, or he was getting weaker. But there was no time to worry as several more of the dogmen came bounding over and dodging between clouds. Cole caught one of them in the shoulder mid leap. It was enough to take it off balance and send it sprawling into a cloud. As it burned away the cloud it had run into came rolling to Cole's feet. With a flash of inspiration Cole kicked it in the path of the last doglike demon heading their way. It hit the creature in the side of the head while it was rounding another cloud. It burned like the others. Cole may be getting weaker, but the clouds still did the trick.

He sprinted a few steps to snag one of the clouds. Pressure and weakness spiking up his bitten leg made him slower than he would normally be. He brought the cloud up to use as a one-handed shield as a wolf man reached him. He managed to get it between them but still took the brunt of the tackle. They both hit the ground, the creature screaming in Cole's face as its chest caved and burned. Cole put two shots in its ribs just in case. As the creature burned away Cole turned his face away and watched from his back as if in slow motion.

Huon, looking more white than grey now. Tossed the last of the smaller creatures twenty feet into the clouds. But the angle of his throw left him at just the right angle to miss the gigantic sasquatch's charge. It rushed in, receiving only little ember scrapes and singed hair from the clouds it kicked aside. With a grotesque and savage roar, it slammed its shoulder into the great wolf at breakneck speed. The wolf let out a yelping howl that would have broken Cole's ear drums in the physical world. He was sent tumbling, a spray of aqua marine clouds flying off into the black night at the force of his fall.

The monster turned its blazing eyes on him as Cole stood up. With a growl of defiance Cole leveled the berretta.

"You okay big guy?" He shouted as he fired shots as fast as they would go. But they didn't slow it down as it started to run at him. As it took its second running step there was a thunderous roar as Huon leapt from twenty feet away and clamped down on the monster's arm. The wolf turned the creature as he dropped his haunches and dragged him away from his partner.

The sounds of pain, rage and determined strength that emanated from the two monsters was incredible. The force of it reverberated his being from head to foot with so much pressure that Cole almost threw down his weapon and ran. As useless as it had been against the real monsters here. But he knew he never could have done that.

He looked down at the useless berretta. The creature's skin had been too thick for the projectiles to do any real damage. Whatever thoughts and experiences that had given the creature being here, must be rooted deep within the wolf's psyche.

Cole had always taken his inspiration for creating his magic from his favorite set of wizard detective novels. Using the memories of his life as the fuel to power his will and guide his imaginings into reality. It centered around the generosity of the woman who took him in and gave him a life anyone would dream of. His gratitude for the many people who had loved and supported his tinkering. Ann, never treating him as a pariah for his weirdness. From all the knowledge he'd managed to intake through his experience and his studying over his short life. It had worked relatively well thus far.

But as he watched his partner struggle, ripping and pulling at the monster that had held him captive to madness for who knows how long. He came to appreciate that these two beings were one in the same. And what he was watching was the fight for the future of this strange being's destiny. That Huon was bleeding and struggling in order to move toward something better. Something that Cole had promised by taking him in, giving him his confidence and showing him a different life. And that the beast was giving it his all to live up to that confidence and walk that path with him.

He realized that to win this fight, he would have to stop taking that for granted. As when they had jettisoned spirits out of the wolf's domain. He reached out to meld his will with his partners. Something they had only ever done when transferring a spirit or making one of their doorways. Cole felt the great wolf's hope surge into his chest as the sparks of light that ran through his body flared. And the berretta changed.

It shimmered and lengthened as Cole held onto all the memories he could remember of the great beast. Their successes at turning evil spirits. Their conversations at finding and destroying the great hinderance they saw to humanity. All the things the wolf had taught him over the last few years. But most importantly, of Huon's faith in him that they would succeed. The grip of the handgun turned into the wired hilt of a sword as a long blade extended from the barrel. In just a few seconds, a silver blade gleamed. The shining silver 'Ulfbhert' glowed the brighter down half its length.

The amount of energy it took from him made his head feel like it was stuffed with cotton balls for a second. But he took little time to gain his bearings as he heard another yelping scream from Huon. The sasquatch was attempting to rip the giant wolf off its arm with a clawed hand. Cole zeroed in on the bright blood that was starting to run down the side of Huon's face. He followed it up to the jagged piece of what remained of his left ear. Apparently, the monster had taken his chunk of flesh, but the wolf had held on. Chest rumbling, wolf eyes bugging in fear and rage.

Without thinking, Cole bellowed, and charged.

Huon had succeeded in turning the monster away from Cole's position. So, he was out of the sasquatch's sight as he came to a full sprint; ignoring the weakness of his leg. He held the sword in both hands at sternum level and crashed into the monster at full speed. The blade sunk deep into the monster's hamstring. It roared, back arching in pain as Cole hit the hilt of the sword with his chest.

His momentum sent him up and off his toes. He lost grip on the sword and felt the briefest moment of embarrassed disgust as his face smacked against the monster's hairy butt. He was immediately flung back and to the side as he bounced off, trying to catch his balance. His injury not doing him any favors.

The sasquatch seemed to gain freakish strength by being stabbed. It ripped its arm free of Huon's mouth. Twisting, it back handed Cole while he was still stumbling away from it. Cole felt lighting flash through his shoulder. He was flung several feet before he bounced off the top of a cloud, tumbled and lay still.

The monster swung back around. Huon jumped back as it tried to smash him in the chest with a with a curled claw. It landed a glancing blow that still brought out a woof as Huon backed away as fast as his injured leg would let him. He scanned the field for any sign of Cole and luckily the monster wasn't in any shape to follow. Having a foot of sword through its thigh, it merely watched as Huon backed away. Its evil eyes narrowed.

Cole was just barely aware he was conscious at all. He was just marveling at how pretty the clouds were and how much closer to the ground they were that night. When he noticed a little glass ball. A shining nodule stuck in a crevice of the little cloud sparked his memory; he remembered where he was. He lifted his head slowly, unable to do much more.

Huon was circling the sasquatch, a fierce snarl on his face. Both limped, with the monster only able to follow Huon's movement from a standing position. The blade protruding from its leg seemed to have taken at least some of its attention and Cole watched as the monster reached down. It grabbed the blade in a claw and drew the sword out. Where the blade was removed, slow, uneven ember lines burned away at the beasts pitch black and shadowy flesh. The hand it used to draw the blade shown brighter with ember scratches as the monster spoke. Cole was most unnerved by the smooth deep baritone voice. Something he wouldn't have thought it could manage through its crocodile teeth.

"Everything you do…" It said in a low, slow and menacing voice. It threw the sword aside and it tumbled and slid to within three feet of Cole's reach. "Results in death." It continued.

Cole read the inscription on the blade. He had always been fascinated with the making of the Ulfbhert swords. In an age when iron was just coming into its own in the world. And bronze was still being used. Some crazy genius, emphasis on crazy, genius; Vikings. Had thought they could imbue the souls of their ancestors or enemies into their swords. Using their remains in the sword making process, they thought they'd succeeded. With their swords cutting their enemies weapons and defenses into ribbons, it was an easy thought. What they had unwittingly done, though, was add enough carbon to the iron to make a more than passable steel. Cole heaved himself onto a knee with great effort. His head spun as he wrangled the little glass ball from the crevice in the cloud and crawled drunkenly over to the sword.

"Your actions…" The monster purred, lengthening the last word in a loud whisper. "Will bring me back to life." It breathed. Huon froze in place, eyes bugging at the words.

"Hey, ugly." Cole stood. Blade in one hand, little glass ball in the other. It was all he could do to make himself heard after the effort it had taken him to stand. The sasquatch turned; fury written all over its haggard face. The arm Huon had attacked hung limply at its side.

"Think fast." Cole threw the little glass ball at the monster as he said it.

With its good arm the creature caught the grenade before it could hit its face. With a pop, and the tinkling sound of breaking glass. The beasts hand exploded. Replaced by a glowing green-blue puff ball. The flash of light that came with it left slashing burn marks across the monster's face and shoulders.

For a split second they all stared at it, the monster in angry surprise. Huon and Cole with amusement. But when the little cloud tipped slowly off the beast's wrist, leaving only a burning ember stump. It roared in hideous anger and used the last of its rage to charge at Cole.

Its roar was followed by a thunderous, whip cracking snarl as Huon also charged. Cole took a stance. Knees bent, Ulfbhert sword poised at his hip with the tip pointed at the charging beast. He bared his teeth and growled back at the monster as Huon collided with the back of its legs. It pitched forward, only ten feet away. Cole thrust the blade with all the might he could dredge up. That coupled with its own momentum and Huon's push. Sent the blade straight through the base of its throat and a foot out of the back of the monster's neck.

And as his mind had been on the Ulfbhert only seconds before. Cole didn't think he could have stopped the spell from happening. The sword pulsed out a wave of unseen force. The monster gurgled out the last bit of its death roar. And somehow in less than a few seconds. There was an implosive wind, and the beast was drawn and sucked into the blade in a flash of aquamarine fire. Cole felt the last bit of energy he had get sucked into the blade at the same time. He hit his knees as the newly forged black blade tinged with ember and blue-green fire, clattered to the ground.

Cole fell to his side as Huon, now glowing white, did the same. He only had the faintest inkling that his partner seemed to be in massive amounts of pain. He was glowing brighter and brighter with golden yellow light, twisting and writhing as he choked out pained screams. Cole realized he must be losing consciousness because he wasn't seeing Huon anymore. Whoever it was stumbling over to him and examining the snake bite on his leg wasn't his partner at all.

Whoever she was, she was human.

"Oh man…didn't see that coming." Cole said as he fully lost consciousness. The young woman turned a bright golden eyed look of concern on him.

Ch. 5

Cole was comatose for three days after the event. Genie had found him face-down on the ground halfway to crawling toward his bed. After he hadn't shown up to breakfast or her class, she'd come searching for him, and found him cold as ice but sweating. After she had helped him under his covers, he had refused hospital care and assured her he would be fine. She had left to take care of her students.

Cole had just enough energy to lift the leg of his jeans to inspect the radiating pain that emanated from his left ankle. He was terrified to see that the bite had translated out into the regular world. Rather than being silver, the bite was two black pinpoints. Black veins seeped from the two points at a diameter of around four inches. Cole had no idea what to do about the bite as the radiating pain steadily grew worse and the veins leaked out further. Luckily, he wasn't alone.

Shortly after Genie had left, Cole was blithering and sweating with his head back on his pillows. When an apparition appeared from out of the silver wolf bracelet that lay on his bedside table. She was the closest thing to a goddess Cole had ever seen. Golden brown skin shown from beneath her bundled white robe. More blanket looking than clothing. Two thickly woven white braids wrapped from the front of her high brow. Connected behind her head and ran down past her knees. She spent most of the morning sitting at the edge of Cole's bed, leaving no indentation. And she produced no feeling at her touch but radiating heat, to the point of burning.

She massaged the veins of black venom back toward the bite marks. Whispering in the language they'd heard the night before. But from her mouth it was more soothing than fear inducing. When the veins had been coaxed back into the two bite marks. She used a complicated series of hand signs and wrist movements, golden sparks seeping from her fingertips to transform the marks. They warbled and extended into what looked like an elongated version of the number eight. An infinity sign, Cole noted. She finished by adding a circle of gold around the new mark and stood up with a deep breath. When the process was complete, she stood breathing heavily but with obvious relief.

The pain subsided quickly but Cole only felt himself coming back to his senses by a degree every hour or so. He was still near unconsciousness when the goddess apparition was taking her last deep breath and he tried to address her.

"Thanks." He said in a whisper. The loudest he could manage now. She turned to him and smiled. A bright and glorious smile that lit up the area surrounding her so that she almost looked as if she had a halo around her head.

"It is I, that should be thanking you." Her voice was a melody of low Alto. And the sound seemed to melt him as it entered his ears. Filling him with warmth and comfort. She moved over to stand next to his shoulder.

"I have contained the curse, when you are back on your feet we will discuss it further. But for now, it will not hurt you." She placed her burning hand to Cole's forehead. He sat in confusion and awe at what he was witnessing.

"For now, we need to rest and recover our strength." Cole didn't have the motivation or time to argue as he felt heat radiate from her hand and he slipped into unconsciousness again.

For the next several days Cole slipped in and out of consciousness like this. Periodically waking to assure Genie he wasn't on drugs. At separate times, to assure the new apparition that he was fine. And after the first day; to watch the goddess meander around his room. Taking excessively long moments to run her fingers along the polished redwood walls. To inspect the spines of the books on his shelves. To sit in the spot Cole usually used to enter the wolf's realm. And in one instance, to stand at his window for hours. Hugging tightly to herself with her beautiful eyes observing Genie's classes and the stillness of the forest when they were over. Intermittently on the verge of laughter and sobs in equal measure. Tears running down her dazzlingly beautiful face.

When Genie had come to talk to him on several occasions. The sprit had been present, but only stood in the corner of the room. A slight smile on her strawberry lips, her golden eyes glowing. As Genie expressed her concern and Cole managed to convince her not to not to worry. That he must have eaten something rotten or caught a virus at the fair he had gone to sell his wears.

On the fourth day Cole woke with a start, sitting up quickly and flexing his fists. All the strength had come back to his mind and limbs, and he quickly scanned the room. There was no sign of the apparition, so he turned his eyes on the wolf bracelet. If it wasn't just his imagination, he could have sworn the aquamarine had added a light shade of golden light. Though it could have just been the gleam of morning that shown through his window. He meant to reach for it, but the rumbling in his stomach made him pause. He hadn't eaten in over three days, that had to take precedence. Figuring out what had become of his wolf partner wouldn't go well if he couldn't do anything to help anyway.

He felt emaciated and weak as he put on a set of the same plain cloths he usually wore. A thin grey t-shirt and dark jeans. He re-checked his room and in seeing only his bookshelves made his way to the kitchen. As he came down the hall the smell of heaven reached his nose, bacon. He came running into the room to see Ann sitting at the counter and Genie over the stove. They were obviously mid conversation. But they both stopped when they heard his quick footsteps entering. Genie turned to give an exaggerated clapping cheer. Ann turned and flashed him a radiant smile. At the sight of

Ann Cole felt something warm stir somewhere behind his sternum. It confused him, as he wasn't used to it. Though she couldn't possibly know that he'd felt it. He tried to hide his embarrassment behind the cheer Genie was giving his entrance. He bowed and thank you'd.

"You gave us quite a scare there kid." Genie said as Ann patted the seat next to her. It took only a second longer for him to respond than usual. The strange feeling in his chest churned and bubbled as he took his seat avoiding Ann's eyes. Genie was giving him a sly look when he'd sat and made to look at her. How did that woman always know? He wondered. Ann gave him a quick side hug and Cole felt the heat in his cheat rise.

"What happened to you?" Ann asked in her familiar, even tenner. Cole turned to answer her but only found himself staring at her. Had she always been this vibrant? He asked internally. Her green eyes so deeply interesting? He was just thinking that the ring of yellow gold that surrounded her iris' melded perfectly with the light shade of green. When she gave him a quizzically humorous look. She did it so well, he thought.

"Are…you, feeling better yet?" She said it through a light laugh. But whatever look he was giving her made her high cheek bones redden slightly as she did. She shifted slightly in her seat. Even the little movement excited him and Cole mirrored her laugh while his face also reddened. Genie leaned over the counter and laid two steaming plates down in front of them. Each was piled with bacon, eggs and a mix of Cole's favorite fruits. It would only be a few milliseconds before his sudden fascination with Ann turned into actual mouthwatering.

"Maybe he just needs to eat something." She said loudly in this ear. Cole blinked stupidly and the hunger pangs from his stomach made him come back to his senses.

"Yeah." He said shaking his head. Genie rolled her eyes, turning back to the stove as Ann was giving him a skeptical look.

"Yeah, I'm…good. Thanks, I'm starving." He wasted no more time in stuffing bacon and eggs down his throat as fast as he could. Ann slowly turned away from him and did the same. Though in a much more dignified fashion. Genie continued the conversation they had been having before Cole entered the room. It faded into the background of Cole crushing down as much food as he could. Until Genie answered something Ann said unnecessarily loudly.

"So, next year then?" She asked as she tipped bacon grease into a glass container beside the burners. Ann cast a sidelong look at Cole when she answered.

"Yeah." She sounded a mix of excited and scared.

"Dad says he's ready to retire…and I should be ready by then." She didn't say the last part with much confidence. Cole stopped shoveling food into his mouth and thought about what she said. Next year…by that time the entire landscape of the world would probably be different. But he didn't think that was proper breakfast conversation. He swallowed hard; half chewed bacon scraping as it went down.

"That's great!" He choked with tears coming to his eyes. "I mean, there's no pleasing your dad but I'm sure you'll do amazing." He amended. Ann looked amused as she gave him a consenting look. The roiling in his chest felt a thrill of rejoicing.

"I'm sure you'll do your dad proud." Genie said. "But that means you only have the rest of the year to be a kid?" Genie glanced at Cole over her shoulder as she said it. Her suggestion to take Ann on his trip crossed his mind and the roiling in his chest became a steady boiling. So obvious, he thought as Genie raised an eyebrow at him. But out of his control, the boiling in his chest seemed to send a mass of steam up to his throat and out of his mouth.

"I'm going on a trip soon. You should come with me. We can be kids for the last time together." Cole was horrified at the outburst and his eyes widened.

Ann's face went from mock surprise, she and Genie had obviously been talking. But when Cole didn't take it back her look changed to an "Oh are we done playing?" sort of gesture. Leaning one shoulder and cocking her head slightly. Cole felt color rising in his face and he turned to keep shoveling food into his mouth. Ann continued to look at him for a long moment as Genie gave them a triumphant look over her shoulder.

"Is this why you were acting so weird the other day?" Ann asked genially when she was done glaring at him. It wasn't but telling her he was getting ready to purify an angry sprits brainscape wouldn't go over so well.

"I know how busy you are..." He dodged. He knew it made him look weak. Maybe she would say no because of it. That would save them both a lot of trouble, but the boiling in his chest hoped otherwise no matter the complications.

When he'd fully examined the contours of his eggs and she hadn't said anything he looked over at her, meaning to be defiant. Ann was looking at him as if calculating a math problem, the playfully sly note in her voice disarmed his defiance.

"Did you worry yourself sick about asking me to go with you?" She beamed as she pushed his shoulder. A gesture she'd done countless times before. This time though her fingers lingered just a little longer. Cole felt the boiling heat in his chest flare out to meet the touch. Impulsively and seeming without his control his hand reached out and stopped hers from falling away as she drew back. They both froze for a moment, fingertips to each other's palms. The heat from Cole's chest spread down to his fingertips. Ann's expression was bemused by the action. But as the heat reached her palm her green eyes blazed, and she raised her eyebrows and leaned in a bit, Cole copied her impulsively.

They stayed like that for a few seconds, staring each other down before Genie cleared her throat. Her eyebrows were raised too but she was holding back a smile. The two pulled their hands back and Cole turned his attention back to his plate. Ann took just a second longer to turn back to hers. A small smile touched her lips, a triumphant gleam in her eyes. It was followed by a look of calculation that stretched for another half minute.

"Well...so." Cole said after another few seconds. "Do you want to?" He stuffed several pieces of bacon in his mouth. The question had come out a bit more exasperated than he would have liked. In the intervening moment of Cole's chewing and Ann's deliberating. Little tiny bubbles of electric suspense were running through Cole's body down to his toes. Finally, Ann huffed out a tiny laugh.

"Well...I can't have you running around by yourself." Cole's inside sang, Ann continued nervously. "We all know what kind of weirdness your family brings back with you." They all laughed, relieving some of the pressure.

After all, they all knew that Genie had left home as a young programming prodigy. Only to come home toting a little refugee and becoming a yoga instructor. As well as she'd done with it, there were many in their small community that valued a different kind of work ethic. Ann's father being one of them. He had spent most of his life buying, selling, and building commercial real estate. So that almost every business in town had once been or was owned and built by his company.

"No offense Genie. I just don't know if he could pull it off as well as you did." Ann seemed to realize her statement could have been taken very badly. And was trying to make amends. She was teetering on babbling as she started to continue to apologize but Genie saved it again. She merely turned away from the stove with two mugs in her hands and bowed. She set her traditional steaming mugs of Masala Chai between them with a brilliant smile.

"No offense taken Ann, hush." She said imperiously. "I have twenty minutes before my first class. Are you still going to help me set up, or do you two need to do some last-minute planning you need

to do?" She directed the first part at Ann and the second at Cole.

Evidently, they had arranged something Cole was unaware of. Ann

looked at him with bright, expectant eyes. His heart almost leapt out

of his throat.

"We've got some time." He said quickly. Shooting himself

in the foot as Ann looked a little disappointed. But he still had a

situation that he needed to figure out as fast as possible.

"It'll be about a month before we go." He finished. Ann

wiggled a little in excitement, beaming at him. She grabbed her tea

and headed after Genie who had already started down the stairs. As

she passed, she ran a forefinger over his arm. This was an unfamiliar

touch, it left a line of electric heat that lingered long after she'd gone.

"Feel better soon." Ann said under her breath as she bounced

away on her toes. Right before she hit the first step, she twirled to

see Cole following her with his eyes. She gave him a wicked smile

that made his insides light up.

"Oh, wait." She said innocently. "Where are we going?"

Cole had a frantic moment of trying to remember exactly where they needed to go. And the nearest place they would even be allowed to land.

"Armenia."

■■■

Cole entered the wolf's domain in a mixture of bemused excitement and dread. What had come over him when he saw Ann? What had made him think it was a good idea to bring her along with him? He had no idea how he was going to keep the objective of his trip a secret while trying to behave like a normal tourist. But he couldn't stop himself. Whatever it was that he had been feeling had taken care of that. And he couldn't deny the excitement he felt at the thought of her coming with him, and the heat that seemed to be taking on a will of its own.

His confused and mismanaged plans were all driven from his thoughts when he stepped into an unfamiliar, familiar place. The wolf's domain had done a complete overhaul. There wasn't a sun in the sky, but the entire plain was bright as a midsummer morning. The grey moldy stone looked as if it had been power washed and polished to new. What had once been a foreboding dark castle now looked like a warm and inviting grey palace. With turrets made to be a good place to sit and read a book. But the most impressive change was the fountain. No longer thickly grimed and muddy. It was now a magnificent white marble, lined with gold writing in what looked close to ancient Hebrew. With golden depictions of a story, written in picture form underneath. Golden clear liquid, thicker than water but less thick than syrup flowed straight up and out of the tower at the center in a rushing torrent.

As he listened to the happily garbling, sprinkling fountain and admired the landscape. One of the shining gems that ringed the outer edge of the courtyard flared brightly. The affect was much muted by the brightness that was now the main feature of the landscape. But it could only mean that one of the spirits he and the wolf had turned was coming through.

Sure enough, a small Siamese cat flowed onto the grey stone gracefully and seemed in a hurry. Cole had named him Talos after he had found the little knee-high goblin. Running circles around, kicking the shins of and stomping on the toes of an insurance agent. Suggesting how to get away with fraud and drug other people's drinks. He had been one of Cole and the wolf's first jobs together. Talos didn't even notice him though. The cat ran swiftly behind the fountain as if he had a plan when he entered. Cole followed leisurely, taking in the new scenery. A few moments after Talos entered, Cole heard the sound of laughter from around the edge of the fountain.

It was the laughter of a young woman, high and soft. Yet it carried weight enough to make Cole want to sprint to find its source. To dance and revel in that joy and hear it play on forever. There was a different kind of warmth spreading through him now. An electrifying, energetic warmth that coursed through him and vibrated in his every cell. What was with him today? He wondered as he ran the last few steps to see what was going on. Even though he had no idea why they were laughing Cole felt a childish giggle escape his lips as he came up on them.

It was the Goddess apparition that had been wandering around his room and crying. The one who had kept the snake venom from taking hold. There was only one real explanation as to who she was. He just had to make sure before he believed it.

She was sitting with her back against the side of the fountain. An excited Talos playing at her feet. She was beyond beautiful. At a level of perfection untouchable by human comparison. Vitality and strength radiated from her as she poked and played with the happy cat. She turned to meet Cole's eyes as he neared. Her golden yellow eyes bright and expectant. He slowed to an immediate stop and cocked his head at her. She mirrored his movement, looking amused at his reaction while still smiling. The move was more pronounced on her part. As one tall ear, and one quarter of an ear turned toward him as she did so. She must have had them tucked under her braids when he had first seen her. Or he would have recognized it at once.

"Ba-Huon?" Cole asked incredulously. Her smile went a bit more devious, and she scratched Talos behind the ears as she answered.

"Not anymore." Her voice was high and clear. Pitched to make a shiver go down Cole's spine.

"But…I've never seen a transformation like this before." He said wondering. "Not even for the spirits we had to take down together. It…doesn't make any sense."

"I am not your typical spirit." She said as Talos purred. "In fact, I am not a spirit at all." She let the words hang in the air. Cole didn't know how to respond so he merely raised his arms in a failing to understand gesture. In response the young woman politely pushed Talos back and leapt to her feet. She spun gracefully on the ball of her foot and sunk into a perfect curtsy. Though it was a silly and childish gesture the grace by which she did it and the fire in her eyes as she introduced herself, turned it into something else entirely. And Cole was struck to chills by the power she seemed to hold reserved. She rose from the curtsy, and the shade of the golden halo he'd seen after she'd contained the snake bite, shown around her again.

"A pleasure to again make your acquaintance, young creator." She locked eyes with him, and Cole felt his insides turn to jelly at the force of her gaze. "My true name." She straightened. And the austerity she managed in just the simple gesture. Made Cole feel like he was looking at Joan of Arc before she broke the siege of Orleans.

"Is Sachiel." Cole felt his knees wobble a little and he sank down into a crooked sitting position as his eyes bulged.

"But…that's not…" He tried to get more words out but they failed him as he shook his head. The Siamese cat and the goddess both looked pleased at his reaction. They looked at each other, amused.

"He's not as dumb as his generation would suggest." Talos said. His voice was between a young man's baritone and a cat's purr. The goddess gave him a tutting glance.

"A few millennia of storytelling and the invention of writing gave him a leg up." She said it, not unkindly. "Besides, I am almost positive he is who I think he is. So, it will be more review than new information, once he accepts it. If only we had not been crushed so thoroughly." She sighed.

"But…" Cole had not heard any of this. He was still trying to get out what he was sure couldn't be true. "Sachiel is supposed to be an angel…" He blinked hard several times.

'An arch angel, depending on who's telling the story." Cole's incredulity was met by Sachiel's amused sort of grimace.

"It is not so much who is telling the story, as when they were telling it." She gave a graceful half shrug and waved a flippant hand. "I got demoted. Do you…by chance, remember the story?" She looked like she hoped he didn't. So he kept it as short as possible.

"You fell from grace. But wouldn't that make you a demon…or something?" Cole tried not to offend her, but she had led him on. Sachiel just looked amused, indeed, she seemed to be amused by everything now.

"Well, the semantics of what you understand is very short sighted…for now." She bent back down to scratch Talos behind the ears again to the cat's pleasure. She continued. "It is better to say that I was on my way down. Then we met."

"But that story is hundreds…thousands of years old." Cole said flabbergasted. His eyes darted back and forth when Sachiel gave him an "and?" sort of look.

"Shortsighted…" He said to himself. His eyes bulged again. "Wait…Does that mean the spirits." He looked at Talos.

"That all of you are…angels?" Talos and Sachiel exchanged amused looks and seemed on the verge of laughter.

"Not so much." Talos replied. "I was the lowest level of demon apprentice. A dark spirit, under orders to spread pessimism and iniquity where I could. Though I appreciate the sentiment, consider that your fight with me didn't force a doorway into *my* mind and take years to flesh out." Cole nodded thoughtfully, though he still didn't know if he really understood. Under his breath he rambled.

"Still don't know how I did that…haven't been able to do it since." The two inhuman beings exchanged looks again.

"You see why we chose to follow him?" Talos asked.

"Indeed, I may see better than you." Sachiel said smiling again. Talos' eyes went a little wide and he gave a slight bow in her direction.

"Forgive me."

"I am not offended little brother. If my sight were true, we would not be here." She indicated Cole and herself. He watched the exchange with confusion again. And thought he should at least try to find something he could get a footing on.

"You want to fill me in on that? Why do you guys follow us? I tell you all you're free to leave." He interjected. Sachiel gave him a reassuring smile. She put a hand on her curved and tightly muscled hip, visible even through her blanket robe. And took on a pondering look. Cole couldn't help the jaw drop that proceeded the gesture. He had to remind himself that this was his wolf partner. His buddy he'd known for years. That up until just hours previously, was his very much inhuman male buddy. Right?

"Can you explain why you turn spirits, rather than force them under your will?" Sachiel's question didn't help.

"Well, what else would I do?" He asked while his eyebrows furrowed, and he tried to refocus.

"Take me for example." Talos tried to help. "How you found me. You and I could have gotten away with all manner of mischief, if you had said the word." The cat took on a playful stance to extenuate the words.

"Imagine if instead of turning me you used me like he w-"

"No." Cole trumpeted the word involuntarily and waved his hand. Talos rolled with it, getting louder.

"What prompted you to have me stay with a man you did not know. To change his life and rectify what we had done to people you do not know?" Talos said amused. Cole shook his head as if shaking off a nonexistent fly. He didn't seem to be able to put together a good answer for this.

"I mean, what else was there for me to do? Yeah, other people might use it for...other stuff. But I just...couldn't think of anything else to do, I guess." He trailed off. His answer made the two others laugh. Though in more of a joyful tune than ridicule.

Sachiel offered him a hand up. But Cole was feeling like the butt of a joke he didn't understand, so he stood up on his own. Looking between the two with a mixture of confusion a chagrin.

"I think its time you head back little one. We have much to discuss and less time to do it in." Talos responded by bowing.

"Of course, ma'am." He shook himself out vigorously. Becoming completely animal in the action as he licked his chops and bounded away. Before he passed around the edge of the fountain, he called over his shoulder. "I expect our next conversation will be…engaging. Farewell, creators." And he disappeared around the fountain.

Cole watched the spot he had disappeared from. He had always taken pride when any of the spirits had called him a creator. Though he hadn't been able to create much without study and elbow grease. But he was now feeling a sense of foreboding at having it used with he and the being next to him in concert. He cast a sidelong look at Sachiel, but she wasn't there. He turned to see that she was already ten paces toward the grey palace and he quick stepped to catch up.

"He called us both creators." He said it half as a statement and question.

"Felines are more talented than subtle." She said not looking at him and bouncing gracefully as they walked.

"Right." Cole's eyes darted around the grounds. Still searching for some footing in the new landscape. "So…does that mean I'm an angel too?" He laughed out the question. Feeling ridiculous even as he said it. Subtlety wasn't his forte either.

"It…would be safe to say. You have a spark of the divine. And are perhaps, again, very young." Her light tone was obviously meant to make it easier information to hear.

It didn't help. Cole's head started to feel like cotton balls were being stuffed inside it again. Not only was he not finding any mental footing to stand on. His actual footing seemed to fail him, and he tripped over his feet. Sachiel caught him by the arm.

Her touch was like fire and the nodes of energy that flowed through Cole's body shone many times brighter and went flowing through him at ten times speed. Lightning pulsed from every one of them and Cole popped back up to his feet rubbing himself up and down and wiggling stupidly.

"Wha-a-at the hell?" He asked accusatorily. When Sachiel just observed him in mild surprise, he rephrased. "Heck…What the heck?" Sachiel just looked amused again.

"One of my powers." She said through a stifled laugh. "That which is, becomes more of what it is. It has been many years since I have been able to use it. Forgive me if my control is a bit…off." Cole thought about that for a moment before he looked at her accusingly again.

"That wouldn't happen to apply to…feelings would it?" Her eyes twinkled and she answered innocently.

"Why do you ask?"

Cole recounted the mornings events leading up to the moment he'd come into her domain. Sachiel's eyes blazed for a moment. Cole paled at the look but after she blinked heavily, it had passed, and she just looked puzzled.

'I do not have enough power to radiate that far now." She smiled sadly. "It must be due to the darkness I exuded, it is no longer affecting you. You made the point yourself. Why would it be any different for you?" Cole gawked at her. He had been carrying the bracelet around with him for the better part of four years.

"You said you weren't a spirit!"

"Indeed, I am many times over and again what they are. That you were able to be who you are with my fetid energy on your person day in and day out. It is quite impressive." That did nothing to make Cole feel any better.

"Wait…so does that mean Ann and I would've…could've been." Sachiel raised her eyebrows at him.

"Memories are to learn from. Do not fret on the past or curse your destiny. You will fall before you have even risen." She was stern in this pronouncement and Cole felt as if he were being chastised. He made to argue back but she cut him off.

"But what if-"

"Could have, would have, should have. What if this or that? All paths to stalling what can be, what should be and what will you do next." The fierceness of her words caught Cole by surprise. Even her golden glowing skin seemed to radiate with more light. He didn't have anything to say so she continued. "The work you have put in has saved many from darkness and the spreading thereof." She gesticulated at him to give her words more weight. Cole felt a warmth in his cheeks and a fire in his heart. If he'd had the ability in this place, he thought he would have tears in his eyes listening to her. "Would you give all that up? When this thing, you did not know you would wish you had been, is only one step in front of you?"

Cole felt as if he knew what it felt like to be a soldier spurred to battle by a competent commander. He thought about each of the spirits he had watching over their people. Keeping an eye out for darker spirits they could gather and turn together.

"No." He answered strongly. Under his breath he said. "You had that ready, didn't you?"

"You were asleep for three days." Sachiel mirrored his undertone. They both laughed softly. There were a thousand questions racing through his mind. The most glaring of which came out. Even though he was beginning to be intimidated. For entirely different reasons by this new version of his old friend.

"How do I explain what I'm doing? Ann's coming with us. How do I hide what we're trying to do while also going on a holiday?" At this Sachiel seemed to lose a bit of her steam and settle down. Even she also seemed to be a bit ashamed as she spoke.

"The first thing is…you don't." She held up a hand to stop him from protesting. "Before we discuss the next step on this journey there are…a few things you need to come to an understanding of. Items of information that were lost to me as I was." Cole looked at her quizzically.

"Normally we would let time and suggestion lead you to your evolution. But it seems this world has gone too far off track to let it be. We are too far downstream…the enemy has taken advantage." Cole didn't understand that, but they were just coming up to the palace entryway. Where it had once been flanked by grotesque looking gargoyles. There now stood two statues of what had to be angels. The female of the two was in Sachiel's likeness.

Both were clad in dragon scale armor, standing straight as the spears, the shape of which were called naginatas, in their hands. With large wings tucked behind their backs. So, he tried to bring it down to something he could understand.

"Hey, where are your wings?" He pointed at the statue to confirm he knew she should have them. Sachiel looked embarrassed and by the question and he regretted asking it.

"There is a reason I cannot manifest them at the moment. It ties into the information we must go over. But first," She gestured to an archway that led to a ten-foot-wide circular room immediately to the left of the doorway. A spiraling staircase that led to the top of one of the reading turrets, its only feature.

"We must start at the beginning." And as they stepped up the marble staircase lined with silver banisters. The angel recounted the story of light and creation coming into the universe. And the nature of the congealed and unthinking matter that it had given life and complex form to. That they had coalesced into two beings of unimaginable power. The creators of and yet created by the entirety of two universes colliding and becoming one.

"Not that I ever subscribed to one or the other, but. This goes against all traditional teachings. This is way out there." Cole stared down at the fountain in the courtyard as he leaned on the merlin.

"What you must understand is that your people have been…cut off. Their progression has stalled. They've made sense out of what they had. But as the light fades from this place, so too does their belief in and use of what you would call magic. Your abilities are a miracle. Cut off and without the full knowledge. Merely acting in your nature with the gifts you worked to create for yourself." Sachiel sat on a stone bench near the gazebo-like opening of the stairs. Even she seemed to be having trouble, making so much information make sense in such short time. Talking more toward the sky while swinging her bare, lightly golden feet.

"We've gone over some of that. That's why I want to take out the gate. But…it can't be that bad, can it? We have computers and cell phones and…garbage disposals. Those are all creations, aren't they? We still have plenty of light, knowledge, magic here." Cole defended. Sachiel chewed on his words, thinking how to describe what she had to say in a way he would understand.

"Think of all the imaginings your people have come up with…Gods, angels, demons, witches, mages, succubae, transformations, powers and abilities beyond anything they can accomplish now. That is what your world should be, a world of constantly progressing and evolving beings."

"Everything I can imagine? You're describing gods." Cole said dryly.

"Not so." Sachiel said softly. "I am describing what the imagination of pure light and all energy was trying to achieve when it came into the material plain." Cole turned around to face her as he asked.

"So, you're saying God wants that?" He thought for a second. "That…gods want that?" Sachiel smiled. Seeing that he at least understood part of what she was saying.

"Indeed, they are both made of the matter that first existed here and the light that came into it. Binding imagination and matter onto one plain. Those two at the focal point of both."

"So why don't they just do it? If they're so powerful, why didn't they just make…beings that could do all of that?" Cole asked trying to hold everything in his head. Sachiel gave him a pitying look.

"They are." She sung it quietly as if it would make it easier on Cole's ears. It sort of was. The sound of her voice singing entered his eardrums like melted chocolate vibrating him from head to foot. It didn't stop his mind from racing though. As the weight of her sing song words crashed over him, his knees went weak again and he sank down. His back against the merlin.

"So…they're making gods?" Cole thought about everything she had told him and tried to put it into a timeline that he could understand.

"They are making beings as close to themselves as they can. It…takes a very long time and there are setbacks on both sides." She said the last bit under her breath. There was a long pause.

"Why?" Cole asked feeling his grip on his understanding slipping away.

"They are fundamentally different beings. One wishes to see it happen one way the other wishes to see it happen another way. Same goal, different roads, where they intersect there is conflict." She was saying it conversationally, but it took several long seconds for Cole to grasp what she was saying.

"How long?" Cole asked under his breath.

"How long has it been, or how long is it going to take? I find I get each one equally at this point." Sachiel sounded more nonchalant than Cole felt. He knew it was on purpose as there was still a strained note in her tone.

"Either…both. Does it matter?" Cole shrugged as he imagined how small he was to the information he was receiving. Not just a speck on a speck, as Sagan had once explained it to him from a past that had seemed so long ago when he'd heard it as a child.

As with then he felt like a child. As many people as he'd reached with his projects. Those he'd tried to help with his supernatural work. All he was, only a tiny piece of such a large puzzle that it would take an eternity's forever to put it together. Even if the pieces were set a millimeter from where they were supposed to be placed at the start. And beings he couldn't fathom were already doing the work.

"Cole." The tone of her voice made him look up. Genie had always been a good surrogate mother. But he had always wondered what it would have felt like to be in the presence of his true mother. Somehow that's how Sachiel had made him feel with the single word. As if she were addressing him from a place of innocence. A place that existed entirely of love.

"Of course, it matters." Cole felt a sour energy rise from his chest to his throat. He was almost too embarrassed to choke out the question.

"Why? How? What can I do that they couldn't?" His mind raced again "Do I have free will? Am I just some piece in the thought game of a god I don't even know?" He felt silly. What kind of angel fetus cries about it? Sachiel walked over and sat next to him. Looking up into the brightness of the sunless sky.

"Oh…humans." She sighed. "Always so worried about your freedom. Do you not understand that is precisely what makes you special? That…is what makes you matter. If you could even understand how important every single one of you will be. One way or the other." Cole pulled himself together enough to give her a once over with a questioning gaze.

"You remember that in the last moments that light and creation came into the universe. That it gave the greater portion of power to the being more interested in freedom. Rather than control?" Cole nodded like a child being taught how to tie his shoe.

"In answer to one of your questions. This has been going on for countless time. Time enough for the entirety of the universe to have…for lack of a better explanation. Exploded and imploded in on itself multiple times. Each time creating waves of new creations. Each time, creating beings of almost no power at all, to beings of incredible power." Sachiel paused, knowing there would be a question.

"But if it implodes on itself are those beings…destroyed in the implosion?" Cole asked. Sachiel smiled. This was the question that she had obviously wanted to hear.

"The first time…yes. They were. But let me ask you something." She turned to him. Cole nodded one to lead her on. "Do you remember every creation you have ever made?" Cole didn't have to think about it.

"Of course." He said in short order.

"And if you were a being of unlimited and incredible power, what would those memories become?" Cole chewed on the thought for a moment. Staring at his hands. When a thought came to him, he smiled. He focused a bit of his energy, and in his hand appeared a replica of the seashell necklace that was his first creation. He held it out to the angel. Thinking it might be a less than appropriate offering for the moment. But she took it with a smile none the less and pulled it over her upright wolf ear. She examined it, still smiling.

"…they remade them?" He asked.

"Not exactly. Just as when you use your power instinctually. When you made a door into this place." She waved a hand around. "They created a way for the beings they had made and loved to live on. Because they felt like they had to." Cole didn't say anything. Just waited for the angel to continue, what was there to say anyway? Sachiel looked up from admiring the necklace to level her eyes with his.

"It was the birth of the soul." Again, her words hung in the air. After a moment of Cole's silence she continued. "And where a spirit is the birth and start of the journey, as it becomes more complex, it needs a vessel to learn to evolve and become fully-fledged. Once a soul has reached a high enough evolution, it will no longer shed bodies to continue on that path."

Cole reeled at the day he was having. He decided to think as if all of it was merely a philosophical conversation. Rather than sitting with an ex-arch angel in her brainscape, discussing the life of the universe at large.

"So…were the Hindus right then?" Cole asked at this pronouncement. Sachiel continued to admire the necklace with a little smile. "Souls moving from life to life, body to body. So…they could keep their creations alive?"

"In a way. But the size and scope of it is beyond what humans have gotten to on a large scale yet. And…the nature of what that means to your existence." The angel half explained.

"Such as…that their gods are only demigods. That were once people at…some point?" That was the best he could come up with.

"Such as the fact that this, your world, is not the only place that beings fight for the freedom of their souls, it is a constant struggle for all. That this is not the only place their souls have been. And in most cases, will go. That the beings who created all things, all souls and places they exist. Run along the path that their own creation and combination designated for all of us. Deviance from the path is unpredictable at this stage and creates much conflict. The occurrences within are becoming more disastrous as the beings involved become more…evolved. And thereby that the path to be, will be one of conflict rather than coexistence." Cole didn't understand why but tears had come to Sachiel's eyes as she said this.

"That doesn't sound so bad." He was now thinking that his ghost like being made more sense, that this…soul he was seeing would go on forever. That in a way, even if he couldn't remember it, he would never die. Which meant that even if he was such a small and insignificant speck. He had time to make a difference, to be heard in the in the depths of infinite time and space. And the thought of being loved so much by either of those beings, that his existence merited the creation of a soul felt nice too.

"You do not understand. Most of it is unconscious. Powerful as they are they do not see everything at once." Sachiel almost choked the words out. And she continued speaking quickly as Coles eyes grew wider at each word.

"Neither are truly like you or I. At times they work together, at others they war. They have creations they care for, but not every creation is loved like they should be. Occasionally they play chess with or bestow power on those they deem worthy. But mostly they leave the ones they've given power to squabble with each other, with little help between their new works. The conflict between each other creates conflict between their creations." She looked at Cole desperately.

"US." She said desperately. Cole gave her an open and questioning look. It seemed to take the wind from her sails. She took a few deep breaths and steadied herself to continue.

"They just sound like bad parents." Cole said under his breath. It was almost worse to know that not only did he have free choice. But that it had no real baring on anything unless he was being watched by some unseen force. They wanted him to be, but be on what terms?

Thanks, past me. He thought to himself.

"So, what you're saying is…they don't take part unless we catch their attention?" Sachiel snorted as he searched for the right words. It still didn't sound so bad to him. He thought Sachiel's recent time had probably had something to do with the rueful way she was describing the situation.

"Not so much that you would be aware of it. They are *too busy* most of the time, and each have a retinue of beings for that now."

"Is that what we're *for*? How do they play chess with us?" Cole couldn't help the questions for blurting out.

"Think of how you found me. Do you suppose it was chance? A powerless…" She stopped herself and gave him a sidelong look. He was almost able to, but she continued before he could ask.

"And a mindless beast, tearing apart people's minds. I was being turned…to use on the other side. It was only because you found me that I wasn't. But if I had fully turned, I would have made a great demon. Especially after leaving this place."

"So, does that mean you were being…observed? Does that mean I'm going to be a target? Are you being watched now?" Cole accusatory with the last question.

"Peace. I was…pursued, not by a true god. Merely by those who think they are. To their credit, their captain has the favor of both gods. And we all lose favor when he moves. But remember that you and I have been together for years. With no true adversary coming to find us. We will have the time to do what we need to before they check on my…progression." She showed contempt for her own words. But at least seemed less emotional at this point.

"Or they're so confident they'll win they haven't bothered. You heard the huntress; they think they've won already." Cole said dejectedly. Another thing she said seemed to sink in.

"But…if their captain is so loved by the *gods*. They wouldn't have wanted to get in his way, would they?" She looked at him intently.

"Maybe I didn't find you by chance, but no one guided me either." He gave her a slight smile; he was unprepared for the blazing look and wave of heat that radiated from the angel. It almost blew him backward as she leaned a bit closer to him. Not on purpose, but because he was so shocked and inexperienced, he ruined whatever he'd just done.

"Hey, wasn't…wasn't the story was you fell because you," Cole's face would have gone red if it could have.

"For well 'falling' for a man." Sachiel raised her eyebrows, her eyes faded back to a dull gold when Cole lifted his hands to make the quotation gesture. Her chin dipped and she pursed her lips, looking disappointed.

"Would you *really* like to know the 'story'? Or would you like to get to the part that concerns you and I?" Cole knew he had touched a nerve when she used the same gesture for story.

But after hearing about how large the stories were in comparison to his tiny existence. And not truly understanding what position he held in those stories. Or where he was at the moment, for that matter. He just couldn't help himself. He squinted and scrunched up his face.

"I mean." He dragged it out. Sachiel rolled her eyes.

"Fine, remember that you asked. *Humans* are very touchy about this kind of thing." She emphasized humans as if it would hurt his feelings. But he didn't know it should.

"Not a word of this leaves this turret. Ever. You understand?" Cole nodded, feeling like a preschooler about to hear his first rumor. Sachiel rattled off the story quickly as if she were trying to get past it as fast as she could.

"In the modern version of the story. Eve was tempted by Lucifer. Who slithered into the garden as a snake, he made her eat a fruit. And she then tempted Adam to do the same, they changed, and were cast out. Do you know the original version of the story?" Cole had in fact read the Hebrew version the year before. And he answered as quickly to get to the meat.

"I think the only parts that were different were that Adam had a first wife-"

"Infernal darkness." Sachiel looked aggravated at the mention. He even thought he saw a hint of fear in her eyes. "Lilith...She will be an obstacle if she is still here. The other part." She rolled her hand to keep him going. Cole noted the obvious reaction. Apart from knowing Lilith was a real being. He thought it was very interesting that Sachiel seemed to know her. He was about to find out why.

"The only other part I remember being different is that the de-um Lucifer." Cole used the same nomenclature in case it would cause another interruption.

"Rode a snake into the garden. And that the snake was some other angel in snake form. But that the interpretation of the name of that angel was never consistent..." Cole trailed off as the true meaning of the story rose into his mind. "That was you?"

Sachiel nodded. She gave a tiny smile as she rolled her wrist.

"So he rode you into the-"She shook her head. Cole furrowed his eyebrows. "You rode him?" He cocked his head. She nodded again looking as if she were about to laugh at his innocent face.

"Into the gar-"

"In the garden." She corrected. Cole's eyebrows rose again, and his face would have gone another three shades more red.

"You rode him...*in* the garden." He couldn't keep going. Sachiel finished the story for him quickly.

"Eve was very interested in sharing it with Adam when she made sense of what she saw. Then they could not get enough of it." Cole let out an embarrassed laugh.

"Wait a minute, *that's* why you fell? But I thought you were around for a bunch of other stories after that?"

"Seeing as the focus was on finding the chosen ones running around..." She made a hand gesture and Cole laughed. "We were left out of thought or observation for a while...As it happens, I was demoted immediately...Eve wasn't the only one wandering the garden that day." The angel looked pained as she said under her breath.

"I do not even know why she was there…In any case, I was allowed to be turned later, when Lucifer made it known to the gods." Venom infused the last bit of her words.

"So, I was wrong? Gods do care about people…" Cole made the same hand gesture with an embarrassed look. Sachiel rolled her eyes.

"In that place, and at that time. It was meant to happen. Just not the way it did." She seemed to be reciting something someone else had said to her, but sarcastically overbearing. They chuckled together.

"Wait, didn't you say thinking about the past would lead to darkness?" Cole widened his eyes jokingly as if he worried she might turn on him. He was getting used to this new version of his old friend. He liked this much more than the other, as he wasn't dodging fangs at every question.

"Actually no. All the thoughts that would leave me susceptible to being turned are gone. Now I only have the good parts." She looked very pleased with herself at this.

"Oh yeah?" Cole laughed. "You managed to get rid of all the negativity associated with that?" He pushed lightly on her leg. She pushed his face in return. Her hand was hot as fire and she was stronger than she looked. Cole nearly rolled away at the force of her push.

"No! As a point of fact. You did." That shocked the playfulness right out of him. "And you did it..." Sachiel was obviously holding back a laugh.

"With pancakes and ice cream."

Their eyes locked for the briefest second before they were both rolling with laughter. It felt good to laugh after all she'd told him. It relieved some of the panicked helplessness he was starting to feel. When they had subsided, Cole had more pressing questions, but he found himself too curious.

"So…does that mean I was right about the gate? God didn't do that did…it? He…she?" Cole didn't know whether either would designate as male or female. Beings other than human seemed to do whatever they wanted on that subject.

"It was the very same ex arch angel that led to my fall." Sachiel looked over his confusion as her face darkened and she looked furious at the thought. "The God of freedom would not cast my brother into prison…And he was not 'making angel babies'. He was teaching humans to achieve divine souls. Though it would not have mattered if he were." She had used quotation gestures when repeating Cole's words from several days previous. And said the last part as if it didn't matter at all. He had so many questions he couldn't get any of them out properly.

"Hold on, that can be taught? Why are humans so import- Your brother?!-Just to be clear, the good god. Doesn't care about…but what if-" Sachiel stood up. Cutting off his stream of questions. She answered him quickly. Something must have come to mind at his questions he thought wrongly.

"There were very few high angels here, and he would have been the target at the time. I know it is he that is imprisoned. A divine soul can be achieved between any life…and it is never forgotten. It can only be suppressed. We thought if we worked with humans, we could teach them. It was going well until…" She trailed off in thought for a moment while Cole tried to cram more information into his brain. She picked back up again.

"Humans are important because they are the farthest creations along the cosmic river of light and thought." She took a few steps and turned to face him. Walking slowly back to stand over him as he sat looking up at her. Like a child at kindergarten hearing the ABC's for the first time.

"Which means, in time, they represent the last moment of the creation of the gods. And those of them that are granted power and live on to use it properly. In physical space, will represent the final hope of the god of freedom. And those of them that gain true power." She gestured to herself then to Cole, who felt his stomach drop a few inches.

"Will be instrumental in casting off the chains of control the enemy places on sentient creation." She held out a hand for Cole to stand. The measure of her words were too much to digest all at once. He sat for a moment staring at her hand with a stunned expression on his face.

"Do not fret, divinely young." She almost sang the words. It made him feel a little better. "You found me remember? No one had to teach you a thing in this life. It is in your soul to walk this path." She smiled as Cole took her fire hot hand and she lifted him as lightly as a feather.

"As for..." She gave him a devious once over. "Nobody cares if all parties are willing, and it doesn't hurt anything. It is a powerful ritual for either side, in fact. But...as a weapon against an enemy it can be a devastating tool." She gave a consenting gesture before she looked at him directly. They were only an arm's length away from each other. In so much that he could feel heat coming off her. Her inhumanly beautiful features seemed to glow a shade brighter.

"But you and I could…" Sachiel gave him another once over. This time slow, her eyes glowed a few shades brighter. "If we both wanted to. Neither of us are even in our physical bodies…It would be more of a dream than anything." Her eyes glowed bright. Even in this ghostly state he felt his body match the fiery heat of Sachiel's hand. And since they were still connected as she brought him to his feet and held it there, she felt it too. What he was going to do about this newfound issue, he didn't know just yet. But he knew he must look completely dumbfounded. She laughed her high, warm and energy inducing laughter.

All he'd just been taught, heavy as it was, worried as he should be. The time involved being so incomprehensible. The thought of his soul being immortal. That he had been someone before he was himself passed through his mind. Sachiel's comment, when she'd been Ba'l, if he was who she thought he was. He wondered if they'd known each other before now, before this life. Sachiel's eyes burned as if responding to his thought.

Cole's body responded as if it wanted nothing more than have that dream she'd mentioned.

Didn't they have so much to do? He thought. Plans to make.

What was that she'd said about not being in her physical body? Did

that mean she had one? Shouldn't they be planning to find that too?

Where would it be now? Would it be the same as the one she

occupied now?

Ch. 6

In his research in the years before finding the little goblin made pixy. His newest friend, that had que'd him to the right location. Where he now thought he should have sussed out for himself. Cole had read of several legends relegated to the region. One that had interested him was the story of the ancient King Solomon. Solomon was one of the only people in history that was said to be Maji. Yet also powerful in ability, political and social structure. Other beings possessed of power usually kept to themselves, used it for their own personal gain or showed up for brief moments in other people's stories.

Solomon however, had used his power to make the ancient kingdom of Judah wealthy and powerful among nations. All while using and fighting demons and spirits his people called the djinn. And working with angels to protect and better his kingdom. He had many stories associated with his time as king. Some enlightening and inspiring, others cringeworthy and disheartening. Cole had always admired Solomon, even though he had lost several of his battles with the demons and djinn of legend. Even just a witch at one point. It was the price he paid for not hiding away with his Maji power and being alright with it, something Cole had tried and failed to do. But Solomon became a target none of them could resist.

It was said that the arch angel Michael had given him a ring imbued with a seal. A magic circle laced with angelic script that enacted a spell. That gave him control over all but the most powerful of demons. And he had once used it to force one of Lucifer's own hounds to build his temple steps. But the story that interested Cole the most, now, was the story of the prison Solomon had used to hold particularly unruly supernatural beings. And the demons he had ordered to guard the prison.

The location of this prison was never told in the stories. But locals in a northern region of Azerbaijan, had found it many years later and turned it into a national monument. They didn't have tours or go down into the prison, for good reason. It was said that everyone who attempted to explore it died. The ones who had managed to leave the place after going down. Spoke of demons roaming below that would kill immediately, if you tried to take any piece of the prison grounds with you. They would engage in conversation, but if given offense, would kill the offender. Or, if you were able to hold a conversation and leave, without taking anything. They would find you later and kill you out of hand. The people who told these stories inevitably did die under mysterious circumstances, which only lent credence to the tale.

What the story hadn't gone over was how the jail existed in the first place. All it said was that the king had used his gifted seal, to access angelic power. And he used it to hold demons in a sort of endless abyss that he just sort of put a magic cap on.

Cole now thought it might be that he was able to open and close an already existing gateway. It would be up for grabs to find out whether Solomon knew himself if what he was using as a prison was the mind of an already imprisoned angel. And since Sachiel had remembered and revealed her identity, Cole couldn't help but see the correlation between he and the ancient king.

Also, that being an angel didn't sound at all like sunshine and rainbows.

It was two days after Cole had fully woken from his fight for his angel partner's mind. Gone to eat breakfast and made the impetuous decision to ask his childhood friend. Now turned something he didn't yet understand. To go with him on his angel hunt vacation. That that decision came to a head, and Cole got into his second fight with another human being.

Cole and Ann were centerpiece to one of Genie's classes, as they usually were. When fast moving tires could be heard crunching down the long gravel driveway. They were in the middle of a stretch in which the whole class were silently lunging, one arm forward the other back. So that it was easy to hear the slamming door after the car's tires had come to a skidding halt. As it was something very much a-typical of one of Genie's classes. Everyone was turned to see the man that came stomping angrily toward Cole's workshop from the front of the house.

He was a thick young man in his mid-twenties. With clean cut black hair and wearing business attire. He was a few steps past the edge of the house when he seemed to notice he was being watched. He turned to look at the class, his anger was obvious in his expression and tightness of his movement. It was only exacerbated when he noticed Ann and her position next to Cole.

"Brian?" Ann sounded as surprised as everyone else to see him. That is, she sounded surprised to anyone who didn't know her better.

Brian, Cole knew only by reputation and hearsay. He was the manager of a local shipping company. He led by strict adherence to the rules and had fired many of his young subordinates for the smallest infractions. He was a promising young businessman on his way up the company ladder and had a good reputation amongst the elder businessmen in town. He was also Ann's boyfriend, and had apparently not expected to see her here.

"Ann?" He moved toward the class with rage in his every step. He pointed a full hand at her as he found and took the stone steps that led to the flat area below. "Why am I not surprised your classes aren't at the gym?" He said angrily.

"Brian, don't!" Ann tried to get the young man to stop his assault on the steps, but he kept on stepping anyway. "We can talk about this later. You shouldn't be here!" Ann was only half yelling and Cole could hear the fear in her voice. She obviously knew something about his anger that others didn't. He put out an arm and side stepped so that she was behind him.

"Oh, *I* shouldn't be here?" Brian said as if under paramount incredulity as he came down the last few steps. Cole's position only seemed to make him angrier. "You can't hide her you little nerd, I've already seen her." His head jerked this way and that as he shouted. He seemed either not to have understood the movement or didn't take Cole seriously at all. Cole thought he must be used to people cowering when he yelled at them. But he didn't work for him and he was not afraid of the pudgy businessman in the slightest. He was growing increasingly upset at his attitude toward Ann, and how he thought he could come to Cole's house and charge his workshop unannounced.

"Cole, I'm sorry. I'm sorry. I told my sister I was going with you on your trip." Ann whimpered from behind him. At least that sounded genuine, Cole thought to himself.

If he didn't know her better, he would have been totally convinced by the whole thing. She had set him up, and after all he and Sachiel had been going over, he didn't much care. He was on her side either way and this guy seemed like a jerk. But he wouldn't want to fight him if he didn't have to. The only reason he'd been able to fight Sachiel's constructs so readily was because they were just that, constructs or spirits. He hadn't fought another person in almost three years.

"Yeah." Brian said it around Cole as best he could. He was taller than Cole by about an inch so he could still see Ann standing behind him. "Imagine my surprise when I found out you're running off with this little psycho." He indicated Cole. Cole could hear Genie's sound of derision from somewhere behind him. He didn't care about the slight to him. He had heard many worse things said about him at school and on his early platform.

"Did you think about how embarrassed *I* might be?" Brian looked on the verge of rage tears he was so angry. Cole put his hand up to indicate the driveway Brian had just come down from.

"He's not a psycho, Bryan!" Ann yelled from behind him. That part was genuine too, Cole thought, but so was her fear.

"I think she told you to leave, guy. You're making a fool of yourself." Cole said calmly.

"Now the little ghost freak is gunna try to tell me what to do." Brian's dumbed down voice only served to prove Cole right. But he was still saying it toward Ann. "Is that right? Is that what she said?" Brian said mockingly, turning his full attention to Cole. He postured up to his full height to look down on the younger man.

"That's right. And now *I'm* telling you to leave. Now." Cole put weight on the last word but couldn't help smiling at the man's posturing. What he didn't realize in time is that Brian wasn't just a jerk, he was a violent jerk. The chubby man's eyes grew much too wide and crazed.

"You know what? That's fine you little piece of shit. I came to see you anyway." And since he had come ready for a fight and Cole was still processing the moment. He wasn't ready for the overhand right that came soaring into his left eyebrow.

Cole lost sight of Brian for a split second as he took the blow, but his head whipped back automatically. He immediately sank into his boxing stance as he reassessed the situation. His heart started to race at ten times speed and his brain went into hyper-focus. Brian seemed to think he was only going to need to hit Cole once, so he started talking again.

"You think you scare me, nerd?" He said gesticulating at Cole's stance as if amused. "How dare you talk to my girl?" He shouted and pointed his flat hand at Cole.

Your girl? Cole thought. He was dimly aware of other people around them also shouting. Genie was yelling something he couldn't register as words. *We were friends a decade before she even knew you existed.* He thought getting angrier at Brian's crazy eyes and nonsense. Brian didn't seem to think Cole would swing on him. Like he was untouchable or that a fight only consisted of him hitting someone and them giving up. He continued to shout.

"Who do you think you-" He was cut off by Cole's feint, he moved jerkily to block a jab that didn't come. Surprise replacing crazy as Cole came in with a hard rear uppercut. Brian's teeth clapped together mid-sentence. His head snapped back to his shoulder blades and his eyes rolled into the back of his head. He looked as though he meant to get into a better fighting stance as his hands went halfway up and his knees buckled. He toppled over face first onto the patio concrete.

It wasn't much of a fight, and Cole hadn't ever planned on anything like this happening in his own backyard. Literally. But he would have the scar Brian had given him for years to come. Even as Brian landed, scraping his face on the pavement. Leaving more outward damage than Cole's punch had. Blood started to leak down into Cole's eye and obscure his vision. He wiped at it as Ann rushed in to ask if he was alright. She looked truly horrified at the mass of red on the back of his hand he'd wiped his brow with.

One of the newer gentlemen to Genie's classes had moved in on Brian. Turning him over to check parts of his body that showed he'd had medical experience. Airway, breathing, pulse, and situated him on his back with his head tilted up. He waved a hand at the others who'd gathered. Words were being said but Cole didn't hear them. He paced once across the back patio, his adrenaline only now kicking in hard as he shook his wrist out. Ann seemed satisfied with Brian's care and decided to pull Cole toward the stairs instead of staying next to him.

"Come on. Let's get you cleaned up." *She* sounded tired and hurt, but triumphant in some way none the less. As if she had just finished something that had taken as much as a race out of her, but that she'd won.

"I'm fine." Cole said with a smile as he pressed his palm against his eyebrow to staunch the bleeding. As they took the steps, he looked back to see Genie emptying her water bottle over Brian's scraped up face. A look of impatient nonchalance on her face.

"*I'm* not." Ann said as if Cole were missing something obvious.

Cole thought she meant that she just had to watch her boyfriend get knocked out. So, he spent the time it took for Ann sit him at the island and grab the first aid kit under the counter. Profusely apologizing and making promises to make it up to her. She didn't respond to any of this, as she cleaned and dressed the cut with butterfly bandages. Green-gold eyes focused wholly on the task at hand, while her mind was somewhere else.

She hadn't even looked like she was listening to him. She rolled her eyes, shook her head and huffed at intervals that didn't match with anything he was saying. When she continued doing it after he stopped talking. He realized she must be going through something internally. He was still buzzing with adrenaline and couldn't drop it.

"I mean, what was I supposed to do? He was yelling at you..." He touched the well-placed bandages on his eyebrow. The cut had started to radiate a dull pain now, rather than just heat and pressure. He added as an aside.

"And he punched me in the face!" Ann was just about to throw the bloody rag she'd used to wipe his face and stop the bleeding into the trash when he said it. She did so forcefully to get him to stop talking.

"Cole!" She seemed wholly focused now and he shut up at her look. She was obviously furious. She seemed to have worked out what she'd been thinking about.

"Why do you think I *only* told my sister?" Her fury was lost on him.

Cole had never known much about Ann's sister. She was old enough to have been out of high school by the time they'd gone in. She still lived at home, working at a tanning salon or something in town and living mostly off her dad's money. At his blank stare Ann's anger seemed to break. She put a hand over her eyes and ruefully smiled as she sighed. Her hand fell, she approached him and spoke as though he were really missing the obvious now.

"I told *only* my sister. When mom and dad are at work and don't answer their phones." She nodded slowly trying to spur his thought. "And *he* knew I'd be at yoga…not at home." She pointed an angry finger toward the back yard from a foot away from him. She added the last part with a clawed hand, exasperated and on the verge of tears. When Cole obviously meant to ask why Brian had thought her class was at the gym. The light came slowly into Cole's mind.

"Ohhh…" He didn't really understand why girls got so angry about a lot of things, but he reached out and grabbed her hand to pull her into a comforting hug all the same.

Not under the strain of having to explain anymore. Ann let her emotions flow for a moment with her head against his shoulder.

Adding her silent tears to the drops of Cole's blood on his ruined grey shirt. There was something other than just the friendship they'd had since childhood in that embrace. Something had changed in both of them in the last few days. Gone was the side hug and strength demeanor she'd always given him. She folded into him, and he accepted her.

"I guess it's not unreasonable they should be talking to each other though, right?" Cole said stupidly. "Maybe he was asking her about a birthday gift for you or-"

"Oh my god!" Ann said exasperated. "They were at my house together, while no one else was there. **On purpose…**" Cole finally got it and it put an appalled look onto his face.

"Your sister? Really?" He asked incredulously.

"I'm not surprised…she's always been like that and he's a piece of work. They're perfect for each other, and being right doesn't make it hurt any less." She said it with a finality that went past him. When he almost laughed at what she said, her anger flared again.

"Ha-Yeah, I'm surprised you chose that guy." He tried to save himself.

"My father set it up." She said angrily. "And it's not like I could say no, I didn't have anyone-" She cut herself off and took a long steadying breath.

This wasn't the kind of moment she'd ever shared with him before. And he tried not to let it confuse him, he just went with it. She seemed so small when she was like this. Nothing of the track star bounding into the corporate world in her now. The faint sound of muffled incoherent shouts and a slamming car door reached them, and she curled more tightly against his body.

She looked up; her green eyes were watery but all business. They blazed with the kind of intensity that prompted action. It was another look Cole had never seen from her. The effect of it did a number on his adrenaline pumped, newly interested body. Cole felt his face go red as heat rose between them like an electric kettle. When it was hot enough to make him start sweating in about half a second. Ann looked supremely and infuriatingly triumphant before she smiled and looked back down. Again, in a little girly way he'd never seen from her before.

He didn't know how to bring it up, but at this point. If he didn't say anything now, he had a feeling his would be the worse secret to be fleshed out. Though he knew what he had to say would most likely end whatever this new phase of their relationship was growing into. He should have known better.

"Ann...I have to tell you something...weird." He said quietly.

"Cole, don't be dumb." She said as though relieved he decided to break the tension that way.

"No, I mean it's really out there. Take left field and Brian all over it." He stammered. That made Ann laugh and it eased him up a bit. "You remember when we were kids..."

"It was me you made those videos with, remember?" Cole was shocked that she seemed to have pinpointed his concerns so directly. He thought he'd been sneaky all this time.

"I was there. *I* never said I didn't believe you…You just clammed up after all that stuff people said about you. And just started tinkering and…reading by yourself. I never left it alone though." She sounded sincere and Cole didn't have anything to say. She unhooked the hand Cole hadn't let go of and ran it down his arm in a blaze of lightning heat. Right down to his wrist and the wolf bracelet there. Cole's eyes bulged. It was only just then, that he realized he may never have given Ann the respect or credit she deserved, and he revered her quite a lot. She sounded like a scientist observing their latest experiment.

"What *is* it?" She asked as she ran her finger along the wolf's back.

"How do you-" Cole started. It was like he was dreaming and wasn't even the main character anymore.

"You don't know how many times I've caught you huddled over this thing." She said as if it were just a throw away comment. "Glowing, with you passed out over it. There *has* to be something to it, I could never get you to wake u-" She stopped when her finger touched the wolf's jade eye. Her eyes bulged and her chest heaved, she looked a mixture of horrified, confused and excited.

"I can hear it…It's never done this before!" Cole was reeling at the thought of Ann having come into his room. How many times? Done this before?!

"What is she saying?" Cole asked apprehensively. He heard Sachiel's voice and he knew she was speaking to both of them.

"I was on the verge of telling her I could show myself. If she wishes it." She sounded amused by the proceedings. Cole wondered how long she'd been paying attention. He and Ann exchanged looks. Cole confused, Ann excited.

"She wouldn't be able to see you, would she?" Cole's eyebrows furrowed.

"As I am now. I can choose to show myself." Cole felt his heart leap. He didn't know what the effect of it would be. But he wouldn't feel as crazy anymore if Ann could finally see what he'd been babbling about all that time.

At that moment, the door at the bottom of the stairs cut them off. Genie took the stairs two at a time. And they were still breaking apart when she hit the top of the steps. Her expression went from worried to supremely and unrepentantly knowing.

"Well." She said imperiously. "I had to make sure that idiot left before I came to check on you." Her eyes traced between the two of them. She was having a hard time not smiling. Her eyes positively glowed. She approached close enough to check the bandages on his eyebrow. "Looks like you were in good hands. Thank you, Ann." Genie did a little head nod toward Ann. Who embarrassingly smiled and returned the gesture.

"Yeah, no problem." She said, red cheeked. Genie turned to slap Cole on the shoulder, though she spoke good humoredly.

"How dare you make her cry." Cole pretended the slap hurt.

"Hey! I'm the one that got punched!" He flinched back but couldn't help but give a pained smile; said punch throbbed a little. Ann lifted a hand, looking even more embarrassed.

"No, Genie. It was-" Genie turned an amused look on her.

"Well, I have a confused and curious class to go reassure."

She turned back to take the stairs with a waving hand gesture. "I'm

sure you two will be fine to talk it out without me."

The two exchanged looks as the door closed again

downstairs. If Cole had thought today was going to go on like any

other. He had been shocked no less than a few times so far. And the

day was only just getting started.

■■

Two hours later, he sat on the edge of his bed, having

changed out of his bloody gym shirt and into his normal thin gray

one. Sachiel was at the sun shining window and Ann sat in the spot

Cole usually used to meditate. Crisscross and staring hard at the

floor, her fingers tapping at her chin.

"You were going to do this without warning anybody?" She

asked Cole with a look that paled him. He answered defensively.

"How do you warn people about something like this?" He

put on a goofy sarcastic voice.

"Hey everybody, it's that tinkerer who sees spirits. By the

way, magic is real…I swear. Guess what? It's been sealed in a prison made out of an angel, those are real too by the way. I think I found it in the ruins of an ancient kingdom none of you remember or care about." Ann smiled and gave him a consenting look. Then she got serious again.

"Still, we could say there was a nuclear waste leak or something. You said everyone will…change? How?" She raised an eyebrow.

"It will not be the same for everyone." Sachiel answered. She'd been giving Ann many once overs and studying her in a very open and peculiar way since they'd greeted each other.

"The level of the change will depend on the person. But there is…potential within all human beings." She glanced lightning fast at Cole. It was not missed by Ann, who was in a better position to see it. "Some are sleeping legends, drained of their power. Some have forgotten who or what they are...others. Stuck in a world they do not belong in, waiting."

"Waiting for what?" Ann asked suspiciously. In answer Sachiel merely half turned and extended a presenting hand at Cole.

He was more interested in who these beings were and what their potential might be when he noticed them both staring at him.

"What?" Cole asked. Ann scanned the room. Eyebrows furrowed so tightly she almost looked as though she had a unibrow.

"You said your brother is imprisoned in this place we're going?" She asked, still looking at the wall.

"He is the prison." Cole stated, trying to get back into the conversation. Ann still seemed deep in thought as she asked.

"And is he…like you?" She waved a hand up and down at the angel. Sachiel regarded Ann in a way that suggested she may want to tread lightly around her. But she did answer.

"He must still have his physical body; else the prison would not be possible." Ann took a moment to digest this and looked hesitant at her next question. And when she said it, Cole understood why. It wasn't as if he hadn't wondered. He just didn't know what the information would have gained him. And didn't want to bring it up if he didn't have to.

"Then are you...dead?" Ann asked softly and looked as though she were expecting the angel to attack her. On the contrary the angel looked rather fearful herself at answering the question.

"If that were the case, my soul would have found another vessel." She indicated herself then seemed to be remembering something dreadfully poignant in her past. Her eyes widened and her glow seemed to dim several shades. Even the room seemed to lose some of the sunshine coming in through the window. "I was betrayed. Torn from my body...left to drain away and turned into a monster." The last part came out in a whisper.

Cole felt his insides go numb and rage filled his heart at the unseen enemy that could commit such a foul act. Ann's face had gone pale, her eyes roved around as she tried to take the information in. Her eyes slid to Cole's look of fury. When he noticed her looking, his face changed into a sad smile, and he motioned for her to come sit next to him. More for his own comfort than anything else. Ann's eyes widened after she sat and laid her head on his shoulder. She seemed to realize something that only Sachiel could see the signs of. Her eyes closed and she nodded to herself, lips pursed.

"What can I do to help?" She asked. Sachiel was taken out of her reverie and the room went back to normal. She looked at Ann with a new air of fondness and respect.

■■

The day after Cole's fight with Brian. Ann mentioned casually that she had told her parents she was going on a trip with him. Cole had almost fallen out of his seat, imagining he would have to fight her dad now. To the contrary, after hearing about what had happened with Brian. Ann said her dad hadn't put up too much of a fuss. And had given his blessing...after several hours of Ann's promises to be good. When Cole asked if he should reassure him in person though, Ann thought that might take a while.

Also, that he had fractured Brian's jaw and broken three of his teeth.

The next few weeks went by in a flash. When he wasn't busy packing, unpacking. And planning what he thought he would need. Planning with Ann what they would do after they'd landed. Trying to figure out how to make the trip down to Azerbaijan seem like a normal tourist destination. Taking Genie's classes in order to be as fit as they could for the trek they would have to take. Genie herself, adding in all kinds of suggestions as to what they should take with them. And selling off some of his projects to a few particularly obsessed fans.

For some reason, it had nothing to do with his sprint and subsequent faceplant into incipient demon butt, he was sure. Sachiel had insisted they go over some proper weapons training. Just in case they ran into anything on the way to finding her brother. He had taken to it like a duck to water.

He had spent many hours practicing with the swords, knives, shields and spears he'd made. And since those were the weapons she liked. Sachiel merely had to teach him the proper timing for the movements and situational awareness. He was by no means an expert. But she'd said he would at least not make a fool of himself again. His hand to hand, however, went even better. Having had more hundreds of hours at practicing this and having had recent experience. He was ready when the angel had suggested it. And found the training much easier than weapons.

"I've been wondering." Cole said as Sachiel side stepped and caught the spear, she'd had him practicing with. He ducked as the tip of her thin rapier, stabbed where his nose would have been. He pivoted and pulled the spear from her grasp and jabbed toward her chest from a knee. She leapt back and took a sideways stance, swishing the sword in a finishing salute. Poised and still as a statue. Her eyes bored into his with an intensity that made him feel as though she were staring straight into his soul. Which in this case, he thought she probably was.

"We have very little time. It would be best to focus until our mission is completed. Ensuring mission success should be our highest priority." She said impatiently. She'd seemed distracted since the talk on the turret and their chat with Ann.

"Yeah, I know but, I'm more concerned with..." There had been many thoughts weighing him down the past few weeks.

"Well...what will happen when we do." Several made more poignant as he'd been planning out the trip. "Will I become like you? Live forever? Will I remember people who...don't remember me?" Cole felt like a child again as he asked. Sachiel observed him with a mixture of sadness and understanding.

"You are worried?" The angel lifter her chin as she said it.

"Of course…" He thought about how best to speak the roiling thoughts that were leaping to and fro in his mind. "What if they don't make it, and *I* do? I thought we'd all live or die together. I would do what I could and…it would be an adventure." He trailed off.

"This *is* what you can do. You see why we wait for the knowledge to come naturally, more slowly? We cannot afford hesitation now, of all times." The angel schooled. She was bristling more than Cole thought his questions warranted.

"But you didn't wait." Cole answered waving the spear. His feet fretted as he thought about living on without Ann or Genie. If he would be able to find them again or how he could even do that, or if they would be the same if he did. Cole felt heat rising in his cheeks. He gesticulated toward the angel with the spear as if it were a conductor's baton.

"Even when you were a half-turned demon, you had reservations. But now…" Cole felt as if there were an answer swimming through his thoughts. But like a wary fish it didn't want to take the bait he offered it. But it swam, just near enough to see.

"This is what it means to be one of us. You need to be brought up to speed with no time and less power. I had reservations *because* I was half-turned sha dim. If you could even comprehend the numbers of those we have had to-"The angel broke off. Her eyes darted back and forth as if she'd almost said something she shouldn't. Her poised position faltered as she too gesticulated as she spoke.

"All we can do is put our intention and will into giving them the best chance. To protect them, but we will not be able to do that while we waste away." This was the argument Cole had been using on himself for the last three years. Of course, not for the same reasons. But the angels dodging words brought forth the idea swimming in his mind. Sachiel cut it off.

"I can tell you this. Before this world met this schism. Many souls traveled here." She looked up and seemed to be remembering with fondness. But it faded quickly. "All of us wanted to be…" Sachiel's shoulders fell as she said words that she was obviously reciting from someone else's long forgotten speech.

"Instruments of freedom's hope." She halfheartedly waved her hands as she said it. "We thought we would come here and turn them all into paragons." The Angel snorted at her own words. But it wasn't humor she saw in her own words.

"A world of angels that would turn back and..." Her eyes grew bright as she stared at the grey stone at her feet, the muscles in her jaw working. Cole's eyebrows furrowed at her words, and he tried to get her to meet his eyes. But she seemed to be lost in thoughts that had been long suppressed. "He betrayed...all of us." The words seemed to rip at something in her throat as she said it. And Cole felt another realization coming.

"It's...not just your brother, is it?" Her eyes grew wide. "What happened to the others?" She still didn't answer. Cole made a frustrated noise and scratched at his head as if going crazy.

"What else is going to happen when we take down the gate?" He stared at her, demanding answers with his gaze. She met his stern, questioning gaze. With a look that turned from fierce and ready. To a measure of pleading. Then to his surprise, she seemed to wither. Her poised posture shrank, and tears filled her eyes.

"There are many possible outcomes. One of which...if it happens."

"You want that to happen?" Cole again failed to get her to meet his eyes. He moved over to her, unthreateningly. He reached out and brushed at the tear that threatened to slide down her cheek. Her eyes lifted to meet his, they were soft and spoke many words that she seemed unable to say. That was all the confirmation he needed.

"You...know me." He voiced what he had been suspecting. Her eyes flicked away, confirming his suspicion. "I mean you knew me before this life. And not just from a distance. That's what you've been trying to get me to realize, isn't it?" He was still not used to thinking of himself as anything but what he remembered being. And still didn't know what they could have been to each other.

"When we destroy the prison gate." She gently took his hand away from her face. She moved away from him and turned to take a seat on the edge of the fountain. Her voice wearier than he'd heard it thus far. Even as she sat it seemed as if he were watching a much older version of the goddess that had appeared weeks before.

"Apart from the power that will be afforded to you. You may gain…memories." Cole nodded. It was as he suspected. Cole followed her to the fountain but sat as he had first found her. With his back to the golden depictions on the ground.

"Will I know you?" He asked his feet.

"I do not have that answer." Sachiel looked toward the sky as if asking for strength.

"I have to help them." He said it quietly, she would know who he meant. "No matter who I was. I won't forget about them."

"I know." She said it just as quietly. "I am not close to the strength I should be, or I would give you more answers. Much the same as you, my power is cut off. But…my memories are coming back. I have been outside of goings on far too long to help much further."

"If we get your body…" Cole looked up at her. She turned to him, eyes blazing into his soul again. "Would it help?" He blinked stupidly at the force of her gaze. It took her a moment to answer.

"Maybe…we are on unsteady ground." She waved a hand around to indicate the domain they were in. "No one has ever been this close to turning and come back. This place should be the size of a planet, a solar system on my good days. With what the enemy has done to this world. It is keeping me from gaining much power." She looked angry at the thought but continued.

"Memory, knowledge, power, they are all linked in ways that are hard to explain. You may have taken in enough knowledge to have reached some of your power. And you may become powerful enough to reach some of your personal knowledge." She sighed and pushed herself off the rim of the fountain. Coming down to sit next to him. When he looked over, she was leaning, forearms on her knees and close, staring at her palace. He asked.

"Then, it all goes back to the gate? We can set the world straight; give what strength we have to our people…and get back what we lost?" Sachiel had turned her blazing golden eyes back on him, nodding at what he said. The effect was so that he trailed off.

"You already knew what we had to do." She sang under her breath. She poked a fiery finger to his forehead. "I should not have tried to cram all that information into your little human brain. I thought I might be able to force you to remember. You are an anomaly in current conditions after all…I thought it might work." She shrugged and raised her eyebrows.

"Hey, look who's talking." Cole said as his forehead continued to burn. It made him wiggle his eyebrows stupidly. "Didn't you say this place should be the size of a galaxy?" He waved a hand around only to have Sachiel slap it back down. A look of over offended humor on her face.

"How dare you speak to me like that, human. When I get back to my full power you will see how beautiful this place usually is." Her playful tone belied the anguish in her eyes. He knew she was doing it for his sake. But the importance of their mission still hung over the conversation. And the slap hurt. He wondered if it had something to with her power that he could feel it, even in this place.

"I'm…guessing we were friends." Cole said through a pained half smile, his hand still stinging. Sachiel almost met his gaze this time.

"Something like that…" She was almost inaudible.

"Is it…" Now he couldn't meet her gaze as he spoke to his feet. He felt awful he couldn't remember who she was, or what he had been. That he had been voicing the fear of becoming what she had been experiencing for longer than he could imagine.

"…Hard?" He could see the angels slight nod in his peripherals.

"It is not the first or the last time for either of us. And there is still work to do." She said aloud. Cole nodded too and took a deep breath.

"Then let's go take back what's ours, stick a finger in the enemy's eye." He gave her a wolfish grin. "And get your brother back." He met Sachiel's blazing eyes. The heat that emitted from her washed into him as if he were standing a foot away from a bonfire. He felt as if all the cells in his body had a new current of electricity going through them. He even seemed more solid, more real, than he ever had been in this plain as they stared each other down.

Though what they meant to do was the only hope this little world had left. Little could he realize where his journey was leading him. And though Sachiel knew more than she was telling him. She couldn't bring herself to tell him what had happened. All she knew was that the rightness of his soul had lived on. Even in his weak and foolish state, he would still take on the same powers that had ended them at their peak. But this time, they would be together. This time, she thought, would turn out different.

Ch. 7

The process of airport travel had never been fun for international travel. Even on a journey to save the world as they were. It was no different that day. The long lines and strange looks Cole got at the TSA check point for his pocket full of handmade jewelry only made it last longer. But in between, it went as smoothly as correlating numbers to numbers could.

Sachiel seemed to want to be out and walking with them. Even around the airport, after Genie had dropped them off. Cole was the only one who could see the angel, as she had not decided to manifest herself to anyone else, so he didn't see this as a problem. And in fact, it had been rather fun, as she had not seen much of the modern world with sane eyes. Her wonder at everything people had managed to create above the level of a waterwheel. Was making the rising level of anxiety in his chest feel more like joy than panic.

There were several moments that seemed to stick out to Cole on their opening journey. One happened on their layover in London. Other than the heightened level of anxiety in his, Ann's and Sachiel's every word and movement. Cole could have sworn he had seen someone follow the angel with their eyes. But he managed to convince himself that it wasn't possible. As the angel had gone to marvel at one of the giant screens on the wall that depicted all the flights.

There was a woman, blonde hair in a tight bun in a business suit and wearing it very well. Mid-thirties and looking as anxious as he felt when not being distracted. Who watched Sachiel, wide eyed and amazed from her seat at the nearest gate. When Cole had done a double take to make sure it wasn't so, the woman was heading toward the bathroom, not looking in their direction anymore. Even so, Cole had convinced Sachiel to go back into the bracelet while they boarded.

On the flight there were the regular passengers. Looking bored and as if they were either headed home or to some work destination. But as he and Ann took their seats, Cole caught the eye of a girl who was alone and looked too young to be so. She had dyed black hair and sat with her knees pulled up to her chin. She was dressed in all black with stocking like black socks and boots that looked like they'd make her several inches taller. She also had on a pair of large headphones a black band t-shirt and black fishnet sleeves. She met Cole's wandering gaze and they held for a second. Both noticing each other's displacement among the other passengers. The moment was broken when, yet another strange passenger entered the plane. His suave southern drawl and over six- and half-foot presence, drew the attention of nearly all the other passengers.

"Thank you kindly, miss." Came his smooth baritone voice in answer to the stewardess' welcome. Cole broke eye contact with the girl and Ann took the window seat in their row. Cole expected the man's voice would have carried over the length of a football field without rising. He took his seat in the aisle and looked to make the man. As he was also a strange presence among the passengers, it might mean something. They were on a quest after all.

If only he had had that thought from the beginning.

The guy had a carryon bag that looked like it cost the same as most people's cars. He had rugged, sunbaked skin and looked to be around forty or so. He was forced to hang his head as the ceiling was too low for him to stand upright comfortably. He wore a button up white shirt with just too long collar tips. Blue jeans, and a gold belt buckle that looked like the real thing. Oval, with a depiction of a horse on it.

"Now, I don't mean to be rude." He was saying to the stewardess. "But if I could get a seat with either somebody very small or no one at all next to me, it would be very much appreciated." He indicated himself and the stewardess gave him an understanding look. She glanced around the plane and pointed to the seat next to the girl in black.

"Much obliged." The man said seeming satisfied. It didn't take him long to get to where Cole and Ann sat. When he saw Cole watching him, he nodded. Cole nodded back, but when the man saw Ann, he looked as though he'd been slapped. He slowed his step to see if Ann would notice him walking by.

She was too busy watching the luggage handlers on the tarmac. Without looking, Cole placed the back of his hand to Ann's. She took it, also without looking, though a small smile touched her lips as she did so. Cole's chest boiled with satisfaction though he didn't see the smile.

The big man watched the interaction. Looked at Cole and up to the newly minted scar on his eyebrow. His eyes glowed with some sort of satisfaction or amusement Cole didn't understand. But when the man gave a more friendly and deeper nod Cole returned it. The rest of the boarding went on as normal. The man's baritone reverberated around the cabin as he engaged the tiny girl in black in friendly conversation. Cole was feeling his curiosity grow at these strange passengers as he heard their conversation. The man speaking loudly in his confident baritone and the girl in a halting, flat, mousy voice.

Both, it seemed, had dropped everything in their lives to come on this trip. Cole felt excitement ramping up as he listened.

They were past taking off before the two had gotten into the meat of their conversation and Cole let his curiosity get the better of him. He excused himself politely from Ann to get another look at the other two. The girl had already described in her small, mousy voice. That she was coding specialist that worked at home and hadn't had a vacation in a long time. She attributed some algorithm to understanding her needs. As her inbox had been flooded with suggestions to go see old Armenian architecture. Cole was just passing them on his way to the bathroom when the man answered as to why he was there.

"On my life, I didn't know where I was going when I got to the airport. I've been having these…freaky dreams for weeks." He looked as though he were trying to figure out a hard crossword. "And when I got up this mornin' I skipped right out and booked the first trip they had available. And here I am…my wife's gunna kill me." He shook his head mournfully and seemed to mean it.

"That's weird." The girl said nodding and staring off into the close distance. Cole passed them and they were too engrossed in the conversation to notice him.

Barring their strange appearance on this particular flight. Cole didn't see anything about them that would blare any alarm bells. If he had not been too engrossed in them. He may have noticed there were two more sets of eyes. One in the middle aisle, the other on the farthest. Following him all the way to the bathroom. One the shade of cool, milk chocolate brown that had been the first to board the plane. And had opened his laptop to hide behind, ignoring the flight rules, as it hadn't been on most of the time. The other eyes that followed him were the shade of blackest night. Connected to a very pretty, dark-haired woman.

All those on the flight went their separate ways after they had picked up their luggage. Cole grabbed his one large suitcase and backpack. Ann, her several suitcases that Cole was inclined to take one of. He gave the strange passengers one last glance as they left. Thinking that he must have been over hyped on the conjoining quest idea as he hadn't found a good time to engage them in conversation.

They hitched a cab on their way into the city and were greeted by a very old looking woman with a shawl draped over her head. She spent most of the ride giving suggestions as to where they could go to enjoy the night life. Cole and Ann were asking where the old woman thought they should go to find a tour guide that knew the countryside. When she started making comments that were the prevue of someone her age.

"What do young people care about history?" She asked in a thick Armenian accent. "Look at me!" She turned and gave them a wide, wrinkly grin they couldn't see.

"You have seen all the ancient sights in my country, now." She laughed and turned back to the road Cole and Ann exchanged amused looks.

"We did want to see some of the old churches in the mountains-" Cole started.

"Churches?" The old lady exclaimed. "What kind of young people are these?" She turned away from the road again to look at them. Her height only allowing for her eyes and forehead to look over the seat between them. Her voice took on a mournful tone as she turned back.

"My son, very much like this. Caught up in ideas, too big. I have no grandbabies now." Her mournful tone took on a touch of incredulity. "Now look at me! I will never have them." Her two passengers exchanged unknowing looks at this.

"Oh, I'm sorry." Ann said.

"Don't be! He lived how he wanted." The old woman said. "You want to make old woman happy?" She egged them on and dragged out her words.

"Be young…. Who cares about marriage?" she waved a wrinkly hand. "I marry, look what happens, no legacy. Be smart, just make the babies." She laughed heartily as Cole and Ann both went bright red and laughed nervously. Just to be safe, they turned the conversation back to the countryside. The old woman still throwing in vulgar comments every now and then.

■■

They were in their room on the third floor of the Grand Hotel in Yerevan. The window of which overlooked a large, circular courtyard with couches and a bar. And several other stations where people were enjoying games, the weather, and the historical center the hotel doubled as. The girl at the front desk had suggested they come down before everyone got too drunk and rowdy. But that seemed to have passed while they were shaking off jetlag. It was only then Cole remembered to ask about the strange moments on the journey.

Ann lay on the king size bed in a bath robe after having showered the travel grime off. The look on her face reminiscent of the look she used to save for after winning a race. And not at all troubled by the thoughts going through Cole's mind. When she opened her eyes and gave him a once over. Standing at the window, watching the high level of activity that a balmy early summer evening always warranted. She seemed to catch on.

"Kind of a weird flight though, right?" She asked seeming to step right into his train of thought.

He just rolled with it, after having seen what she was capable of on and off the track. What with her twenty gold metals to setting up her sister and ex to out themselves. And taking on world changing events with cool and poignant questions. Not batting an eye when a glowing ghost soul popped out of a bracelet. He wasn't surprised that she was on the track she was in life. Or that she seemed to read him like a book.

"Did you know anyone that was on the plane?" Cole asked turning away from the window. He was slapped by the figure Ann struck. Turned on her side at the edge of the bed. Dark wet hair in a tangled mess. One lightly tanned leg halfway out of the robe and dangling over empty air. Her eye that wasn't buried in pillow searching over him. It made his body heat rise to measures on the kelvin scale. He was hard pressed to keep his mind on anything else.

"You mean the big southern guy who couldn't keep his eyes off me? Or the little tech girl you were so interested in?" She gave him a devious smile. Cole's eyebrows rose as he realized she had been paying a lot more attention than he thought. He was even more surprised when she said. "No… but I was paying more attention to that lady with the dark eyes. She stared you down almost the whole flight."

How much attention did she have? Cole thought. He hadn't even noticed that part.

Ann seemed troubled by the thought of the woman. Remembering the blank look of hunger she had given her when their eyes had met, she shivered as goosebumps rose slightly on her visible skin. Cole was distracted from the distraction that was Ann's body, by an itching sensation on his ankle. As he sat down on the bed next to Ann's outstretched foot, he heard a voice in his head.

"Can I come out now?" Sachiel sounded impatient and angry that she had been made to wait all day while there were goings on. Cole gave her an affirmation as he lifted his pajama pant leg to inspect what had been a snake bite. Now, seemingly…a cheesy looking tattoo.

"Wow…how have I not noticed *that*?" Ann said mockingly and smiling broadly as Sachiel appeared looking worried. She inspected the wiggling curse mark with an air of apprehension.

"I didn't get it on purpose." Cole said defensively as he scratched at it. Ann's look changed from humored to slightly grossed out. Sachiel bent over the curse mark to inspect the change.

"It's moving!" Ann exclaimed and leaned in to get a closer look. Golden sparks of light reflected in her eyes as she watched in stunned amazement at the proceedings. Sachiel had started to whisper in her flowing language as she waved over the bite. Dripping more power into her circle around it. After the mark had ceased its fussing, she looked at Ann. Even the angel seemed momentarily distracted.

"This…woman you spoke of. Describe her to me." Ann seemed troubled again at having to remember the woman thoroughly. Not nearly as troubled as the angel, as the features became clear to her. Sachiel's eyes went into some middle distance and her breath came fast and shallow as the description ended. Both Ann and Cole watched her apprehensively as she stayed silent for several seconds afterward. In a whisper, almost beyond audibility, she said.

"Lilith." She seemed to deflate a little as memories unknown to the others came back to her. She let out a soft yet furious moan.

"So soon?" She asked to no one in particular. "Will she never cease to haunt me?"

Cole and Ann exchanged looks of curious apprehension.

"I'm guessing there's history between you two?" Ann asked. In answer Sachiel first pointed to the mark on Cole's ankle. Then answered.

"Some of the thoughts you helped me to destroy were made from memories." She bit her lip in concentration. "Memories, that involve other beings…powerful beings, can take on a life of their own."

"So, that snake was made from memories of Lilith?" Cole asked also looking at the mark.

"Yes." Sachiel said quietly.

"And she…bit him?" Ann asked quizzically, her face flushed. Cole looked horrified at the thought. It was then that he started to grasp the measure of the actions he'd taken in helping the fallen angel.

"She tried to kill him…and almost succeeded" Sachiel said mournfully. "I can only hope when the gate is breached, or when I get my body back, I can bind and remove the curse completely." The news that he had been on death's door slid down Cole's spine like an ice cube. He felt a wave of gratitude for the angel but was more concerned with the present.

"Why is it…active?" He and Ann looked toward the door as if they expected her to come through.

"I cannot answer that." Sachiel said sorrowfully. "I am a husk of what I was. It could mean she is close. Or that I was thinking of her. Or that she is nearer and using her power and you are merely feeling the resonance."

"She could already be onto us." Said Cole trying to think of all the implications. He stood up and walked slowly back to the window.

"Could? She was on the flight; she could be on top of us for all we know." Said Ann, also troubled.

"We'll have to cut out some of the touristy stuff." Cole thought out loud.

Armenia had been the first country to declare itself a Christian nation. And had some very old and very interesting churches along their countryside. Since there had been recent conflict between neighboring Turkey and Azerbaijan, the latter being where they planned to go. They had plotted to visit some of the churches. So as not to look as though they were defecting to go fight a war.

"We'll have to find someone who can get us over the border fa-" He stopped talking when the scene outside came back into view. What he saw took a moment to sink in.

Where there had been the normal bustle of a summer night. There was now something strange and eerie going on in the courtyard. The people who had been cheerfully talking and laughing. Were all still, hunched or looking as if they had fallen over mid action. This did not strike Cole as drunk and rowdy. The torches that had been lit for the oncoming of the night flared larger and brighter than normal. Casting a strange glow to the scene.

"Get dressed." Cole said in a low voice, but there was no time for that. Right after the words had left his mouth. A youngish woman with black hair in a black business suit. Looking exactly like the one Ann had just described from their flight. walked casually into the courtyard. With pitch black eyes, she observed her surroundings, seeming satisfied with herself. Cole swore loudly as Ann slipped on her second shoe. She'd always been very fast, and she seemed to have the where with all to grab the most essential thing first.

Sachiel was at the window faster than a physical body could move. And she let out a stream in that strange language. No longer sounding terrified or mournful. Only cold, contemptuous fury mingled into her tone at the sight of the woman. Cole didn't know what kind of power this woman had. If she was superhumanly strong. Or if she had magic that he wasn't capable of understanding yet. But what she was displaying now was already beyond anything he'd seen done in the outside world. As if to add to the thought, her eyes shot to the window as if she'd heard it. Cold dread creeped up his spine.

She smiled, not the kind of smile you would expect someone to give an old friend. It was more like the smile Cole imagined Captain Ahab gave when he finally found Moby Dick. Equal parts ecstatic, sinister and insane.

She reared her head back and let out an ear-splitting noise. It sounded like a mixture of screeching car tires, a bald eagle, and the elongated sound of breaking glass. And from out of each of the people around her rose black smoke. It quickly resolved into figures that resembled the spirits Cole had spent his life hunting down, only bigger. They were not as big as the Sasquatch had been but were easily of a height with Cole.

They fully formed, each into grotesque looking monsters with long arms. Strong looking bodies and ember eyes set within almost perfectly round heads with no neck. Lipless mouths wrapped around jagged teeth and they had no noses. To his horror, Cole noticed by the indentations on the couch cushions. And a drink table tumbling to the ground, as one of the monsters stood and turned its too wide body. They weren't the ghostlike beings he was used to; they were solid. Cole counted around ten before Ann spoke from behind him. Having run over to see what was going on.

"Time to go." She said as she shoved Cole's backpack into his arms. He swung it over his shoulder as he followed her toward the door. Her bathrobe whipping at her speed.

"Where do we go?" He asked incredulously as she pulled open the door.

The deep sound of impact, coupled with a slight vibration resounded from the wall behind them. A half-dressed man with poofed, curly black hair stepped out into the hall from directly across from them. A quizzical look on his face at the commotion. Ann caught the man's door before it closed all the way and went barreling through the room. The sound of breaking glass sounded right from where they had just been. The man they were invading his room let out a horrified scream as Ann picked up his ice bucket.

"Anywhere but here." She said as if stating the obvious. She threw the ice bucket as hard as she could, and it shattered the window.

On the front of the building was a light blue awning that stuck out from around halfway up the second floor. It had ivy growing around the sides and top and was used to cover a little restaurant that ran year-round. The quaint little restaurant sat across the street from a wide river. that bent and turned through the city and reflected the failing light in dazzlingly pretty shades of pink and orange. The little eatery was popular among the locals and visitors. And it was being enjoyed by several families and couples. They were lucky the awning was made of sturdy material. As, after several very loud, very strange noises the sound of breaking glass could be heard twice.

The second breaking glass was followed by several stranger things. The first was what sounded like quick rain fall and a thumping sound. Followed by a clinking ice bucket bouncing off the ground in front of the restaurant. The second and third were much louder thumping noises followed by quick footsteps across the awning. Then, seemingly the strangest thing the restaurant goers thought they would see that night. Two young people, both looking as if they belonged in the movie they thought they were in. Dropped the twelve or so feet from the top of the awning onto the cobblestone and took off, fast as Olympic sprinters.

The restaurant goers looked around at each other. Several men and women with red faces, as neither of the young couple looked ready to be out in public. The boy in house shoes, pajama pants and no shirt. While the girl in nothing but a pair of shoes with no socks and a loosely flowing bath robe. They looked as if they were settling in for the night. Not gearing up for a flight for their lives.

But as the cacophony of noises and sights that followed, started. They all realized that is exactly what it was.

A two-foot-wide section of the edge of the awning exploded in a shower of wood shards. As a monstrous black figure came hurdling down toward the fleeing couple. It tumbled, out of sorts from its flight from across the hall and clipping its wide body on the edge of the window. The sound of more commotion and screaming was soon followed by more breaking glass and drywall.

Several monsters, the same as the first. Came hurdling through the front of the hotel, literally. They streamed out in a shower of glass, debris and earth-shattering noise that scattered all throughout the now unhappy restaurant goers. Leaving cuts, scrapes and memories that would haunt them for the rest of their lives.

Cole heard a hideous lion's roar trumpet from a hundred yards behind him. As the sound of tinkling glass over cobblestone subsided. Ann was several feet in front of him and adding to the gap. He pumped his legs faster to catch up, but she only added more speed when she felt him closing. Had she always been this fast? Cole asked himself. She had used him as a practice opponent when they were growing up, but she'd never outstripped him like this. She didn't even seem to be trying that hard while he was pressing his limit.

"We are near the gate." Sachiel said quickly as she erupted from inside the stone where she had apparently gone but was now keeping pace. She was no longer in her blanket like robe. She now wore lightly glowing, golden white battle armor made to look like dragon scales. She wore no helmet, and her long white hair was curled into a giant braided bun. On her hip Cole was surprised to see that she did not wear the thin rapier that was her practice sword. But the black Ulfbhert sword tinged with ember and aquamarine waving lines. Each shown separately and brilliantly in the failing sunlight.

"Your power should start manifesting." She finished, indicating Ann. Who was not only outpacing him, but was doing it while trying to hold her bathrobe together. Cole thought about this as the sounds of their pursuers gained on them.

Ever since they'd landed, he had been feeling a rising tension within himself. It was shadowed by the goings on that followed. But as it had been brought to the forefront of his mind and he was seeing it with his own eyes. He decided to focus on his energy as he usually did when creating something in Sachiel's space. He was unprepared to feel such a difference. Where before, he had felt flowing sparks from fist size clumps of energy. He now felt as if the mental picture of his energy was focused on a being that had to be at least ten times his size. He did a mental zoom out to realize that the energy stores within him had just gotten that much bigger.

"Cole!" Shouted Ann over her shoulder. The sounds of stomping feet, growling breath and terrified civilians started to fill the air around them. "If you have anything up your sleeve, now would be the time." Ann looked as terrified as he felt as she looked past him.

Several of the beasts were overachievers, far ahead of the rest and were almost on top of them. Cole felt the same sense of life or death that had gripped him when the sasquatch had charged him, four years previous. Leading to the creation of his first enchanted jewel. And a month earlier that had resulted in the new Ulfbhert.

Sachiel gave him a hopeful glance as she stopped abruptly and turned around to face the oncoming threat. They were only a stone's throw away as Cole skid to halt as well. Focusing all his might on something, *anything* that could save them. Instinctively he thrust his left hand over Sachiel's shoulder as she brandished the Ulfbhert. Knees bent and poised to strike.

The narrow street, now dark as they had passed into an area with buildings on both sides. Lit up, like an aquamarine spotlight had just been turned on and pointed at the three beasts that had caught up to them. Cole's palm shown with unfocussed energy. And as the monsters neared, every step brought them closer. Closer to being the charred remains of monsters.

The first two were moving too fast and hadn't seen it coming. They passed through the edge of the light and the first two layers were immediately seared away. Within two steps, they were crumbling charcoal, left to tumble toward the two combatants' feet.

The last in the line had gotten smart quick. It had leapt as soon as Cole's spell had gone off. Catching dexterously to a windowsill to their left. And out of the beam of Cole's energy blast. It hadn't waited for him to turn toward it and was now soaring through the air to catch his flank. It was caught mid-air by the first three inches of the Ulfbhert. Which greeted it from clavicle to groin. Cole managed to roll and only caught a desperately weak hand to the back. As the beast dropped past him and landed face first on the street with a huff. They both turned back to where Ann was standing. Looking stunned and breathless but satisfied.

"Yeah. That works." She said shortly.

Without waiting to see if the others were catching up. Or if they were towing their master along with them. The three turned back to sprinting down the street. There were several people who had started running in the same direction and the three's appearance only seemed to make them panic even more. Aside from the monsters they may or may not have seen. Apparently, there was something going on that was sending people out of their beds and into the street. They were screaming, and though Cole didn't know the language. He heard some measure of coordination mixed in with the fear. This wasn't their first rodeo.

The civilians seemed to have communicated something to each other. As the people that were running with them abruptly stopped and changed direction. Being added to by the people who had been further down the street. The people who passed them had looks of confused terror on their faces. Ann slowed, coming to realize what it meant. Sure enough, as they came around the light bend in the street. There were two monsters, heaving breaths, gurgling loudly at every exhale.

They stood on either side of the street. With a monstrous tiger's roar, the third made itself known from the top of the two-story building to the left of them. Cole and Sachiel overtook Ann and directed their steps off the sidewalk toward the monsters.

They were too far away, and too far apart for Cole's new weapon to be of any use. He merely lit up the street and sent their ember eyes to glow with reflected light. But he could feel the edges of the power like a giant cone that extended from his palm. Mechanically, he focused on concentrating the light into the smallest point he could.

In answer to the monster's roar. Sachiel let out battle cry that was one high, pure single note. The sound of which shattered the nearest windowpanes and sent electrifying clarity through Cole's entire being. The Angel blurred, taking thirty yards in a single stride only a foot from the ground. The monster on the farthest side of the street tried to catch her as she reached it. It's dying hands clutched onto her shoulders as the Ulfbhert extended a foot out of its back.

The monster let out a pained roar as it clutched tighter to the angel's shoulders. It shifted so that Sachiel's back was turned to the monster on the other side of the street. That one turned away from Cole as he realized what they were planning to do.

He pulled back his aqua lighted hand as if he were about to throw a baseball at the beast. The energy, prompted by Cole's desperate need and the Angel's clarifying scream. Coalesced into a beam half an inch across. And followed his arms movement like a giant shining whip. The beast was only a foot away from sending a knife hand through the back of the struggling angel's armor. When a ten-foot bolt of shining blue-green energy burned its way through its hips and into the ground with the sound of a swishing clap of a whip, only more electric. Its body jerked to a halt and bent almost in half. The power behind its strike was ripped away. So that the pointed hand that meant to go through the angels back only crumpled against the scaled armor.

Sachiel took the blow with a huff of expelled breath and wrenched herself free of the other monster's grip. She ripped the Ulfbhert free from the monster's body twirled it fast as lightning and beheaded the beast in one swift motion. Its head tumbled to the ground and deflated in a whisp of black smoke.

The beast Cole had stopped in its tracks roared and tried to push at the bolt of energy that held it to the ground. The sound of sizzling hit the cooling night air and half the monster's hands were seared off to tumble to the ground and turn to black smoke as his partners head had done. Sachiel swiftly pivoted and sent the first six inches of the black blade through where the monster's nose should have been. It melted away in black smoke as the beast on top of the roof roared again.

The Bolt of glowing energy faded as the beast disappeared.

"This way!" Ann shouted. Cole turned to see her waving an arm. Standing at the opening to a narrow alley.

She was opposite a tall, long wavy blond-haired, blue-eyed man. In a black button up shirt, black slacks and a brown leather shoulder holster. The monstrous gold-plated gun he held was pointed toward the roaring beast. The man's blank eyed, blank faced focus preceded his firing. A deafening deep sound and wave of tiny explosion blasted through them in three quick waves as the man let loose on the beast. One of the down sides to being solid, apparently. Was that solid objects influenced this new kind of monster.

Cole ran toward Ann; he heard the whump and crash that was the falling beast as if it were further away than it was. The shots stopped and left a high pitch ringing in his ears. And from the distance somewhere ahead of them came an answering roar he could barely hear. The tall man ushered them into the alley with one hand as he put the golden gun back in its holster with the other. Sachiel had apparently gone back into the jewel as she was nowhere to be seen.

"Who is this guy?" Cole shouted above the ringing in his ears.

"Paul." Yelled Ann as if only his name would explain. He hushed them and his voice was deep and thick with a Greek accent.

"Hush, you two. They still come." He dashed beside them and led the way between business and apartment buildings.

The sounds of regular folks as they transitioned between their regular lives and wondering what the commotion outside was.

Mixed with the noises of roaring beasts echoing above and around them. Getting closer as they closed in. Paul seemed to know where he was going as he didn't pause once in his tracks. Cole thought it may be smarter to be wary of the strange man, but it had seemed as though he wanted to protect them and they didn't have much of a choice.

They came out onto a dark empty street. The civilians all having found somewhere else to be after the noises of what sounded like escaped tigers and gun shots had started resounding. The only thing that seemed alive were two red brake lights attached to a tiny white truck that sat running and waiting. The cab of which looked like it would only fit two small people. Paul rushed them over to it and insisted Ann take the second seat in the cab.

When Cole heard her exclaim at the driver, he pressed his face to the glass as he tried to make himself fit in the bed with Paul taking up most of the space.

It was the old woman who had been their cab driver earlier in the day. Her eyes were only an inch from his with only the thin glass separating them. Once she saw they were stuffed safely enough to drive she hit the gas. She laughed maniacally at Cole's dumbstruck face.

"You've met my mother." Paul said as they exchanged a quick handshake. Cole pulled his backpack onto his lap. It was filled for a hike. With two pairs of extra clothes, a pair of hiking shoes, three pairs of socks. And energy bars and water bottles stuffed everywhere else. Yet again Cole was struck by Ann's ability to take exactly what they needed.

"She uh…made it seem like you were dead." Cole said as he took out the items he wanted.

He leaned over the side of the cab and knocked on the window. Ann thanked him as he passed her a set of his clothes. As much as the patrons and citizens of Yerevan had enjoyed the skin she'd been flashing them. He had a feeling she would rather have been dressed for the scene they'd just caused. He turned back to Paul to see the big blonde man looking exasperated.

"She is always doing that." He said as he rapped the window with his knuckles. "I get turned down one time-" The big man started but his face turned instantly serious as he pulled the gun from its holster. From a kneeling position, he fired. The start of a tiger roar was cut off by the sound and shockwave of three large booms. Cole was prepared this time and took his fingers from out of his ears to scan the rooftops. He let the backpack fall to the cab floor. He took to a kneeling position as well and held himself down by grabbing at the still open windowsill. Ann's hand grabbed his wrist to steady him as he tried his whip bolt spell for the second time ever.

Standing on top of two buildings ahead and on either side of the street were two more of the troll-like monsters. Cole lit one of them up with a spotlight. It roared and leapt down at him in a headfirst dive. Cole drew back the light and with the sound of an electric whip he sent a bolt straight through its forehead and down it's spine. It hit the side of truck bed with a soft thump as it turned into black smoke. Cole quickly pressed the hand Ann wasn't gripping against his ear. As three more booms filled the air. The last of the beasts was nowhere to be seen.

They sat back down in the bed, Cole felt immensely drained. He took three long deep breaths before he grabbed his last grey shirt and threw it over his sweaty body. Letting go of Ann's grasp long enough to do so but taking it back when he was done.

Paul looked him up and down with curiosity etched all over his face. He dropped the magazine out of the bottom of his monstrous golden handgun. Taking another from a belt on his waste, he slid it into the bottom of the gun and pulled the slide back. All while staring at Cole, who laid back with his grey eyes closed, he turned his arm and gripped Ann's wrist back.

"That move…" Paul said bringing Cole back to reality. He looked at the big man, who was still oozing curiosity.

"Could it be?" The man said as he searched over Cole's features as if hoping to gain some sort of answer. Cole just looked back with slight puzzlement. "But you are too old…we only lost him a few years ago." Paul said to himself as Cole had no idea what he was talking about. Paul shook his head as if coming to some sort of conclusion and shrugged.

"Ach, we will get more clarity when we get there…but" Then he looked excited as he asked. "Where is she?" Cole glanced toward the cab.

"No no no. The Angel! I saw her." He insisted. He leaned back against the cab wall. "Oh, so beautiful. I have not seen her in so long. Where has she been?" Paul seemed wholly earnest.

Cole couldn't help the disbelieving look he gave the strange man. It couldn't be helped as the man didn't look to be over forty and he hadn't gotten used to time dilation amongst long living beings yet. Still, the man had helped them, he held up his left wrist to display the brightly gleaming wolf's eye. Paul returned the disbelieving look but seemed to somewhat grasp what Cole was saying. He made to grab his entire wrist. When the man's palm touched the stone, his eyes widened, and he almost shouted in joyous surprise.

He laughed for a second, but it died quickly as he grew more focused and concerned. A long moment later his face flushed in anger and his grip on Cole's wrist turned into a vice. He growled in a furious rage that rumbled the entire cab. Cole pulled at his arm and the big man lightened his grip. He gave Cole an apology then started speaking a stream of Greek that could only have been curses.

"Damn that woman." He hissed in English. Cole knew Sachiel had continued whatever she had been saying as Paul went back to listening. He nodded several times as the redness drained from his face. Cole wondered why he was being left out.

"Well, we fill you in on that." Paul said out aloud. He nodded several more times and hummed.

Then his eyes bulged, and he stole a glance toward the cab. Ann was on her knees and fully turned around to see what was happening. When first Paul's, then Cole's eyes flashed at her she gave them a look of surprise. Her grip on Cole's arm tightened, and for the briefest span Cole was genuinely worried his wrist might break.

Luckily it was only the flash of her surprise that caused her to clench up uncontrollably. Cole almost leapt from his seat. Both his wrists had apparently become at risk in such a short period. Ann seemed to realize and shouted an apology over the wind that was picking up. The truck had left the cramped streets and made its way to a quieter area of the city mostly filled with living spaces.

Ann's apology was followed by her jerking her chin toward Paul. She was obviously more interested what she could glean from his reactions. And his next reaction didn't disappoint. He had gone back to listening carefully. But then his eyes positively bulged out of his head as he looked up at Cole.

"HE'S THE T-" He stopped as Sachiel's voice came through to both of them. Apparently, she was not holding back now.

"STOP!" She shouted. She continued speaking to both quickly with a hint of apology. "I apologize for the secrecy…now is not the time to figure out why your memories have not returned." Paul gave a consenting look.

"We are close." He said, checking their surroundings. "We discuss more there."

The rest of the ride was spent mostly in silence. Cole was running through the events of the past day. He and Ann passed as much silent information between them as they could. While holding onto each other for the rest of the ride. They were both realizing there were greater powers at work than they'd expected on this trip. He was distracted several times by Paul sneaking glances at him.

And subsequently trying to hold back excited looking smiles. After the third time Cole couldn't take it anymore.

"What?" He asked twitching his head and sounding more defensive than he meant to. This night had him more adrenaline pumped than he had expected or been prepared for. Paul held up his hands.

"Oh, nothing." His suspicious little giggle said otherwise. The truck bounced as they reached the parking lot of a restaurant bar. The glowing sign out front read *Nikon Bar and Grill*. Cole rolled his eyes; he wouldn't have to wait much longer for some information anyway.

They piled out of the truck and Cole almost laughed at how Ann looked. He couldn't tell before, but the oversize grey shirt and her holding up baggy rolled up jeans were comical to say the least. Ann usually wore high class stuff after all. The look she gave him killed his laughter in its cradle. He turned it into a question instead.

"Ha-how-w, you OK?" He tried to save it. Ann took a full three seconds of staring him down. Before she laughed at the ridiculousness of his question and the look on his face. She presented herself with her free arm. Cole tentatively laughed with her. Then the absurdity of what they had just been through seemed to wash over them. Then they both laughed emphatically while Paul gave the little old lady an update on what he had learned.

"Ha!" came the old woman's wheezy bark of laughter from behind the truck. "I tell you." She said wagging a finger at Paul from around his hip level. She held out a hand and Paul pulled out a brown leather wallet to slap a bill in her hand. Annoyance written all over his face.

"How could I know? You picked them up. What were the odds?" He shrugged and threw them a brilliant smile. Now they weren't running for their lives Paul's striking, chiseled features became more prominent. The old woman presented a hand at Cole and Ann. Their laughter subsided as they watched the scene playing out.

"Just look at them. Kids!" The old woman hobbled toward the bar entrance. "Talking about churches…What else would they be? This is why I have no grandbabies." She flung her hands up in annoyance. Paul rolled his eyes and gave her a rude hand gesture.

"I felt that." The old woman responded. The interaction made them want to laugh again as Cole and Ann looked at each other, so they did.

"Hey, wait." Paul called after the old woman. "Did we get the others?" The question roused a sharp interest and made their laughter die down quickly. Cole and Ann followed the two when Paul beckoned. As the old woman opened the side door to the bar she called back.

"A little…weird girl come in just before I come to get you." She waved a hand over herself to indicate the girl she spoke of must look weird in some way. "A vegetarian." She made a disgusted noise.

"I tell you, Greek salad was good idea." Paul ducked slightly to get through the doorway.

"Bach." The old woman spat as they entered the bar. "You have good idea? Give me grandbaby." Paul looked up to the roof as if asking for help and shook his head. This was obviously an argument they'd had many times.

The restaurant bar looked just like any other. They had a seat yourself sign written in several languages, one of them being English. Light brown polished wood was the most prominent feature to the place. It made up the ten or so tables and chairs that occupied the main seating area. Half the seats were occupied by happy looking patrons.

There was also a bar that took up most of the back wall. Manned by a wizened old man with such bushy grey eyebrows you could hardly see his sharp dark eyes from behind them. And French doors to a parlor off to the right that stood ajar. Off to the left were two pool tables. One being played at by group of drunken looking couples, the other by a single tall blonde woman in biking leathers with a cohort of young men holding pool sticks. All of whom looked to be much less invested in the game as they were in her.

There was one large booth that sat next to the edge of the bar, and it was occupied by a single good looking young black-haired man in a smoking jacket. And several very good-looking young women that were fawning over him.

When the four pair entered the bar they caught the eye of the barman, the woman in biking leathers and the young man. All at once they excused themselves from what they were doing. Ann noticed this as Cole was still taking in the atmosphere of the bar. It seemed like a homey place to spend a fun evening.

The barman put the glass he was cleaning on the counter. Filled up everyone's drinks who sat in front of him and flipped up a small sign. The young man feigned needing to use the bathroom. Apologizing to his harem in a thick Italian accent.

What Cole did happen to notice was that the woman in biking leathers. After catching Paul's eye, turned, and in one shot. Sank every single ball left on the table except the white ball. She even called and hit the eight ball last as the first of seven balls sunk into their holes. She left the group of young men debating whether they still lost. Seeing as how she had sunk more of their balls than her own.

Ann and Cole were being ushered into the parlor as this was happening. Paul slid open the double doors and smiled as he lifted a welcoming hand. The old woman went to greet the barman as he crossed the table floor. Ann and Cole decided to trust it as they looked at each other and shrugged. The look they shared was: their night had already gone so awry. It couldn't get much worse.

Or so they thought, as they took the closest seats at a large round table that was made to seat at least twelve. The room was lined with booths but none of them seemed to be occupied. Paul hung back to talk to the woman in leathers. Cole set his backpack on the ground next to him and took out two water bottles and passed one to Ann. She took it gratefully and downed most of it in one. Cole did the same.

"Well." She said afterward. "I guess we were a bit optimistic about how this trip would go." Cole snorted and spat out the last drink he was gulping over the table. They laughed again, it felt better to laugh than to lament.

"So much for being a kid for the last time." Cole said with an apologetic look.

"You kidding?" Ann said looking aghast and raising an eyebrow. "I spend most of my time going over market data and watching my dad do sales pitches." She rolled her eyes. "Getting chased down by a witch and her demon pals…with you? Meeting helpful strangers? That's better than childhood. I just had to trust you weren't spying on me with mirrors back then." She gave him a devious smile.

Cole had only a moment to really grasp how lucky he was to have her there. If not for her quick thinking he probably would have been mincemeat at the hotel. Adventure over. That coupled with how well she was taking all of this in were…something he really didn't know how to thank her for.

"I was spying on you…just not with mirrors and not when you thought." It was a joke, they both knew it. Ann put on a scandalized look, but it was tinged too heavily with amusement to be real. She never missed a thing. Especially not when it came to him. She pushed his face away as she had done so many times before. But this time Cole caught her hand as she pulled back, intentionally this time and pulled her into him.

Ch. 8

"Well, this is new." Paul said as he entered the room flanked by the woman in leathers. "It usually takes a while longer. But considering…." The old woman and the barman followed. The young Italian was the last in the precession. He held a giant bottle in his right hand. It wasn't until he crossed the threshold that Cole and Ann broke apart.

"Bach. What do you know about that?" The old woman said giving them an approving look. Paul rolled his eyes again.

Immediately after the young Italian closed the doors Sachiel burst from inside the jewel. She was in her regular blanket like robe again. Perhaps too excited or disheveled to keep herself from being seen to the patrons, she had waited. To some surprise, when she came hurdling out of Cole's wrist. She made a b-line straight for the barman. His body untensed from initial shock and he hugged the angel back. His dark eyes gleamed from far under his bushy eyebrows. He patted her braided hair and whispered something in the angelic language Cole hadn't yet been able to understand. He sounded consoling, like he was speaking to a daughter. Sachiel was racked with sobs. Before Cole could ask what was going on, the angel spoke.

"I'm sorry." She said in a tiny voice. The old man hummed in an, it's ok, sort of way. "How did you escape?" She asked. Cole looked around the table. The group were looking at the two like this was a meeting that should definitely be happening. And that they were a mixture of happy and mournful at it. The old man answered, his voice was gruff with emotion and had a hint of a German accent.

"I was…the only one who got away." He had a soft, breezy and gentle voice. Cole thought this would only intensify her sorrow. But the angel let out a fierce growl and stopped herself from crying.

"I have met one of our faction…recently." Sachiel said, trying to bring herself back to the present. At this the old man raised his bushy eyebrows.

"How? They were being turned when I was forced to flee." Sachiel turned a hand to Cole.

He smiled apprehensively. The old man held out his hand to shake Cole's. Cole stood and when their hands met. He saw in the old man's concentration, that there was something other than just a handshake going on. His dark eyes shone brightly, after a few seconds he chortled.

"So…you came back together? Good." He nodded his head in approval. Cole and Ann looked at Sachiel. She only glanced at them but couldn't hold either of their gazes.

"I knew it." Ann said with a triumphant look.

"Hey…I got that one too." Cole said in an attempt not to look completely out of the loop.

"Oh yeah?" Said Ann playfully, pulling a face. "Why don't you tell me *why* she won't tell you who or what you were?" She pulled another face that said she knew exactly what he was missing.

"Well." Cole said trying to think on the spot as all the others took seats around the table. Ann looked more amused by the second. "Something must have happened…" He said dumbly.

"Actually." Said Sachiel in an undertone. "I am more interested in confirming who *she* is." Sachiel indicated Ann. The old man gave her a small toothless smile as he extended a hand. All the humor dropped out of Ann's face, and she looked as if she very much did not want to know.

"I am surprised you could not get the information for yourself. After all, you are my superior, are you not?" Asked the old man gently as he waited patiently for Ann. Sachiel answered in an embarrassed tone.

"I am without most of my capabilities and power, it took...a while to confirm with him." She glanced at Cole then gave Ann a once over.

"I am willing to confirm but...they didn't ask. And are without perspective." All faces went red, and Cole didn't meet Ann's eyes. Ann looked at the angel haughtily, eyes blazing as she slapped her hand into the old barman's.

"What kind of angel are you?" She asked half amused half incensed as the old man clasped her hand.

"You see?" Sachiel said. The old barman chortled again. He stopped as his eyes grew bright, his chortle turning into exclamation. "My question exactly." The angel added to herself.

"Ohh…" The old man said quietly.

"Laphaliel." A look of determination crossed his face and he bowed his head respectfully.

Ann nodded back confused; there was a familiarity to the name. She did not feel surprised, only, *right*, somehow. There was so much more she wanted to know, but held her questions, for now. Her eyes darted around the room to see if there were any reaction to his words. Sachiel scrunched up her face and nodded slowly, her shoulders fell slightly. But she seemed to steel herself and took on a poised, soldier-like stance. Hands by her sides and a stern expression. She also gave a little respectful bow. Everyone in the room gave the old man and angel impatient and excited looks. All accept the old woman, who was close enough to hear. She looked at Ann with a mixture of triumph and satisfaction.

Ann was looking back and forth between the two and a nervous little laugh escaped her. Cole, on the other hand, was looking at her in a whole new light. So much about her made sense to him that he couldn't have placed before now. And he felt a little sense of satisfaction that he knew something she didn't. He didn't have the time to gloat as the sounds of the patrons outside the doors were muted by a new sound. There was half familiar voice near the door that made them all perk up.

"I appreciate y'all helpin' me." Came a smooth southern baritone. "And I could sure use a glass of whiskey, but this don't look like any hospital I've ever seen." The moment was broken by everyone's eyes turning toward the French doors. An old man's amused basso voice, heavy with a Native American accent answered.

"Don't you worry, pale feet. Do you not want to know what's going on?" The southern baritone answered impatiently as the voices drew closer to the French doors.

"Man, ain't no mystery to gettin' attacked by a crazy bum. You comin' outa nowhere is the only-man I don't even know your name. You tryna take me out to dinner?" There was a deep chuckle in response.

"My name is Flying Falcon Claws That Runs with Wolves and Tames the Bears." Silence met the old native voice.

The doors opened and the big man they'd seen on their flight turned to look inside with a flat expression. He locked eyes with Cole and Ann for a second each as they were the closest. He looked like he'd been through a similar night. The sleeve of his white button up was torn, and he was holding an ice pack to his cheek. His shoulders fell when he saw Ann, as well as the hand holding the ice pack. There were four blood lines underneath, the second from the top being deep enough to start bleeding without pressure. As if someone who had visions of cat status had slapped him across the face.

"Aw hell." He said exasperated. "This night couldn't get any weirder." He said wrongly. His attention turned to Sachiel and his eyes went large as dinner plates. The vision of her heavenly beauty and one wolf's ear took up all his attention for a brief second.

"Tell me about it." Said a flat mousy voice from the back corner of the room.

Where they had thought was an empty booth was the small girl in black that had also been on the flight over. She was peeking out from behind the seat. Her large headphones making up most of what she was revealing. They all spun around to look at her. This seemed to be too much for the big man.

"What the hell is goin here?" He looked ready to fight again as he put up the hand without an ice pack in it.

"Calm down, young man and take a seat. All will be explained when the others arrive." Said the old woman.

When the girl in black seemed to take the advice readily. Jumping down from her bench to take a seat at the table. The big man's eyebrows unfurrowed, he looked at each of the people at the table one more time. Eyes lingering on Ann for some reason. Before he went to take a seat next to the girl in black. She had taken a seat next to the tall woman in biking leathers. She was about the size of one of the blonde woman's legs and looked even more like a child next to her.

"I'm Kenzie." She said in her mousy voice. "Am I-I'm supposed to sit here, right?" She looked around the table quickly. No one objected. The woman in biking leathers looked amused by the question. She stuck out her hand to greet the girl and held it for a moment.

"You call me Tema." She seemed satisfied with the handshake after a moment. She also had a Greek accent that matched Paul's.

"Another angel." She said to the room at large. "I don't know which." She looked at the old barman and indicated the surprised looking smaller girl.

"Lucy." Tema invited with the wave of a hand. The old man chortled again as he moved slowly to the back of the table. Kenzie's wide eyes following him.

"Impertinent girl." The old woman spat from across the table. The younger woman blew her a wink and kiss.

"Sorry mama." She didn't sound sorry at all. But now that she'd said it Cole saw the features that made it very clear that she and Paul were siblings. Both had the same austere, chiseled features and looked like they belonged on a movie set, rather than in a dive bar.

"You alright with this?" The giant southern man asked as he took his seat next to Kenzie.

"Shut up, Brad. I'm super into it." Kenzie said breathlessly as the old man extended his hand to her. She took it while Brad shook his head but continued speaking to the table at large.

"This may sound a little crazy...well maybe not. But the reason I'm gunna stay..." He said looking around the table. "I've been having some messed up dreams this last month." He gesticulated while the main cut under his eye started to leak a little.

"And in every single one of em. Is that perty little lady right there." He pointed to Ann.

Again, Ann looked shocked by the proceedings as she looked at Cole. So far on Cole's trip, she seemed to be getting more attention than he was. When they locked eyes there was something unspoken in both. Under the table Cole grabbed her hand and squeezed for a moment to make it more real.

"You want to explain that?" Brad asked to the table at large. No one answered.

The Native American straightened from where he'd been listening to the old woman's whispers. He wore a midnight blue suit that looked as though it had been expensive. As it was scraped, and dirt smudged now. It looked like the Bolo tie he wore clasped with a gold falcon and gold talon aiguillettes… was the most expensive thing he wore now. His long black hair was pulled back into a ponytail and held together at intervals with colorful leather bands.

"Mm. Not surprising." He pointed over to Brad. "Him too."

"Me what?" Said Brad defensively.

The old barman next to him chortled rather harder that he had before. Even so much as to call it a laugh as he unclasped Kenzie's hand and said something to her in a low voice. She looked mildly surprised at first, but it turned to slight excitement. Her voice still flat.

"You want to see?" She asked him. In response, the old man held up a bracing hand, which he then extended to Brad. Brad didn't take his hand but looked at Kenzie and shook his head again.

"Look I don't know what kind of weird culty stuff you guys got goin on here. But I'm gunna need some more from you if I'm gunna be shakin strange old guy with glowin eyes' hand." That got a laugh from all the bars regulars. Which did nothing to make Brad feel any more comfortable about it. He took his hands from the table and put them in his lap. The old man put his hand down and went to take a seat.

"Now is good a time as any." The old Native American said. "Start now. Catch the stragglers up when they get here. We have a couple of days"

"How many more people are you expecting to show up?" Ann asked.

"There are always seven. Some come thinking they will find treasure, others, their soul path." The old native made a wave with one hand. "Some don't know why they get here but get here, they do." The old Native glanced at Brad. The young Italian in the deep purple smoking jacket snorted, but he had an impatient and annoyed look on his face.

"Well where do we start? These are all angels." He said. He indicated a hand toward Sachiel. She was standing on the other side of Cole to Ann. "Even a *fallen* has returned. This is angel business, is it not?" Cole didn't like the way the man emphasized the word *fallen*. Mocking, with a hint of laughter.

"Don't be jealous, Dice. It makes you ugly." Tema said with a half-smile. The Italian gave her a long-suffering look and pulled the cork on his giant wine bottle. Tema turned to Sachiel. "He always wanted to be an *angel*." She said it with the same mocking hint of laughter.

"Perhaps, he has a point." Paul said when he saw the look Cole was giving Dice. "Where do we start?" All eyes in the room turned to Sachiel, who turned to Cole.

"Uh…well." He said when she gave him a look. "I guess I can tell you all what I know." And for the second time in his life. He went over everything supernatural he had ever experienced.

This time he added Ann into the story. Who added in bits about watching his progression, details even he hadn't been aware of. And Sachiel filled in explanations of her own actions as a wolf. By the time it was over, Brad had two glasses with only ice left in them. And Dice was mostly done with his giant bottle of wine.

Still, no one else had shown up.

Brad had spent the hour or so, looking less and less incredulous that everyone seemed to be on board with what he was hearing. The whiskey had probably helped with that. Kenzie not only looked on- board but grew more excited as they spoke. Even adding in exclamations at some of the more harrowing parts. The regulars of the bar were catching each other's eyes and making expressions that indicated they were having a silent conversation as the story went on.

"So…" Brad said after Cole finished. "The takeaway from…" He waved his hands around wildly. "All this weirdness is that you want me to come with you to…unlock a gate to let all the magic out? All kinds of messed up junk is gunna happen to people." He raised an eyebrow. "But it'll be good for us?"

"To be fair, we didn't know anyone else would be here. You could go home right now and we'd still go." Cole said with a shrug.

"Not about good or bad happening if you do it." The native said as if Cole hadn't said anything.

"More like if we don't, most of us die anyway." Paul said looking serious. "Souls, stuck like hers was, only worse." He indicated Sachiel. This was news to Cole and Ann as well as Brad. They looked at Sachiel, who looked guiltily between them. She seemed to have questions that she wanted answered though, as she turned back to the group.

"Have we heard from anyone that wasn't here when…when it happened? Where are the knights? Why haven't any come to help?" At this all the regulars looked like they'd just heard their respective favorite pets had died.

"Before we were cut off." The Italian said quietly angry. "We got word. Gabriel, Barachiel, Michael, Zadkiel. All prisoners. We don't know where. We've heard nothing of Uriel or the big guy but…they haven't shown up."

Cole knew the names but didn't understand what they had to do with their situation. Or what the situation was turning into for that matter. Sachiel looked as if she had been punched in the gut. Her eyes went wide and watery. For some reason, she looked at Cole to see his reaction, her breath, heavy, came with a look of worry etched in her face. When he only blank stared at her she turned back to the barman. As if she didn't want to know, she asked,

"And…the knights?"

Cole didn't understand that at all. As far as he knew, the Archangels *were* the knights. Even the Italian didn't seem to be able to answer. He just looked angrier as his face darkened.

"Gone." The old woman said, sepulchraly. Sachiel looked horrified and disbelieving in equal measure.

"That…can't be." She said under her breath, as though choking on the words. "What happened?" She whispered. In response, Dice slammed his empty bottle on the table.

"Why don't you tell us, *angel?*" He spat the last word. He didn't back down at the angry looks most at the table gave him. "You made promises you couldn't keep. You lost." He waved a finger at the three. His face going red with anger. When Sachiel merely looked at him with a chastised expression he continued.

"Left us all to fight and die…wither down to nothing for thousands of years." He stood up and Paul put an arm out to encourage him to sit back down, but he wasn't having it. Cole also stood but Sachiel and Ann took each of his forearms and pulled him back down as Dice shouted.

"You come back stupid." He indicated at an incensed Cole then Sachiel. "And weak, half dead. After we try to clean up your mess, and you ask *us* what happened?" He laughed humorlessly and waved a hand at them.

"You failed." His anger sounded tight in his throat.

Paul stood up now, but it seemed as though Dice had said what he had to say. He didn't fight Paul, but stomped from the room to acquire another bottle. It took a moment for the room to settle back down. All seemed to be breathing heavier than normal.

"We...pooled communications after everything settled down here." The old Native said calmly, after a moment of silence. "No one could explain. Everyone in panic. But all said the same thing. The knight's world, their entire sector, gone." He said somberly.

"Came in right before they got us." He finished. All the regulars and Sachiel were sharing a moment of extreme sorrow and disbelief.

"Um..." Kenzie broke the silence. "So, then what happened to…us?" She said it as if she wasn't sure if she should add herself into the group.

"Betrayed." The quiet old barman said. "Ambushed. All our captains and generals beaten in the first wave or scattered to the wind." The somber atmosphere of the room deepened.

"He was right…we lost." Sachiel said, staring at her feet.

Ann spoke up. "No. Look, I realize I don't know much about any of it, but…we're still here. That means we haven't lost yet, right? We can still fight." She had a fierce look in her eyes and the commanding tone of her voice seemed to wipe away all the negative energy in the room.

"With what?" Brad joined back into the conversation. At this, Kenzie sat up. She made twinkling eye contact with the old barman, and he nodded to her, adding, "I've seen some action. Buuut it sounds like guns aint gunna do you any good here."

"Depends on the gun." Paul said. He pulled the giant golden handgun from its sheath. Brad seemed to brighten up as it was passed down the table to him. In any other's hands the gun looked made for a giant.

"Is that a Deagle?" Brad asked, excited. At least he was able to hold onto something familiar. Paul smiled at the traditional nickname. Kenzie passed the weapon over, then hopped off her seat to grab the knife and fork off of her booth table.

"Check the rounds." Paul said as Brad took the impressive weapon in a trained hand. He checked the safety and extended it to look down the sites. Pointing it far above Cole's head. It didn't look so big in either of the larger men's hands. But Cole knew it was powerful enough to take down a bear. Brad pulled the weapon down and released the magazine to follow Paul's suggestion.

"What are all these markings?" Brad asked as he inspected the topmost bullet.

"Angelic script. For killing demons and their spawn." Paul answered appreciatively. While they were discussing the meat of how the weapon worked Cole turned to Sachiel and whispered.

"Why didn't you tell us the part where we all die if we don't take down the gate?" Sachiel looked slightly apologetic. But the action and news of the night seemed to have drained most of that out of her. Ann leaned over to listen.

"You seemed motivated enough without that knowledge." Sachiel said, shrugging. "It could only have added to your burden. And I thought you were…alone." Her eyes darted between he and Ann.

"Well," Ann broke in, matter of fact, "Not anymore. But we still have to talk about all the other stuff."

Cole felt heat rise in his chest at her first statement and Sachiel blurred in front of him, as she nodded.

"There is…something else you should know." Sachiel started. The moment was interrupted by the sound of an electric current rising.

They all looked over to see Kenzie holding her knife and fork a few inches away from each other and in front of her. With the sound of a glass shattering taser. An electric current lit up between the two utensils. The power seemed to intensify and redouble as it passed back and forth. Kenzie was soon hard pressed to hold the utensils steady. Her hands shaking faster than the eye could follow. She looked around the room, eyes wide, smiling like a child under the Christmas tree. With a loud crack and sizzling sound her hands were forced apart. They all looked amazed at her.

"I was screwing around before you guys got here." She said, back to her flat voice. As if she had simply found a good skipping rock by the lake. Cole started an applause that smattered around the table.

Cole kept on with the exhibition. Right now, he was more concerned with getting everyone on board. Past events could wait. He stood and lit the ceiling up before pulling the light together. With the sound of an electric charge and whip crack. He brought the tip of the light whip down on the center of the table. To everyone's surprise, instead of leaving scorch marks, the single board that the light had touched, bubbled and turned into the original branch it had been before being cut. Complete with leafy appendage.

They were all staring at it, flabbergasted. When the branch and, indeed, the whole table rose six inches from the ground. They all looked at Ann as she set it back in place and shrugged. Seeming not to have put much effort in to the action. Cole marveled, he had been playing around with his powers for years, getting to know, by bits, what he was capable of. *Ann*, Huh.

"I noticed when we were running through the streets." Ann said, toward Cole and Sachiel. "I could have outpaced those things by a mile." She turned interestedly, as they all looked at Brad. He was concentrating on the branch.

"Well, I guess that's something." He said under his breath. "Now you mention it, I did feel something weird when I was gettin away from that bum. Like I was…" He stood up from his seat still holding the monster golden gun. He took a place in the aisle between the tables and booths. Without warning, he leapt forward. For a big man and the effort he put in, he positively soared. Seeming to hang far too long and going much too far. He looked disbelieving at his own action. After he landed, he started laughing. He jumped lightly and lifted over a foot in the air.

"Oh, no way!" He said as he lifted his knees and came down as slow and lightly as a feather.

From a crouching position he pushed down as hard as he could. He shot straight up and slammed his head into the eighteen-foot ceiling. The thumping crack, that was the breaking dry wall. Was swiftly followed by the thunderous sound of a gunshot as Brad clenched up at impact. Fortunately, the gun was pointed at the ground and didn't hit anyone. But Brad fell like a sack of potatoes, having lost the concentration it had taken to use his new power. As he crumpled to the floor, and everyone put their hands down from shielding themselves. A smooth, cold and clear woman's voice sent shivers down everyone in the room spines. From the area of the French doors.

"Impressive." She said. It was as though, just in the sound of her voice, they could hear the promise of cruelty and bloody, torturous pain and death. And the shadow of countless souls crying for mercy that had never come. The sound of it felt like a curse.

Cole felt his ankle move straight past itching and into radiating pain. It almost crippled him as he and everyone else in the room turned slowly toward the voice.

Ch. 9

Her black eyes scanned the room with an air of confidence that was beyond reproach. If she didn't look and sound like a nightmare, she might have been beautiful. She had a narrow face, full blood-red lips and pale, almost translucent skin. She wore her tight black business suit perfectly. Her thick, slightly wavy black hair fell to thin, strong shoulders. Lilith stood, leaned with her back against the left French door, at her leisure. In her visible hand she held a cell phone. She pointed it at Brad, who was still dazed and crumpled on the ground. After the sound of a quick snapshot, she put the phone back to her side.

"I'm sending that to his wife." She said humorously. Her voice held some accent that wasn't immediately recognizable. Like someone who had grown up in Egypt, learned English in Britain and had spent ten years in the states. No one laughed at what she obviously thought was a joke. "She can see your shame, before I send her your corpse." And she laughed. The sound was equally as disgusting as her voice, only amplified. Most of the people around the table were visibly affected by it.

"Nobody move!" The old woman's voice came harsh and clear over the sound of Lilith's laughter. "You can't win as you are, you'll just die." She finished as Lilith's laughter subsided.

In answer to the old woman's pronouncement, Lilith turned into the room. In the hand opposite to them, as if she were holding nothing but a rubber chicken, was Dice. She held him by the neck like mother lion would her cub. He was barely conscious, eyes rolling as he mouthed words none of them could hear.

The front of his jacket looked like it had been slashed open by some four clawed creature. Too bright scarlet dripped through the tatters and down over his waistband. His feet dragged limply as Lilith presented him to the room. Her eyes took in the reaction with an almost sexual pleasure. Paul and Tema both hissed, standing. If Paul had had his gun, the movement he made would have had it in his hand. The elderly of the room let out moans of agony.

Cole hadn't much liked the guy so far. But he hadn't lived the other man's life. And he didn't think he deserved anything close to this kind of treatment. As he stood there, pain radiating up his leg. his new acquaintance dripping blood onto the carpet, he finally realized just how much this journey was going to take, and that he wasn't ready for someone like this. Lilith peaked her black eyes over Dice's shoulder. They looked merry, like a girl who had just gotten a pony for Christmas.

"Listen to your elders, baby gods. Sit down...or the boy dies." There was no room for negotiation in her voice. Just to emphasize her words, the sharp black nail at Dice's throat extended. Drawing a line of shining scarlet as the tip sank in. Slowly, and with dark looks that would have cowed an elephant, the siblings sat back down. Lilith caught Cole's eye then Ann's then Sachiel's. With that same sense of pleasure, so raw it was palpable in the air, she addressed them. Her tone almost as though she were addressing old friends. "Hey Jo, Laph. Been a while...for you at least." She snorted and her eyes went merry again. Cole and Ann exchanged quick glances. At the look, Lilith almost vibrated she was having so much fun.

"What did you do to them?" Sachiel asked furiously. Lilith turned toward the angel and a truly evil glint flashed across her face.

"Nothing you didn't help us to accomplish. Little.Trusting.Fool." She underscored each of the last words. Then put on a fake but convincing air of mocking desperation.

"Sachiel! There's a new power that has arisen in the east! They've hurt so many people, we need you! Come quick!" Lilith laughed as the horror of what she was implying sunk into everyone else in the room. "Ooo, Saaash." Lilith crooned in an admonishing sort of way. Sachiel was staring so many daggers at her it was hard to believe the witch hadn't started receiving pin pricks on her neck.

"You haven't told them?" She pulled Dice back toward her, so she was truly peeking out from behind his right shoulder. Her black eyes lit up like a beetle's in firelight. "Worried she might kick you out again?" Lilith's eyes indicated Ann as she said it. Sachiel's anger only intensified, the air around her went cold and she couldn't help the growl that escaped her lips. It was matched by Lilith's soft, cold laughter. She added insult to injury.

"You want to know where your body is, don't you?" She asked in a sly voice. Her eyes flashed evil again and she pointed in indication to make them all sit. Against every instinct to attack, they did. "Don't worry, you'll find it." She said dispassionately.

"I didn't come here to fight. Waste of my time, anyway." She had taken on a slow superior tone when she'd gotten what she wanted. "And it has been, oh so long since I got to play with a…" She looked at all the newcomers in turn. Brad had come to and was in a kneeling position, staring with mixture of anger and re-focus. Her smile turned positively vulpine.

"Fully grown angel."

"Woman." The old native said impatiently. "Get to the point, or I'll die here waiting." He shook his head slowly at the floor. Lilith turned her gaze on him, and he met her eyes. Steady and unmoving, the old man held her stare. Lilith didn't show any amount of fear at the look. On the contrary she merely turned her insults in his direction.

"Old Fleeing with Flacons, Runs Away from Wolves, Cowering Under Bears." She mocked him. She held the cell phone up in her free hand as she said it. Sharp black fingernail clicking as she made a call.

"It's a wonder you've been in the game so long and didn't notice." She looked around the room as if searching for something.

"There seems to be something…" She said sarcastically as someone answered the phone. The woman's voice, from the other end, heavy with a British accent, sounded bedraggled and terrified. As if she hadn't slept for a week and run a marathon without any water.

"Hello?" The voice whispered, made louder by way of speaker phone. Lilith smiled again, and her sharp teeth gave the impression of a shark about to shoot for its prey.

"Or *someone* missing?" She said as she tossed the phone onto the table. They all stared, transfixed as it clacked onto the table. The voice whispered through the room.

"I know…" The voice choked as if the woman were holding back tears. There were the noises of other people in the background. The rustling of heavy chains. Her voice lost all semblance of hope as she spoke. Seeming to know no one would go so far for a stranger.

"We don't know each other." She tried again. "She showed me your picture...before. I don't know if you saw me, I was at the airport in London." Cole's mind flashed back to the blonde woman he'd seen staring wide eyed at Sachiel. He'd seen her, he should have said something, should have approached her. Ann noticed his look of comprehension. She watched his heart sink along with his head, knowing what it meant.

"Some leader you are, teacher." Lilith added quietly toward Cole. She still managed to sound amused. Cole was still trying to process this level of hatred and cruelty when the woman on the phone spoke again.

"I..." The woman had been trying to hold back tears, she failed now. As she broke down, from somewhere around but near her, there was the sound of a wet snapping, and a tortured scream. High pitched and grating as if whoever it was, was being split in two. It seemed to force the scream out of the woman's mouth too.

"Please!" She screamed. The tortured scream died down, as did the woman's shaking voice. "Please. Save us...She said if you don't, she'll kill us both." Cole felt his insides turn over. His eyes were blurry again, so that he couldn't see Ann as she tightened her grip on his hand.

"Please." The last word was almost inaudible as the woman's voice died. For just a second longer, before the call ended, they could hear the woman crying. The only thing she seemed to be able to say was the tiny pleading repeatedly. The call stopped. Everyone at the table made to rush the demon at the door. In response she held out Dice's limp form.

"Ah, ah, ah, ah." She crooned again. It was successful at stopping them, but only just. "You'll all get your chance." Lilith said fiercely. All semblance of her humor was gone.

"When you're worth the fight." She spat as she flung Dice as if he were a sack lunch. He soared above Cole's head.

The sound of Tema's voice screaming, "Dionysus!" Was drowned out by the sound of a monstrous boom and a ringing. Brad had the only weapon in the room capable of reaching Lilith. And had apparently been waiting to use it as soon as Dice was out of his firing line.

Lilith's head slightly snapped as the bullet ran across an inch of her scalp next to her temple. Only to bounce away in a whisp of black smoke. It left an inch wide shallow rivet, black as night. And even as she snapped her attention to her shooter, it visibly began healing. Lilith hissed; her eyes flashed with anger so cold it could have frozen fire. Brad didn't pale at her anger, he shot again. The bullet hit the door frame as Lilith moved, fast as lightning, out into the night.

Ch. 10

The next few minutes were a haze and flurry of movement. At Sachiel's swift command, Ann pulled Dice over to her. He had been stopped from sliding off the table by the addition of the new centerpiece. The angel made swift work of tearing open his jacket and shirt to get to work. Golden sparks dripped onto the four deep slashes that went from the upper side of his left pectoral down to his navel. As she whispered in the flowing angelic language, the cuts started to heal, and the bleeding slowed.

Paul, Tema and Brad all ran to the entrance of the restaurant to make sure Lilith had gone. As the older regulars huddled together to whisper to each other. Kenzie walked around the table to take a spot on the other side of Ann, as she and Cole watched the angel do her work. Hope and concern written across their faces. It took a long moment for Tema and Brad to come back from the front. The looks on their faces showing that something was wrong.

"She used her mind-bending spell on everyone out there. They will need help." Tema said pointing toward the door. Cole remembered all the people he had seen in the courtyard of the hotel, fallen and motionless.

"Can't get em to wake up." Brad said looking slightly confused but mostly irritated.

"Where is your brother?" The old woman asked, worry written on her face.

"Preparing the bus." Tema said shortly as she came to check on Sachiel's work.

In only a few minutes, Dice's cuts had healed to the point they weren't going to be fatal. But Sachiel seemed to be running out of juice. The golden sparks were coming out at less frequent intervals. And something of her glowing nature had seemed to fade. Her breathing was becoming more ragged, and she took a deep stomach breath every four or five. But she seemed determined to get Dice as close to fixed up as she could. The old woman nodded at Tema's words.

"Midas and Shiki." The old native said. "We sent them after the last two of our number. We need to find them. You know where they were headed." Tema nodded shortly to the old man. She gave Dice one more long look. She turned and walked briskly out of the room. The old man joined her as they left the restaurant bar. Moving more quickly than his aged figure looked capable of.

"That got crazy really fast." Kenzie said flatly. Her expressionless face matched her voice, but her eyes showed she was shaken by the proceedings. Cole, Ann and Brad gave her haggard nods. The ringing in their ears finally faded, as did the pain at Cole's ankle.

"Is he going to be, ok?" Kenzie asked. Sachiel didn't stop her whispering but nodded once, her focus unwavering.

"I knew it was going to be weird but this…this is." Ann's words failed her as se hiked up her too large jeans. She took in Dice's unconscious and bloody form and looked close to breaking.

"Little girl." The old woman said impatiently. "Get a grip. What matters right now?" Ann looked at her, eyes narrowed, at the diminutive.

"Ya know…" Said Brad steadily. "Sometimes, it's hard to tell who the enemy is. Or when fightin' needs to be done. Lady like that?" He shook his head. He still held Paul's monster pistol. And as they all turned to him, he lifted it as if reexamining it. "She makes it easy. Wants the fight too bad. Gets off on people's pain. She's got to go. I couldn't face my boys if I didn't do what I could here." It was a simple statement.

But everyone at the table seemed to agree as they nodded. Brad gave them each a serious look in turn. Making sure they were with him. He didn't need words. Likely, it would have been only him that needed convincing in the first place. Lilith had gone too far, overdone what hadn't needed to even be done. Pulled them into a fight they hadn't known was waiting, but wouldn't have hesitated to join in.

"That was a good shot." Cole said as they all turned back toward Sachiel.

Brad snorted. "Obliged. I probably shouldn't have shot her but…I just couldn't help myself." Everyone silently agreed with him.

"When do we leave?" Cole asked toward the old man.

"When everyone is prepared." The old barman said quietly. Cole nodded and exchanged looks to confirm with Ann that they agreed. She seemed to have gotten over her initial shock as she nodded.

Sachiel was still moving her hands across Dice's body. There was a fiery look in her eyes, it had never been a question as to whether she wanted to fight. And they all took heart at her determination that was her answer. Dice's cuts had finally stopped bleeding. He took his first full breath, and his eyelids fluttered. She gave it a few more seconds but then fell back into her seat and looking withered. Her breathing was ragged, and she had all but faded to a ghost. Cole knelt next to her, Ann taking a spot at his shoulder.

"What do you need?" He asked. His mind searched empty places as to what a raw soul would use to heal itself. It turned out to be quite simple.

Sachiel looked back and forth between him and Ann. She was gulping breath as if she'd almost drowned. Cole thought it must be a symbolic gesture, as a soul couldn't need oxygen. But it was the only thing her body knew to do to outwardly display the dire need for something to obtain equilibrium. He took her hand, it felt weightless, cold and hollow. At his touch, her eyes closed, and a small bit of her warmth came back. Her breath came easier, but she was still struggling.

"I…" she said hesitantly, her eyes opened and met Ann's for a second before darting around at nothing in particular. Not losing any of their desperation. They flitted to Cole's hand several times as she searched for an answer. Their interaction with Lilith seemed to have robbed her of the boldness she'd had beforehand.

"Stupid boy." The old woman said from the other side of the chair from Cole.

He looked up at her, she was watching Sachiel's eyes. So too, apparently, was Ann. Cole heard her sigh heavily behind him as the old woman made to speak again. She stopped as Ann stepped around Cole and moved to scoop up the angel form her seat. Cole had never tried to touch her in the real world. He hadn't known it was even possible until he touched her hand. Ann showed that it was more than that as she lifted the angle to limp feet and pulled an arm over her strong shoulder.

She guided Cole with a swift nod toward one of the booths. He took a seat and Ann laid the angel against his shoulder. She curled into a ball against him. It was an eerie gesture as he could feel almost nothing at her touch. It was like touching a hollow, soft, papier-mâché person. He put an arm around her and gave Ann a questioning look. She gave him a queer little smile.

"Just…be yourself." She whispered. If the situation weren't so dire Cole would have felt more confident. He had no idea how to heal her. He turned his attention to the weakened angel. Her eyes still looked desperate and had filled with tears.

"Hey." He tried to sound lighthearted, but the nights events had made it sound as hollow as Sachiel felt. "I'm right here." He said and pulled her in closer.

Her warmth was so slow to return it was imperceptible. Cole had a thought spring to his mind. He focused his energy so that his palm lit up. He ran the hand over the angel's white hair. He could feel his energy being pulled into her as he did so. After Lilith's appearance and in her weakened state, Sachiel finally broke. The strong visage she'd shown him till now was gone.

"I'm...sorry." The angel said with a slightly stronger voice. The progress was muted by her ragged tears. She repeated the words several times. "It should have been me." Tears started to fall down her lovely face in earnest. Disappearing as they left her cheeks. She turned slightly so she could address the room at large.

"All of you should have lived...and I should have died." She said in a tiny voice. Everyone in the room looked as if she had just stabbed them in the heart. And though many in the room looked as though they understood her plight. In none was the pronouncement so affecting than in Brad. He looked at the angel with a mixture of sadness and insight. The look made Cole think the big man knew exactly how she felt. Sachiel looked up at Cole and there was pleading in her eyes.

"We were never soldiers, you and I. Not like the others...you heard her. You were..." She looked back down and the pain in her voice was palpable in the air. "The Teacher, Jophiel. I was The Healer."

Were, she'd said. They *should* have lived. After everything he'd heard. Cole took only a second to realize that it wasn't just memories or a fight they'd lost. It meant they must have all died at some point in *this* story she'd been holding back. Guessable, still, not comforting.

"When I got demoted, you wouldn't allow me to be sent down to grunt. You took me as your second." She heaved a ragged breath. "I failed you. They made me trust them and they…"

"Stop." It was Ann. There was something hard in her eyes Cole had never seen there before. She came to kneel at the booth. "I've already seen enough of both sides to know better." She placed a hand on the angel's curled leg.

"Besides, if we were the soldiers then we failed you too. I don't speak for everyone." She looked around the room. In response to her words, Kenzie and Brad both stepped over to the booth. "But I forgive you." She said.

Brad put a hand on her head and his voice was gruff with empathy. "It's alright, girl. All I've known is a good life."

Kenzie put a hand on Sachiel's shoulder, and she said flatly, "It's ok. Let's go kick her ass."

Cole squeezed the angel in a tighter embrace. Her warmth and light returning steadily now. She seemed to gain something of her solid weight back. He whispered. "You've saved my skin more times than I can count. What's changed? I still wouldn't take anybody else as my second." He tried to take on a lighthearted tone. "You did say I wasn't taking this seriously enough…message heard." He laid his head on hers.

He didn't know how the rest of the trip would play out, but he hadn't come to this place to lose anyone. What she had done or been tricked into doing had no bearing on that. Not when it had been so long ago, in another life he couldn't even remember. As the broken and fallen angel regained her strength, she wept. Tears, a mixture of grief, joy and redemption, that were many, many years overdue.

Brad and Kenzie stepped back after a moment to talk in low voices to the elderly. They had been watching the proceedings between checking Dice's injuries. They didn't seem to think he was ready to be moved just yet. But his breathing was coming deep and steady now. They had somber but satisfied expressions for Sachiel.

Brad looked as though he were asking about the layout of the plan. His hands making jerky leveling movements as if laying out steps. Periodically taking glances at the three in the booth.

Kenzie listened to the questioning, and at one of the old man's answers, she fixed Ann with a long stare. Ann looked as though she were chewing on a question herself, with a look of trouble on her face. She didn't want to pressure their exhausted companion any further, but she it was time to know some things.

"So. The old man called me..." She started.

"Laphaliel." Sachiel whispered. "Your people would say, Raphael. You were...The Protector. I could not be sure. I do not know how you two found me but..." Sachiel said in a tiny voice and curled herself a little tighter. Ann sighed again.

"Fate can be cruel." She said and then smiled. It was a toothless smile but warm. "But sometimes...it can be good too. You've gotten us this far, let's do the rest together. You don't have

to carry everything on your shoulders anymore. And we need you."
Sachiel nodded. There was a sliding noise as one of the French doors slid open further.

"Dry your tears, angel." Paul had returned.

He had a platter stacked with sandwiches and fries. Cole hadn't realized how hungry he was until he saw it. Paul set the platter on the edge of the table; his face somber.

"She's right." Paul said nodding to Ann. "I have never seen Lilith so excited. Coming out of her hidey hole isn't normal. She must really like you."

Sachiel snorted. She took one long deep breath and seemed to gain strength from it.

"The feeling is not mutual." She said in a slightly stronger voice than before. Paul waved a hand to Brad and Kenzie. Brad came and grabbed a handful of sandwiches with no hesitation. Kenzie went to grab the rest of her Greek salad.

"All of you get your strength," he continued. "I want to wait for Tema to get back. You're two people short, and we have no time to prepare. I'm sure Tema will agree, her and I will stand in." When the old woman made to interject the barman put a hand to her forearm.

"But, what about the ones she took? Shouldn't we be leaving as soon as possible?" Cole asked, worried and responsible. He had finally come back to the realization that their would be companions lives were on the line.

"That's what she wants. Take deep breath. Take the next step calmly." Said Paul. All the newcomers tried as he suggested. "Divide, break, conquer. It is her joy. Gathering our strength to go *is* as soon as possible. If we want a chance to win." Paul said, while they did as he suggested and breathed in deeply.

"He is right. She has only started to play." Sachiel said, disgusted.

Ann looked at the former god as if sizing him up. "How many times have you tried?" She asked.

"Many, though never with so many angels. Maybe you can get Gate to spew something out instead of holding it in." Paul said shrugging.

"If we have the time, can we clear one thing up before we go?" Cole asked as he took a sandwich with his free hand. Paul locked grim eyes with him.

"What are everybody's actual names?" Cole said through a huff of anxious laughter. Paul smiled at the request. He indicated each person in turn.

"I am, Apollo. Called Paul in this age. The old man, our barman is Aeoles, called Less, and the nagging old lady is Leto. Just call her Mother. Maybe *you* give her the grandchildren she desires. My sister, Artemis called Tema. The old Indian is Silap Inua. He goes by many names. Dionysus, we call Dice now. And there are Midas and Shiki, who you have not met."

"Aren't those all…God names?" Cole asked with his mouth full of turkey, cheese and bread. The simple food; bringing some semblance of normalcy to him like Brad's gun had done earlier.

"*God* is subjective." Paul said shrugging. "To normal person, the smallest thing can make you a god and we used to be better. This is as far away from the gate we can go to stay…" His eyes turned to Dice with a dark look.

"Undying." He finished in a low undertone.

"How do the gods match up to an angel?" Ann asked. Paul gave her an imperious look.

"Human god is lower level of evolution than angel. But there are many paths of power. And dead angel can take many lives to get back up to speed in these conditions. You'll have to get back to my level. Getting nearer the gate will awaken some potential. Which is, admittedly, very high. If we were in natural conditions, chances are good you would have been reborn more powerful than you will be standing on the gate itself." All the new rookies in the room took in this information with nods.

"Stronger than an archangel? I didn't think there was any such thing." Cole asked interested.

"Hold your horses, cowboy. In normal conditions, reborn stronger than you are *now*, with the world and your bodies drained and beaten." Paul said. His Greek accent making the initial phrase sound funny.

"You could live and die many times as angel or archangel. There is…was, only one being higher than that on our side. We called them The Knights."

"Seems like a downgrade as far as names." Kenzie said, poking at the plate she held in one hand. Paul gave her a weird look.

"The other side had a name for them." He said with a lifted eyebrow.

"What's that?" Asked Brad on his second sandwich.

"God killers." Paul answered shortly. It hung in the air for a second before Kenzie's flat voice answered,

"That's way cooler." Her face showed slight interest at the name. Paul laughed a little.

"Who knows?" He said. "We finally win this fight; someone will need to take their place. Maybe you'll be one someday. You don't turn into one of the gods they hunt down."

"I thought there were only seven archangels?" Cole asked, his mind still on them, eyebrows furrowed.

"Seven, in command of thousands." Sachiel said. Cole's eyebrows raised. "Knight prospects. When ready, they become the generals of legions, the next to become the best, under the battalion of knights." She finished.

"How many knights were there?" Kenzie asked, at the same time Cole asked.

"How do they do that?"

And still at the same time Ann asked. "We're supposed to go up against whoever beat them?"

Paul gave them all a long-suffering look. "Not many, few hundred at most, in all of time. I have no idea how. And have some faith, our god is better. Getting them to look away from their work that is the real hard part."

"There were always three hundred. One will step down if there is another to come. That must be where the others are." Sachiel whispered. "I am sure of it. Metatron, Uriel. They could have been knights but chose not to be." He eyes flashed up to Cole again. "They are either making an appeal. Or making the change."

"Makin an appeal? You mean to God?" Brad asked wide eyed as he grabbed a handful of fries, his mouth full of sandwich.

"Making the change?" Cole asked. Paul gave him a long look before he turned his eyes to Sachiel.

"Yes…I am curious how it is done. Oden tried to skip the angle part, but he only made it halfway." He said looking interested.

"I do not know either." Sachiel said. "Our work was focused on other problems. They would never tell me if I asked, and I have never seen one make the change."

"What were they like?" Cole asked fascinated by these strange new powers forming in his mind.

"They were…well, more like Laphaliel used to be. We always said she was next in line." Sachiel gave Ann a quick glance.

"What was *she* like?" Cole asked, unable to stop the question. He winked at Ann who gave him a foreboding look. Sachiel took a moment to answer while Ann looked as if she might rather not know.

"Distant…cold when she thought no one was looking but, kind if you spoke to her. And always happy when she was…when she was around Jophiel." Sachiel added the last bit at Ann's look of embarrassment.

"So, not much different." Cole said jokingly. Ann slapped him on top of his head. With her newfound strength, it hurt quite a lot. With a tear in his eye, he gave her an apologetic look. There was commotion at the front of the restaurant as the door opened. Tema's voice came through to the parlor.

"Paul!" She called. Everyone moved immediately to go see what was going on. Apparently, they hadn't been as calm as they were pretending to be. Before Cole moved to slide off the bench, he turned to Sachiel.

"You ready?" He asked. She took a deep shuddering breath.

"I am going into the jewel until we are on our way." She said it almost as a question. Cole nodded and she vanished into his wristband. He scooted out, taking a handful of fries and a sandwich with him.

Most everyone was standing by the front of the restaurant when Cole made his way out. He was met with a strange scene. The pool players were all hunched by the tables, either on the ground, or slumped in stools, propped against each other. Dice's girls were all hunched over in their seats, as were the other patrons. Even as the commotion at the door was happening. Cole saw Aeolus, *the barman*, and Leto, *the "mother"* of the Gods start working on their guests. Checking their vitals and preparing to reverse whatever Lilith had done to them.

Tema and the old Native were carrying a woman between them. She was gorgeous, of a height with Ann. Similarly, all tight curves, with waving black hair that curled in ringlets around her thin face. She wore a tight black skirt and tiny black tank top. Neither leaving much to the imagination. It was only off set by the half conscious look in her eyes and drunken, wobbly steps. Lilith had apparently been very busy that night. Or she had help with a similar ability. He could only pray that wasn't the case.

"Midas." Tema said jerking her head toward the door. Paul immediately rushed through the door to retrieve their member. Brad followed in case he needed help. And since there wasn't anywhere better to put her, Tema and the old Native dragged who Cole guessed was Shiki into the parlor and laid her next to Dice. Only a few seconds later, Paul and Brad came in. A man held between them in similar state to Shiki.

He was dark, tall as the men who now held him up, but thicker with muscle. That was saying something, as they weren't weakly built. It was a good thing Brad had gone to help as he was so gigantic. The man wore the ugliest fitted suit Cole had ever seen. Mustard yellow suede with a velvet button-up underneath and shining black dress shoes.

He must have a real good personality, Cole thought.

They laid him on the table with the other two. He was so large, when they rested his head against the branch at the center, his feet still hung over the edge. When they had all been set down, Paul and Tema exchanged looks. Both nodded and they beckoned to the others. There was no time for half-conscious greetings.

Brad grabbed the platter of food on their way out. He held the large plate in one hand. Cole just noticed he must have given Paul's gun back at some point as he was grabbing fries with the other. Tema gave Ann a quick once over and ran behind the bar and grabbed something from underneath. She tossed a set of clothing at her and pointed to the bathroom.

"You can't fight like this." She said as Ann caught the clothing with a relieved thank you. As they waited the few moments for Ann to change Paul went on ahead. Cole watched the old barman with his hands to one of the young pool players temples. He was whispering inaudibly, a look of concentration on his face.

"Are they going to be able to wake them up?" Cole asked. Tema gave him a proud look.

"Don't underestimate them." She said, either referring to the older Gods or the people, Cole didn't know. "These people aren't like us. They will need help in waking, but they should be ok." Cole felt relief rush through him. He didn't like the idea of collateral damage, now he'd seen it.

"When Lilith first found us, she…made shadows come out of people." Cole didn't know how to form the question he was trying to ask. Tema gave him a disgusted look.

"That curse." She spat. "She takes all the evil within a person and creates a living being with it. Animals, she controls, only capable of terrible things."

Cole had no time to think about this as Ann came out, ready to go. The warning look on her face took the words out of Cole's mouth. He was left to have his face go red and his body temperature spike again, despite their dire situation. Though Ann had always been athletic, and logically, he knew her body would reflect that, she usually dressed modestly.

"Don't you dare." She said when she noticed Cole's eyes roving. Her cheeks flushed, which took away some of the imposition of her words.

The clothes must have belonged to Shiki as they hardly did anything to be called clothing. A black low cut, long sleeve belly shirt, showed off Ann's lightly muscled midriff. And a pair of cut up daisy dukes showed off all her work as a track runner. She had tied her dark hair up into a ponytail. So that she looked more ready to go out to a club than to a fight.

"Nice." Kenzie said appreciatively. When every conscious person in the room agreed, even the old ones, Ann went beat red and buried herself against Cole's chest.

"Must be nice, pretty boy." Brad said smiling, and he stuffed some more fries in his mouth. While chewing, he indicated the scar on Cole's eyebrow. "Worth it?" He asked, still smiling as he chewed. Cole gave him a broad smile and hid Ann in his arms. He answered as if Brad were crazy for asking.

"Hell yeah."

Ch. 11

They all stood at the back of the restaurant, staring into a
large open garage behind it. Paul was in front, facing the rest of the
group. The cool night air was still, and quiet. Not at all in compass
with the raging that was going on in the people he was addressing.
What they had witnessed that night had shaken each one of the
merely human of the group. But each had no intention of letting it
make them run. None of them had any visions of being a hero. There
is no glory in setting a truly terrible situation to rights, it's something
that needs to be done. They couldn't let the monster that had forced
her way into their lives have her way.

"So, when you said bus, you weren't making a euphemism."
Kenzie said. For behind Paul was indeed a half sized white school
bus.

"No. And I need to warn you…" Paul said with a look. "If
we had more time, we would be able to get you closer to the gate in
stages. But this time we are going straight there, top speed. It might
be, uncomfortable, to say the least." He said. At everyone's confused

looks he gestured for them to follow him aboard. It became apparent what he meant when they stepped onto the bus.

"It will be more clear when it happens.'' He tried to explain.

The bus was set up with seating along the sides. So that everyone would have their backs against the walls. It was also set up like a prison bus, as if each of them needed to be in solitary confinement. Cages of thick metal occupied most of the space inside. They were etched with similar symbols that had been on the bullets of Paul's gun, and the fountain in Sachiel's mind.

"Since we don't know what will happen to you as we get closer. You will each need your own space in case your power goes out of control." Paul explained as he took a seat at the back of the bus.

They all took him at his word as they chose their seats. Opening the cage doors in turn, to stay out of each other's way. Cole examined the cage as Ann sat across from him and Brad beside, with Kenzie diagonal to him. Each of the cages had spiraling hand holds welded onto the side walls. They were also inlaid with row upon row of the angelic script.

"The cages should be enough to absorb any excess discharges. If it's too much to handle, hold tight." Paul said as he saw Cole examining the handholds. The engine fired up as Cole touched the jewel on his wrist.

"Any idea on whether memories will be coming back as we do this?" He cast his thought to Sachiel.

"I am, not sure…" She sounded timid, as if the thought of his memories returning now had her worried. "Cole…" She said slowly.

But Paul was trying to catch his eye, unaware of the conversation going on silently.

"Did you by chance notice when Lilith greeted you, and made it seem as if it had not been long since she had seen either of you?" Sachiel continued.

Paul was leaning forward now, his gaze intense.

"I just thought, maybe, because you guys remember living forever, a couple hundred? Thousand? Years here and there didn't mean much to her." Cole said. The bus rumbled a bit as Tema took them out of the parking lot.

"Perhaps…" Sachiel didn't sound very convinced.

"Malaka!" Paul said loudly over the sound of the bus rolling down the street. Cole turned his attention to him, surprised "Ask the angel to be present. I want to inquire about something." Cole nodded.

"You hear that?" He asked flatly to Sachiel.

She promptly appeared, half sitting on him. The script on the cage wall lit up bright blue where she touched it. Not used to actually touching things in the physical world, Sachiel made a panicked noise and wriggled. Paul looked satisfied, as there was some jostling and scooting for her to squeeze next to Cole. She hastily opened the door to the cage once they had situated themselves. Ann gave her an appraising look.

As Sachiel bent forward to open the cage, Cole noticed that she had changed. Her blanket robe was now a hooded white cowl over a tight snow-white long sleeve onesie, made of a leather looking fabric but softer. And her wolf ears had vanished, to be replaced by uninjured human looking ones. Her white hair was shorter, though still very long, and had turned into loosely curled ringlets.

Cole hadn't realized how much the night's events had affected her. Paul watched her mistrust with a sad smile.

"You are not a prisoner." Paul said, pointing toward the open cage door. "They are for my protection." He said, holding a hand to his chest trying a warm smile.

When Sachiel only answered by making and embarrassed noise, he continued, "It was your kind that made these cages in the first place…Anyway." He said. His face had gone serious, but somehow in a positive way. "We had a hundred groups pass us by. Some with your kind mixed in. None could reverse the gate, it only goes in. That is still our problem, but now…" He indicated the group. They all watched him. "Two archangels and their seconds. Others, archangel level. Lilith coming out of her lair to wreak havoc on the city. Tell me there isn't something different." He said it as if he were ramping up inside. The gleam of hope in his eye.

In response, Sachiel turned to Cole and held out her hand. Still not happy at her entrance she didn't speak yet. Cole spent a moment trying to reach into his pocket without dying under Ann's stare. He put the dove necklace he pulled out into Sachiel's hand. She leaned out of the door and tossed it out to Paul. He caught it deftly with a quizzical look on his face. Sachiel closed the door to the cage and turned her bright golden eyes to Cole.

"First test, no pressure." She said so only he could hear. He smiled broadly at her as she disappeared into the bracelet on his wrist.

It took several seconds in which everyone looked silently between each other. She reappeared, outside of the cage, emerging from the necklace in Paul's hand. Before Paul could fully grasp the concept, she disappeared into the necklace. Reappearing several seconds later next to Cole again. Paul looked back and forth between the necklace and the bracelet, then at the cage, calculating. Suddenly he gave a monstrous growl of excitement. He pounded on the roof and addressed his sister.

"You see this?" He shouted up at her. Tema had been watching the proceedings periodically in the rearview mirror. Her eyes reflected the same look of glowing hope in them. They both let out primal yells of fierce joy that no one else in the bus really understood. But it made them smile anyway.

"I should not be surprised." Paul said looking at Cole as Tema went back to focusing on driving as they had veered while she shouted. "You know what they used to call you?" Cole gave him a wondering look as he gained his balance from swerving back onto the right side of the road.

"The...teacher?" Cole asked hesitantly.

"No, not our side, the other side." Paul looking rather manic. Cole just shrugged. "They call you The Teleporter. Though it is different this time. You may have to re-learn." Cole didn't know how to take that in. Paul seemed to be in a mood as he pointed around the bus. First to Sachiel then to Ann and Kenzie.

"The Hope, The Psychic, and the Thunder Goddess. I have never personally seen any of you in action before now, but...It would be an honor to fight with you." Cole was reeling at Ann's old nickname as she went wide eyed in comprehension. Suddenly, her ability to read body language and catch onto people's wavelengths was making more sense. Kenzie looked satisfied with her naming. She turned to Ann.

"I'm your second, by the way. The old guy told me." She gave a little awkward wave. Ann merely nodded as she was still pondering the implications of what Paul had said.

"What about me?" Brad asked getting into it.

"Aeolus did not read you so…" Paul shrugged but his demeanor had gone no less intense. Brad looked disappointed. "We have fought our way to the gate several times." Paul tried to explain through a fierce glare. Remembering the hard-fought battles.

"But always for naught. Or to lose another who goes in and can't come out." He shook with anger as he said it.

"Are they all still in there?" Kenzie asked. Paul nodded angrily and turned to Sachiel.

"You should know, the last time we speak with your brother." Sachiel's attention spiked and she unconsciously turned her full body toward him. Her hands reached up to grasp through the thick links of the cage.

"He is alive?" She asked desperately, giving away she hadn't known when she'd told Ann he must be.. Paul nodded but his look went grim.

"The last time we speak with him, his was…setting. With that much power being held within him, the effect is changing him." Sachiel made a growling noise as Paul continued. "The beings in him are…petrified. Eh, solidified, almost stone. And that was years ago." Paul tried to find the right words.

"He can't transfer enough power out of himself. Especially with the black stone encasing him." Paul raised one hand and lowered the other bringing them together as he spoke. "Where the river connects to the mouth of the lay lines. Is where his prison sits, his body is focal point." He clasped both hands together to give them a visual.

"Encased in black stone, to keep him in and so he can't send power very far." Sachiel let out an angry noise at the treatment they had all been subjected to. Paul held up the necklace, the silver dove swinging back and forth. "Even with this. It will only be good enough for…slow release. So, if you were hoping for reinforcements…." Paul shook his head.

"I will do it. We will share the burden." Sachiel said fiercely. Cole thought about the name Paul had given her, it started to make sense after he applied it to her.

Paul gave her an appreciative smile, saying, "In your state, with the time we will have, it will only be enough for one. Choose well…" Sachiel sat back down, thinking hard.

"Do you have any suggestions?" She asked after a few seconds. Paul also thought for a moment.

"I say you all get rest." He addressed the rest of the bus "My help will be to get you to your brother. He will have the better idea than me." He said to Sachiel.

"How long will it take to get there?" She asked.

Paul gave her a wobbling hand. "Six hours, give or take an hour or so." She nodded slowly and excused herself to go back into the jewel. Some of the light leaving with her as she disappeared.

"Why such a big difference?" Cole asked.

To that Paul smiled and indicated the handholds next to him. "You will see. Power has to go somewhere." Cole reexamined the hand holds as Paul seemed done with his inquiry. He sat back, blue eyes gleaming, while staring at the floor.

As most of the other passengers hadn't been able to add anything, they agreed to resting. Kenzie curled up in the back corner of her cage with a faraway look on her face. Sachiel went back into the jewel and Brad put the empty platter under his seat to lay back. Something in his posture belying his disappointment at not getting a nick-name.

(I'll let you in on this little secret, Brad had been called "the lesser dragon". But only because the other dragon didn't like competition. When "the other" dragon wasn't around, they merely called Brad "the dragon".)

Ann sat back, staring at him as Cole stared back with a smile.

"What am I thinking?" He asked playfully after a minute of silent staring. Ann smiled slyly before she rolled her eyes.

"I never needed ancient powers to know what you were thinking." She spoke. Just to test her, Cole cast his thoughts to the memory of the moment before Lilith had shown up the first time. It may have just been the look on his face, but Ann went red, and gave him a devious look. She opened her cage door and stepped over to his. As she opened the door to his cage, Paul made to protest.

"That's not a good-"He started. Ann silenced him with a look.

"Who's the angel here tough guy?" Ann said in a light playful voice, eyes flashing. Paul rolled his eyes as his cheeks went red. He muttered under his breath as Ann entered the other cage.

"Dead angel…don't blame me if you kill each other." He repositioned himself so he was facing Kenzie and struck up a conversation. Kenzie, peeking out from behind her knees, answered Paul's questions in her flat voice. This conversation blending in with the background noise of the bus's massive engine.

Ann, unlike Sachiel, dropped sideways right down on Cole's lap on purpose. Since he was still pressed up against one side, she was able to lay back against that side of the cage. She gave him a "you still want to play" sort of look. In answer to his thoughts.

It could have been the adrenaline, horror filled night that instead of backing down, Cole focused on her green eyes, brighter than they should be in the dark. Made brighter still, as streetlights passed them by. He ran his fingertips over her exposed belly.

Ann gave him a surprised look, as she had expected him to lay off quickly. She leaned in closer to him as his fingertips slid past the shorts and down her leg. Neither wanted to give in but Cole knew how competitive she was. So, he squeezed lightly above her knee where he knew she was ticklish.

She shook her head violently and huffed out a goofy, squealing, laugh. Cole broke too, and they both laughed. She gave him a quick peck on the cheek and laid her head against his shoulder, her eyes already closed. The contact and joking were necessary for them both. Neither had been prepared for just how intense the trip had gotten.

And it was only going to get worse.

It wasn't until they had been traveling for around three hours that anything happened. Cole and Ann were fast asleep against each other. When the sound of Kenzie's horrified voice woke them. They both looked over to see her in the same curled position she had been. Yet her eyes were now wide with terror and seemed to be seeing something that wasn't there. Her voice went from a whisper to screaming in rapid succession.

"No, no, no. Not like this, stop it. No, not like this." She repeated it as electric lines of energy ran along the lengths of her arms and legs. Everyone sat upright and watched her.

She made reverberating noises akin to standing under a torn powerline. She started heaving breaths as if she were having a panic attack and repeated the phrase again and again. It ramped up to the point that Paul had to shout over her.

"The hand holds!" He was just in time.

Fortunately, Kenzie still had the mental fortitude to follow the instruction. Her hands shot out as her three-inch heels hit the floor. Her cage lit up in light blue angelic runes that ran down through the floor. The sound of a thunder bolt and the flash of lightning blinded them. Kenzie's small frame was wreathed in and seemed to be made of charged electricity. With a jolt the bus jumped forward, its speed increased by taking in Kenzie's energy. They were all rocked by the force. But above everything was Kenzie's scream.

"NOOO! HOW COULD YOUU!!" Kenzie's voice came out as if through a megaphone, pained at the same level as their would be companion in Lilith's phone call. And warped by the power running through her and into their mechanical steed. Words seemed to fail her as she screamed with such force everyone had to put their fingers in their ears or risk rupturing their eardrums.

"Holy Hera!" Tema yelled as she struggled to keep in control of the new speed.

Cole gave Ann a panicked, worried look. He mouthed. "Read her mind." Ann looked hesitant and terrified for a moment. But she took a deep breath and focused all her attention on Kenzie's screaming form. Trying to use her power intentionally for the first time. As her eyes grew wide with terror, Sachiel erupted from the jewel on Cole wrist and sat next to him.

"No, don't!" She tried to warn. Ann's eyes filled with tears as she seemed to be trying to tear her eyes away from the scene.

She twisted and writhed, her face turning into a mask of horror. Finally, when a scream started to erupt from Ann as well, Cole grabbed her by the chin and pulled her gaze into his. She didn't seem to be seeing him. The horror subsided but her breathing came in huffy and ragged. She seemed to also be going through a change. Her legs kicked out faster than Cole's eyes could follow. Bending the thick links at the force, even as they lit with blue light.

Cole tried to lay across her to hold her down, but her arms shot out. With one hand she grappled the links, bending them again. And unbidden, for she was not in her right mind, her other hand slammed Cole against side of the bus. Her fingernails raked into his chest and if the breath hadn't been shoved out of him, Cole would have screamed in pain. As it was, he could only give a horrified grimace as blood started to leak down his shirt, his vision blurring.

It felt as if she were near digging into bone as she twisted and writhed. Her face racked with silent screams as she crushed him against the bus wall. Sachiel wrestled her writhing form off the cage and barely managed to stuff her into her own. She placed Ann's hands against the grips, one slippery with blood, before rushing back to Cole. He was sitting in shock, heaving breaths, and starring at the chunks of flesh hanging from his body. He was quickly relieved when the Angel of healing placed a hand over the wound. In a shining flash of golden light. Cole's chest was back to normal albeit tingly and traumatized. Sachiel had had an upgrade as well.

He hadn't even realized the back of his head had taken a blow when Ann had shoved him. Not until Sachiel took his shoulder and bent him forward to place a hand on the spot. In another flash Cole felt a heavy pressure relief and most of his shock wear off. Sachiel turned a worried look on Kenzie.

There was a huge metal thumping noise and a huff of expelled breath from where Brad sat.

"Aw shit, not again." Came Brads voice. They turned to see him pressed up against the roof, straining to reach for the hand holds. Even as he did it, the entire bus groaned and lifted slightly.

The radical lightning surrounding Kenzie, pulled together slowly and loudly. Getting thicker as it formed into the shape of two curled wings. And wrapped around Kenzie's huddled form. Just for a moment as they unfurled, Kenzie struck a truly angelic form only the gods and Sachiel could ever remember seeing. Wreathed in flowing electric light but formed in the shape of a winged human. As they marveled, the electric energy faded, drawn back into Kenzie's body. Her screams died down with the transformation.

Kenzie hadn't been ugly, but she would never have won any beauty pageants. Now however, as the lightning faded, she reformed into a being that was not wholly unlike Kenzie had been. But was on a new level of beauty. A level Cole had only ever seen in the angel next to him. And when she wasn't ripping apart his body, the one sitting across from him, now in fits of silent mania.

Kenzie's black attire had also changed to match Sachiel's white leather onesie and cowl.

Without his calling for it, though he should have expected it, Cole felt the power he usually had a cap on, start to take hold of his body. Perhaps it had been due to the excitement, or that he had experience using it before, that his had taken longest. But as he tried to control the energy ramping up inside him, he understood what had taken place with the others. It felt like explosions of heat and light were taking place over and again inside his body. From head to foot, he felt his clumps of tangled energy inside him tightening in some places, becoming more closely coiled. And in others lengthening and thickening. At the centers of each cluster, they seemed to be trying to break through to something they knew should be there but wasn't.

His hands lit up with bright aquamarine light and he immediately grabbed the hand holds. As he did so, his mind was transported into the glowing metal. His mind flowed in a wave across the entirety of the bus. Scanning each piece down to the mixture of its molecular structure. It was some mixture he had never been aware of until now. That made for a substance twice as strong as steel. He felt each of their separate powers raging though the system of metalwork. His predecessors had connected and molded it in place to transfer the excess power into the drive shafts. What a thought.

He didn't have to put forth any effort for the magic to happen on its own. He watched as his power reformed the rest of the structure of the metal bus. To mimic that of the angel made cages. So that it wasn't just the added system reinforcing the bus. But the entire bus itself that was now tank tough. He felt massive amounts of energy flowing forth during the process and worried how much it would take. He watched Ann bending the bars and links of her cage with the same worry for her.

The new Kenzie observed her surroundings with the same calm, flat expression they would have expected from the old one. The bus creaked and groaned as Cole's magic ran through and transformed it. And Brad lifted it slowly from the ground. Kenzie raised both of her hands.

"Calm down." She said and lowered her hands to sit in her lap. The whole process hadn't lasted more than ten minutes.

Her voice had become more melodious, if no less flat. She turned her gaze into the middle distance as the raging in Cole's body settled down. The power he felt coursing through the lines of cables inside him no less present. But now felt as caged as he was. Ready to be called upon in an instant. Brad fell slowly back down to his seat giving Kenzie a wide stare. Ann stopped writhing and trying to rip her handholds free of the cage.

"Carlel?" Sachiel asked toward Kenzie in a hesitant voice. Kenzie turned to her and nodded once before turning back to stare at nothing. Sadness radiated from her in waves.

"Woh." Brad said appreciatively. "Did I get a new look too?" He asked. Turning to try and see his reflection in the window.

"No." Kenzie said shortly. Brad looked disappointed again.

"Your memories…" Sachiel started but couldn't go on. Kenzie, now apparently Carlel, turned to her. And surprisingly to half the bus. There were tears cascading down her cheeks. Lines of electricity flowed down the lengths of her arms again and the power held within them vibrated through the air.

"It is as I feared." Sachiel said quietly and her eyes also filled with tears. Ann, having looked inside the old new angels mind, knew what had happened. She leapt from her seat and grabbed the handle to her cage so forcefully it broke off. Undeterred she simply shouldered her way through it. It took some effort, but it shouldn't have been possible. She leapt over to Carlel's cage and more gently opened her door. Carlel didn't protest as Ann sat next to her and pulled her into a hug. Sachiel did the same, only more hesitantly as the others watched, dumbfounded.

"What happened?" Cole asked somberly. Knowing the answer couldn't be any sort of good. Ann gave him a look and he took a deep breath. Preparing to hear what she had to say. He wasn't ready, but no one with a simply human mind could be.

"They..." Carlel started, holding back mightily as she tried not to lose control. "The sha dim, find us." She said in a shaking voice full of terror and fury.

"It is a game to them." She said disgusted. "The younger the better, so we won't become a threat. They find us when our power manifests...and *kill us*." The information hit Cole like punch to the gut and an ice-cold bucket of water over his head. Brad's face went pale, and he looked as if he was going to be sick. Paul's face went even darker in the shadow of the night. So that he looked as though he were wearing a black mask.

"We were, *are*..." She referred to all those in the bus. "a special focus. They, don't just kill us...It...what they do...it makes us weaker every time."

"I don't want to know any more." Brad said hoarsely, leaning his elbows to his knees and hands to his forehead.

"If you want to get back some semblance of your true form, not just partake of raw power...You will have to remember." Carlel said. Brad looked up at her, understanding what she meant. In order to gain their old powers back, they would have to get through the memories of being hunted down and killed for millennia. Carlel's electric power surged around her hands. Flashing lines accompanied with flowing electric noise filled the cabin again. "In order to remember, to get back what small power these weakened bodies can handle. They have...made it so you will have to go through hell."

Ch. 12

According to Paul they were nearing their destination. There were no more power surges to be had. Paul explained that they usually went back and forth across the area where the output from the gate was strongest, as they had just done, in order to avoid someone losing control and killing everyone right off the bat. But this time there had been no option but to push forward. And possibly because they'd been angels, it might have been easier to handle. It had been for a few of them. After Sachiel and Ann had left their cages, Paul had humbly thanked Carlel for the assist. She had simply nodded and went back to staring at some middle distance.

Ann and Sachiel were now both in Cole's cage. Ann was sitting on the ground with her head laid against his knees. While Sachiel was beside him making sure his wounds were healed. Ann let out another apology every few minutes. She had looked at the holes in his shirt and the blood on her fingers with horror. And not for the first, or last time this trip, her eyes had filled with tears.

"It's alright." Cole said trying to smile as Sachiel poked his back to see if he would respond in pain. "Ow, hey, not so hard." Cole said wincing. In response, there was another flash of golden light.

"I hardly touched you." Sachiel said in an undertone. "Cracked rib most likely." She said, to Ann's deflation and watery eyes. Cole gave her a not worried sort of look as his breath came in deeper. With everything they had been exposed to, he hadn't noticed that either.

"Hey, it's ok." Cole said wiping a tear from her face. He took on a more somber note. "Now we know their game, I'm sure we're in for far worse than accidental injuries."

"Do not doubt that." Paul said as he handed out water bottles and bagged lunches from under the back seat. It was still dark outside and the expenditure of energy that they had all gone through had left them hungry. They took them gratefully.

"My takeaway." Ann said after she drained some water. "Is that they do the worst possible things imaginable. Not just to do it, they enjoy it." She said revolted.

"But they do it for the affect it will have on us. To make us slip up." Carlel nodded somberly to her. At the gesture, Ann continued more confidently. "So, we need to expect the absolute worst. Think of the worst thing you can. Then make it worse."

"You mean like…kidnapping and torturing an innocent girl and her friend…just to get us to fight em?" Brad said not jokingly.

"How can we make that worse?" Cole asked. Paul answered as if he knew exactly what could be worse.

"They wait for you to think you will win, then kill them both in front of you. Then do the same to you. Rinse, repeat. We are not the only ones who wait for newcomers to show up." He said quietly as the bus pulled off to the side of a dirt road. They all pondered on his words grimly as they came to a halt. Then exited with grave looks on their faces. Seemingly prepared for what they were about to meet.

"Hey, why didn't we run into any border guards or anything between countries?" Cole asked as Paul handed out backpacks from the under carriage. There was more food and water, along with rope, a harness and carabiners inside them.

"We have our own way of getting here. Far away from guards and police." Paul answered. Cole wasn't surprised he hadn't noticed. There had been too many things going on.

They all strapped their packs on while Paul and Tema talked at the front of the bus. Something struck Cole as he watched them, neither had shown any signs of strengthening as the journey had gone on. He was just beginning to worry about this, when out of nowhere, their cloths changed. Not like they took them off and changed into something else. Their cloths simply melted into, no joke, fluffy white togas with laurel leaves poking out of their hair. Tema, whose blonde hair had gone slightly curly. Even bent down and grabbed two very beaten looking bows from the undercarriage. Their leather quivers had the same angelic markings as the bus, carved into them.

"We felt like going old school." Paul answered Cole's look, as Tema pulled out a massive sniper rifle that she slung over her shoulder. The quivers they both had strapped to their hips.

"Well, mostly." She said as she pointed to the gun under Paul's arm with a slight smile.

"Hey uh, you got any weapons for us...or are we bare fistin' this lady?" Brad asked also with a slight smile. His eyes darted around to see if anyone would laugh. No one was in the mood.

Tema pulled out a hidden shelf from the under carriage. There was an arm load of items that looked like they had seen several centuries. And a rack of pistols and smaller automatic weapons. The older weapons included a bastard sword with a razor-sharp blade and blue leather grip. That was Ann's choice. Along with an mp-5 she checked and slung over her shoulder as if practiced. Cole gave her a quizzical look.

"No offense, but you don't know anything about conservative dads." She said in explanation. "I've been shooting since I was little." She shrugged. Cole raised his eyebrows.

"Well, you're right. The only father figure I ever had." He said smiling and scratching his head. "Was a giant wolf that turned into a beautiful woman. After I stabbed and blew up her demons." Ann gave him a look and shook her head as Sachiel blushed.

"Thank you." She said as Brad selected a handgun akin to Paul's, only silver. And another mp-5 that looked like a child's toy in his hands. Cole was struck by sudden inspiration. With his newfound power he thought he could make it happen.

"Hold on." He said and walked over to the big man.

He placed his hand on the small weapon. Scanning it with his new power came naturally and made the transition easier. He even got all the markings on the rounds copied as he focused on one of his many projects. Slowly, he unleashed the raw power that was raging to get out of its cage. The weapon shimmered with aqua light and lengthened. Molding into a full-size M249 machine gun and made of the angelic metal. It was still only the same size as Ann's was to her, but Brad whistled at the slightly heavier new weight.

"Now that's what I'm talkin' about." He said looking the weapon up and down.

Everyone watched the transformation appreciatively. They had no choice but to become used to the use of power. Cole turned to Ann and indicated her sword. He didn't change it into anything different, other than to switch the metals. Ann didn't even notice the slightly heavier weight. She swung the dully gleaming grey blade inexpertly but appreciatively. He hadn't planned on taking any weapons with him. But as she swung the sword, a battered old berretta caught his eye. He took it and noticed that Carlel took no weapon.

"Everybody ready?" Paul asked. They all agreed and followed the siblings into quickly cooling night air.

Cole stuffed the berretta into the holster on his hip. It was old and worn as the weapon it had sat underneath. He wondered how many people had used it before him and hoped he would be the last new one. It was now as easy for him to use his power in the real world as it had been in Sachiel's realm. He also hoped that would be enough.

They hiked for a half hour through a baren rocky mountain path before stopping. Periodically they ran or jogged when the path allowed for it. Their faces were slightly sweaty and gleamed as the sun started peeking out over the horizon. Throughout the swift journey they had all been mostly silent. Steeling themselves for whatever the demon witch had planned.

Paul and Tema both knelt on the closest side of a bend in the mountain trail. They unzipped their bags and took out binoculars.

Cole hadn't seen any in his bag, so theirs must be the only ones. They inched over to the edge of the path and stared through the binoculars for a moment before beaconing to the others.

"Not many, considering." Paul said to Tema.

"She wants us all to herself." Tema said half sarcastic, half determined.

"I could take a lot of them out in one go." Paul said as they turned to the group. He handed his binoculars over to Brad, who was closest. Tema handed hers to Ann who was closest to her.

"What are you going to do?" Cole asked interested. Paul gave him a broad smile.

"I've been saving something just for them."

Cole had been with Ann in the middle. While the two white cloaked angels were out of earshot and taking up the rear. Now, he hung back as Brad and Ann inched forward and peaked over the edge of the path. Both tried to take in what they were seeing without fear. But Cole could read Ann's body language and heavier breathing. That mixed with Brad's glistening sweat, turning into dripping sweat, gave Cole preparation for what they were seeing. Ann gave him her set of binoculars with a pale face and a look of warning.

"Is this what you were seeing all the time back home?" She asked as Cole inched forward.

"Only one way to find out." He said as he placed the binoculars and edged the last bit over the path.

What he saw reminded him somewhat of what Sachiel's mind had been. The path dropped almost straight down for several hundred feet. Then slowly sloped outward for another several hundred feet, reaching out on a slow slope for a quarter mile and into a half a further mile of flat plain, covered in grey stone and patches of sparse grass. It then sloped up slowly in the other direction for another half mile into a volcano shaped hill around one hundred feet high. Complete with a hole in the top.

In the flat space, there were a horde of black shapes meandering around. From their vantage point it was easy to see all that had assembled. Each of them varied from the humanoid beings they had seen the night before only slightly, but there were some differences.

"Nice of em to put themselves in the kill box at least." Brad said.

"We don't know if they're all on this side though." Cole answered.

"We always attack from here, only place to go." Cole could hear Paul's shrug in his voice.

"Then…we should switch it up on them." Ann said. They all looked at her as she turned to Sachiel. "Are you the only one who can move through the gems?" She asked.

"I can only go in as a spirit. And none of us can go in if she's not already in there." Cole answered. Sachiel Corrected him.

"That was due to my lack of power. I believe I could hold you now but…one at a time." Despite their situation the idea excited him. Cole felt his heart leap at the idea. Carlel answered from beside her.

"I will lend you the power you need. Stay close to me."
Sachiel nodded but Ann hesitated as she thought about the
mechanics of her plan. "Just move toward the jewel and focus, I will
do the rest. What do you have in mind Laphaliel?" The new Kenzie
was awesome, Cole thought. Ann seemed weirded out by being
addressed by the name, but she continued.

"Do you still have the necklace?" She asked Paul, who drew
it from his pocket. Cole pulled his eyes away from the scene below
to watch. Ann grabbed an arrow from out of Paul's quiver. Taking
the necklace, she wrapped it around the base of the triangular head.
She spent a moment making sure it was secure before handing it
back to Paul.

"Where do you usually attack from?" She asked. Paul
nodded toward the back end of a winding path with a half-smile.
Starting to understand what she had in mind. The path led down the
side of the mountain and came out about a mile off to their left. As
Cole saw it, he noticed most of the creatures down below seemed to
be gathered around the exit. Ann positioned her arm facing the exit

then moved it in a half circle in the other direction. Paul was already nocking his arrow.

"So if you put us-…"Ann started.

"Way ahead of you cowgirl." Paul said as he drew the arrow back. The dove dangling from under the razor-sharp tip. Paul was already a muscular guy. But as he drew back the arrow every muscle in his body stood out in stark striations. He whispered some spell and the arrow, as well as the necklace disappeared.

"Wait till we're all-…"Ann said quickly.

"Aorato skata." Paul said and released. With a deep twang that was more of a whooshing sound. And a small burst of wind that rattled their eardrums, he let the arrow fly. A light layer of dust lifted and followed the shot. Cole was geeking out, while the last bit of Ann's statement came out annoyed.

"Inside…Right, well. Hopefully they didn't notice that." Ann said rolling her eyes. Cole understood where she was going with it. He quickly took off his wolf bracelet and threw it over to Tema.

She caught it wordlessly and slipped it on, giving him a nod. His wrist felt naked without it, but it was a good plan.

"A pincer move, nice." Brad said approvingly.

Ann pointed at Brad, "With you from above. And them providing cover fire with perfect accuracy…if they live up to their legends." Ann said, now pointing up and then looking at the siblings questioningly. They looked at each other and both snorted.

"Don't worry, we won't shoot you." Tema answered through a wide smile.

"Oh right, I can do that now…I'll get high up as possible, so I'm not shootn at yawl either." Brad said.

Cole put the binoculars back up while they discussed the details. It didn't seem as though there were any reaction to the arrow. He zeroed in on the nearest one, it was larger than the others. And looked hopped up on ten Monsters and three lines of cocaine. It breathed and growled heavily while fixated on the path. It quaked from head to foot as it leaned back and forth, ready to spring.

Carlel brazenly stepped to the edge of the path and extended a hand over the field. Electricity running down her arm and coalescing around her hand. She didn't seem to have much patience for scouting. And the plan had already been made.

"There are one hundred and seventy-three of them." She said from under her hood.

Cole looked back to see that Sachiel had also pulled hers over her head. So that her face was hidden in shadow as well. It made them look more menacing. There must have been symbolism to it he didn't understand yet.

"We do not exist for this." Carlel answered his questioning look. She turned to the other angel; Sachiel hesitated but Carlel gave her a nod. All present could hear how much it meant to Sachiel, to be included in the mantra.

"Killing is the prevue of the fallen and wicked. There is no glory or beauty in the act." They took up the last part together.

"But when demons are at your door, we answer swiftly and without fear." Carlel fully faced Sachiel and positioned herself a foot away from the other angel as they finished.

"For God is with us, and we stand together." They clasped each other's forearms. It was their call to battle. Apparently, the hoods meant the time for talking was over.

Sachiel confirmed this by taking two quick steps and vanishing into the bracelet. Carlel indicated that Ann should follow. Her body moved over to the old Kenzie quickly, but her eyes showed she was scared. To her credit, she didn't hesitate when she turned around.

Cole had another flash of inspiration as she said. "Here goes nothing." She focused on the jewel and moved forward, Carlel sent an outstretched hand at her back. And for the first time Cole watched a whole human being vanish into the brightly shining jewel. So, it was possible, he thought. He was moving toward Paul, reaching for his quiver, when Carlel turned toward him.

"Jophiel?" She said.

"I'll be right there, go on without me." Paul allowed him to grab a fist full of angelic runed arrows as he said it. The demigod seemingly enjoying the proceedings.

Carlel didn't hesitate to trust his words and moved forward to disappear as Cole focused his power on the arrows. A wave of blue green energy ran along the double fistful of arrows. Outwardly, they hadn't changed. At Paul's questioning look, Cole just smiled.

"It'll be cool, trust me." He said as he put the arrows back in place and focused on the gem. It felt like he was being sucked through a straw as he leapt forward.

Sachiel's domain had changed again. The stone had gone from polished grey marble to polished white marble. And was so bright he had a hard time focusing. There were other changes, but Cole didn't have the time to admire the scenery.

Ann didn't seem to agree as she stood right next to the hovering jewel gate, marveling. Cole grabbed her hand and they moved together toward the angels.

"This is where you've been hanging out all this time?" Ann asked in disbelief as they ran.

"What? Are you jealous?" Cole asked jokingly.

Sachiel was just picking up the black blade from where it leaned against the fountain. With Carlel's hand on her shoulder for support.

"How in all of heavens beauty did you get that?" Carlel exclaimed when she noticed the sword. Sachiel pointed to Cole as he approached. Carlel fixed him with a surprised expression. In the blazing light of Sachiel's new domain, he could see her even under the hood.

"What?" He asked when he saw her staring. Both the angels let out a snicker as they turned to continue.

"Leave it to Jophiel, yeah?" Sachiel asked brandishing the sword as they crossed the courtyard in pairs. One pair hand to shoulder, the other hand in hand.

"Indeed!" Carlel answered in the most excited tone any of them had heard from either her or *Kenzie.*

Cole wasn't paying attention; he had seen something at the entrance to the palace that caught his eye. And in fact, it wasn't something, it was someone. Talos sat stalk still, following them with his cat slitted eyes. The most recent little fairy sat on the head of one of the angel statues. When they saw Cole notice, Talos twitched his tail in greeting, and the little fairy waved vigorously. Cole waved his free hand and smiled.

"Wish us luck!" He screamed. The cat didn't answer, but his tail flicked back and forth in amusement. The little fairy laughed and continued to wave.

"Whose cat is that?" Ann asked with a hint of hilarity in her voice. "Is that a fairy?!"

"He's free to come and go as he pleases, he's his own cat." Cole said. Ann just shook her head and listened, as the angel's conversation reached back to them.

"How were you able to acquire a piece of…him?" Carlel asked in amazement.

"Do you recall my demotion?" Both angels glanced back at Ann.

"I see." Said Carlel with dawning comprehension. Cole felt Ann's grip on his tighten painfully.

"Look, I'm sorry alright!" Ann said frustrated as they reached the opposite edge of the courtyard where the dove gem had been placed.

Sachiel positively tripped as she slowed to let Cole and Ann pass through first. They noticed the stunned look on her face before jumping through. Carlel looked supremely satisfied as she raised a hand to assist Ann back through.

They emerged several football fields behind all the waiting monsters, and quicky side-stepped. The other two came through, Carlel leading the way. Cole bent down to grab Paul's arrow to take the necklace as it was a critical part of their plan. He took the arrow with, in case Paul wanted it.

As soon as they'd come out. It was impossible not to notice the strange noise that cascaded down over the valley from where they had just been.

At first it sounded like animal, gurgling, and growling in a chant that set their hearts to boiling and their hair to stand on end. It was joined in perfect concert by another vicious growl and yowling. It was a sort of animalistic song that reached down to the core of a tribalistic and violent nature Cole didn't know he had. It was followed by a scream that came from deep within each of the sibling's guts. Then Tema's voice alone, came out in a high, cold ethereal chant. In that chant, any who heard it were given a waking dream that promised far away treasures and happiness to be found in the blood of their enemies. Apparently, the gods had a more savage call to battle. Those who had come out of the gem felt their feet moving without having to bid them.

"Vrochi thanatou." Paul's voice sounded clearly, even from this far away. And from their spot on the mountain, came a glimmering silver star. It shot high into the sky as they ran over grey stony dirt. And when it reached its zenith, it split into many little stars that came raining down on the field only one hundred meters in front of them. The arrows, aided by Cole filling them with explosives, and Paul's multiplying spell. Rained devastation on the monsters who had been transfixed by Tema's voice.

Deep booming, growls and screams greeted them as they moved closer to the fray. Cole had fallen behind the rest of the group as they were all much faster than he was. Even Ann was left far behind by the two white hooded angels. So, they had a good view of what happened when the enemy started retreating toward them. Through the clouds of smoke, debris and dirt clouds several of the creatures emerged. At seeing the charging crew coming up behind them they were momentarily surprised. Then charged ahead toward the oncoming foe.

The oncoming foe responded in a fashion that would stick with Cole for the rest of his natural life. Ann paused to rattle off a few shots from the MP-5 at the furthest to the left creature. Sachiel turned into a blur as the sound of a massive electric charge ripped through the air.

Electric lines of energy erupted from Carlel's body, forming into the shape of great wings. At one massive pump and the sound of a shockwave she launched over fifty feet into the air. Her wings retracted into her body, and she sent no less than ten bolts of lightning into the same number of monsters. Sachiel took advantage of their paralysis by flashing between all of them. Severing vital chunks away as she did so.

It gave Cole an idea as he neared the place Ann had stopped. She had downed the creature with the mp5 but had several others closing in. Cole knelt to the ground and sent his scanning power as far out as he could. He could feel the beasts beating charge as they neared Ann who was firing shots in threes between them. Cole let loose a pulse of power and one of each of the beast's feet, fell into a deep hole that had just appeared there. As they were either stopped in their tacks or fell head over heels, Ann finished them off.

Another beast emerged from the smoke as they were appreciating their work. Only to have an arrow protrude from its forehead before it could get near them. The gutturally deep sound of automatic gunfire reached their ears from above and toward the entrance to the path. Brad seemed to be busy as well. Cole collected the second arrow from the drifting pile of black smoke. It must have been Tema's as it hadn't exploded.

Just for kicks, he tried to meld the two arrows into one to see if he could.

A resonance of the power emanated from the arrows as they melted and formed into one. Apparently, the angelic carvings and handywork of two ancient demigods coming together was no simple thing. Cole felt the power of the arrow pulse up his arm and into his own power. They connected and shared each other's strength, both being stronger for the binding. At its finishing he held it in his hand like a wand. Which he absolutely intended to use it as. He laughed and rushed to back Ann up.

Despite the enemy's numbers, they were hopelessly out matched as they were basically mindless. The four on the ground congregated and moved together, back-to-back. Cole and Carlel stopping them in their tracks while the other two dispatched of them quickly. Cole used the arrow to create waves of three bolts of energy. Akin to the one that had stopped Lilith's troll in its tracks the night before. But taking a que from Carlel, instead of sending solid bars of energy through them. He focused on giving it a lighter touch and simply froze them in place without impaling them.

Ann switched to her bastard sword when she ran out of ammunition. And if she wasn't graceful with it, she was plenty fast and beastly strong to get the job done. All while arrows rained down from the siblings. Brad's quick bursts of automatic fire that ended rather quickly. To be replaced by the occasional massive booming of sniper and 50 caliber handgun fire. It was gritty, smoking and smelly. But it only took them fifteen minutes to clear the field.

When there were only a few left. There were two whooping noises from above. Cole glanced up to see Paul and Tema, simply jump down the cliff face. Tapping their feet on rock outcroppings like mountain goats. They hit the steep decline like surfers on a wave. It inspired him to go all out, he rent the arrow in a downward slash. A line of blue green energy pulsed forth in a diagonal wave. The charging ember eyed monster took the blast across the face and split into two clouds of black smoke.

Brad came floating down from above, becoming visible through the dust for the first time. And without his machine gun. He landed heavily with a few quick stutter steps next to Cole, waving his arms as he did so.

"Sorry, I didn't get to coverin you." He said after catching his balance. "They all went hightailin' it up the path after all that singin." Brad shrugged after he'd straightened up.

"Made for good target practice though." He finished. Cole was about to ask where the machine gun went, when he saw it in Paul's hands as he and Tema came running at unreal speeds toward them. Their legs looking like cartoon blurs. His eyes went wide as he changed gears, pulling his eyes away from the siblings with difficulty.

"It worked out." He said as they approached.

Tema caught the last of the straggling beasts with and arrow in mid sprint from fifty yards. They did live up to the legends. Paul's quiver was nearly empty, but Cole didn't want to give up his new toy now. When Paul noticed him holding the stray arrow though, he gave it a queer look. He handed the massive gun back to Brad with his eye still on it. Cole heaved a sigh and held it out as Brad thanked the other giant.

"Obliged." Brad nodded to Paul. "It's a lot harder to stay stable while shootn. Sent me doin backflips, lost my grip, good thing I had the side arm." Paul didn't seem to notice him speaking as he inspected the arrow.

"This feels different, powerful." He gave Cole a cocked eyebrow. "What did you do?"

Cole pointed between the two siblings with an embarrassed smile while scratching his neck. He didn't know if he had crossed any sacred lines, so he tried to sound lighthearted.

"I...just put both of yours together." He shrugged and gave a 'no big deal' look. Paul and Tema both stared with intense interest and shining blue eyes at the arrow. "I was using it as a wand." Cole added quickly, as neither Paul nor Tema had shown any signs of fatal line crossings. The demigods exchanged an amused look and Paul handed it back to him.

"You have to get used to that around him." Said Sachiel, her head turning this way and that. Paul nodded.

"We would need time to learn how to use it. Keep it." He said, handing it back over reluctantly. Cole took it back and stuffed it into his belt with a smile.

"Keep your guard up." Carlel said flatly. "We have just started." She started moving toward the top of the volcano shaped hill and the others followed. Sachiel caught up to stand beside her. At this point Cole could hardly tell she wasn't a whole being. It was only her slightly golden aura that gave her away. And though they were in the middle of a deadly struggle. He felt a moment of happy pride that she was able to stand next to one of her own in such a fashion.

"Stop being so looud." Ann whispered from beside him. "Your thoughts are like a blow horn."

Cole smiled at her. In his thoughts he pushed forth the moment he'd realized how lucky she'd made him by coming along. She smiled back, rolled her eyes and pushed his face away from hers.

"Cheeseball." She said under her breath as Carlel and Sachiel picked up the pace, in unison.

There were several large enough boulders in which to tie their ropes at the edge of the massive hole in the ground. The bottom of which was too far down to see in the early morning light. After Paul and Tema gave them a brief lesson on how to repel down, Cole and Ann were on their way into the darkness. They were passing the halfway mark when the two angels and the sibling demigods came raining down around them. Ann thought she could probably have made the leap. But didn't want to leave Cole as the only one repelling. Brad floated down more slowly, he gave Cole and Ann a wry smile as he passed.

"Must suck not gettin a superhero entrance." He said as he passed.

"Don't trip on your landing." Ann sang with false concern in her voice. She released the rope underneath her and fell past Brad. Cole released only a little more pressure but came down in time to hear Brads reaction. As Ann clenched her bottom hand and stopped a foot from the ground.

"Damn, you're competitive." Brad said. Cole made a derisive noise.

"You should see her on the-…" He lowered the last ten feet under Ann's silencing glare.

The darkness of the cave floor had lessened as they got closer. They landed in a dim, circular shaped cavern stretching a little over 20 meters in every direction. There was an underground creek running along the left side that had clumps of the same grass from above at the edge.

The twins and the angels already stood at the edge of the light coming down from above. Paul and Tema both stood with their hands up, facing the three newcomers. The reason for this, being that there were several shadows pacing the ground around them. All but one not paying them any particular attention.

These weren't shadows of the type Cole was used to seeing. For one, their eyes didn't glow ember, but gleamed black even in the gloom, all but the one staring at them., that one, from a wall at the far-right. They weren't of any worldly shape he could place. One being a mastiff sized scorpion spider with six eyes running in a line down its nub of a head. Another with a humanoid body but with arms so long its fingers dragged on the cave floor. With a head like an upside-down A-shape. Conical horns raised a foot from the base of its skull. And still one more that looked like a wild boar with an extra set of legs, bigger tusks and a long pointed snout .

"These are the demons King Solomon set to guard this place from thieves." Paul said quietly. "They will not harm or speak to you unless addressed or attacked." The newer arrivals looked around the cavern with suspicious eyes. There was something else Cole noticed about them, apart from not having ember eyes; these creatures had the air of being more solid than any shadow he'd ever come across. Somehow their bodies, reflecting in purple and red shades against the light, looked more real, more solid, than any he'd ever seen.

"I feel no violent intent, yet." Carlel said, pointing to the one staring at them. "That one has something to say, though."

"The entrance. He is…the servant." Tema said shortly. There was a grotesque hissing laughter that came from the direction of the servant. Followed by an equally grotesque high pitch gurgling voice.

"Come now Artemis, we have been at this too long for you to be petty." He waved a hand and a doorway appeared in the wall beside him. "If treasures you seek down below, just know; no matter how far you run, we will find you." The creature said. Something in his voice begged for them to test his resolve in the matter.

"There's treasure down there?" Cole asked, even though he had felt his stomach go cold at the creature's pronouncement.

"Of many kinds, rotting angel" The creature said. Cole made a grossed out face at the title. "Solomon, King, was not so altruistic toward the end. Though the wretch cursed us to guard this place for eternity before all that. And we have done our job rather well." There was a hint of amusement in his voice.

Like Lilith, there was the promise of misery and death resonating from his words. All the creatures in the room stopped meandering to gaze in Cole's direction. As if they were sharks that had smelled a hint of blood. The servant was trying to get him to say something offensive, so he didn't say anything. The servant at the door lowered his head and looked toward the twins.

"Speaking of, how is your father? I do not see the stalwart among this new batch of sacrifices. Tell me, did he die after our last bout?" Paul and Tema both looked as though they were using all their strength not to reply in anger. But their breaths were coming heavier, and their eyes gleamed in the dimness. The demon responded with its strange laughter.

"None will be your sacrifice today, morning son." Carlel said quietly. The demon didn't let it stop his laughter and let it die down with a humming.

"Mmm, another rotten angel has joined the hapless cause, I see." He pretended to only just notice Sachiel beside her. "Ahh, and Sachiel, too bad you decided not to join us. We would have welcomed you with…open arms." It laughed again, the sound seeping into their ears like oiled millipedes. Sachiel answered by straightening and moving forward, her white cloak waving in her wake. Something in the power of her movement made the others follow without giving the servant any more of their attention. The demon didn't stop as they tried to ignore it.

"I assure you, none of you are a tenth of what you were and not a quarter enough for what lies ahead. To have died by my hands, would have been a mercy." Almost as if it were being forced, the creature bowed as they passed. But the sound of its laughter followed them as they passed through the door and onto a narrow set of stone stairs.

Sachiel's golden glow was the only thing that kept the stairs barely visible until the twins produced flashlights. Even still, the steep stone stairs were difficult for them to manage after talking with the servant. Ann put both hands on Cole's shoulders and shuddered when they'd passed through the door.

"His mind." She said through a quavering choke.

"Was it that bad?" Cole whispered back. Something about the stairs made him feel like he should use his library voice.

"I didn't even hear his thoughts…I couldn't." Ann tried to put the words together. "It was like trying to push against glass covered in soap…I thought I was going to slip and…" She shuddered again. Cole's ankle itched.

"That thing is near enough too Lilith herself." Paul said. His anger was palpable, as was Tema's as she continued. "What Solomon was thinking keeping him down here, we will never know."

"Maybe someday you can ask him." Cole whispered over his shoulder. Paul and Tema both gave derisive noises.

"Not likely. After all Solomon did. *He* sent a few of the enemies best to take the last human with any power and dragged him away." Said Tema with mourning in her voice.

"He?" Asked Cole.

"The morning star." Answered Carlel somberly. Just at the mention Cole felt his stomach turn over.

"I don't know about yawl, but I'm hoping we don't run into the devil down here." Brad said in an undertone. His baritone voice made it sound like a low yell through the clacking of their footsteps.

"It is doubtful. But do not worry, we have the next best thing..." Said Sachiel. "His wife."

They all went silent at the angel's words.

There were passages that led off the staircase, but they kept descending as the path lilted this way and that in slow bends. Cole thought he could feel presences in several of the side rooms. But didn't have any desire to inquire after them. Not after their encounter with the servant. The stairs changed from steep to long and shallow. A least a half mile down the steps the flat stone staircase revealed itself to be a catacomb.

After feeling the difference in the wall's texture, to his great displeasure, Cole pulled his hand back quickly when he'd run it over a set of ancient teeth. Human remains, some glazed in order to preserve them. Others left to deteriorate naturally, peaked out from the walls. Their hollow, empty gazes giving them all the feeling of being watched. He put both of his hands on Ann's which were still placed in either of his shoulders.

The bones became more tightly knit as they neared the end of the stairs. So that as they came to the six-foot-wide doorway at the end. It was bordered by pillars of tightly packed remains. There was a flat space five feet long at the bottom of the stairs. As the others stepped down and through the doorway. The last few feet became more visible. The ground had been scattered with a dripping fluid. Some looked old and dry, turned the color of rust. While there were a few, still glistening scarlet drops. Accompanied by the recent smudges of footsteps.

When they came through the doorway there were several sights that became immediately apparent.

They emerged into a massive cavern, known more by its presence than the sight of it. For most of it was shrouded in darkness. All of them were hit by a dense cold wave of energy as they stepped inside, so thick was it, that it hampered their movement. They paused for a brief moment to observe their surroundings and get used to the new feeling of heaviness in the air. Cole silently bounced on the balls of his feet, physically orienting himself.

There were three shafts of light that shined through small holes in the ceiling. The sun hadn't risen high enough to illuminate what the farthest bar had to show them yet. But see it, and regret it, they would. On the right and twenty yards ahead of them was what looked like a mural carved in dark grey stone. Richly detailed, as if it had been made by a particularly morbid Michelangelo.

The scene depicted two angelic figures. Both wore the same sort of scaled plate armor Sachiel had worn. And were in the throes of a dying struggle. Both looked as if they had been beautiful and worthy of pride in life. All lean muscle and strong frames. The female of the two was on a knee, a pained but determined look on her face. As dark grey blood cascaded down from large slashes across both of her jugulars. She was directly behind the male figure. He lay prostrate, a seven-foot naginata, akin to the ones that the statues in Sachiel's mind held, protruded from the base of his spine. Pain and anguish were his main expression as he reached a mailed hand toward the first shaft of light. The base of which came down twenty feet in the diagonal left of them.

Under that light was a ten foot long, six-foot-wide block of black stone unlike any Cole had ever seen. The surface of which was smooth like granite as if someone had run it over with ultra-fine-grained sandpaper. Where the spots on granite would normally be there were points of light. Tiny, yet shining bright, like that of stars in the nights sky. The effect of the block was that any who looked at it thought they might be looking into a rendition of a dense section of deep space. If their telescope's lens was foggy. Cole shook his head, as the stone gave him a slight sense of vertigo just by looking at it. The power that emanated from the stone was what caused the cold pressure that was making them sluggish.

"Always hard at work." Paul said toward the block. The siblings moved toward the stone, seemingly unaffected by the density of the air. Everyone else moved as if they were trying to wade through mud to follow. It got harder as they got closer to the stone. The cold and pressure becoming almost unbearable. Cole looked to his companions to see them pressing forward as if in a gale force wind. Brad leaned forward on his toes, Ann with her arms up and covering her face. Even Carlel and Sachiel seemed to be having trouble. Cole felt a quick spike of fear as Sachiel dimmed and looked like she had after healing Dice's wounds. But her face was set and determined to get through it.

The twins rushed in, their lights moving with the arch of their steps. When they approached the stone Paul lit up the shorter side of the stone block. It faced the innermost part of the cave. Protruding from the stone, deep in concentration, eyes closed, eyebrows furrowed, and jaw clenched, was the head of a long white-

and wavy-haired man, with more than perfect human features. His resemblance to Sachiel was visible in the shape of his chin and thin pointed nose. When the light hit him, he started and looked toward it with a sluggish gaze. The cold pressure around them vanished as his golden, glowing eyes slowly focused on the group.

The moment the pressure had gone Sachiel turned into a faded gold blur and was kneeling above her brother's protruding head. While the others caught up Cole noticed several other things. First, was the stench. It smelled as if a family of skunks had died and were decaying right under his nostrils. He fought the need to retch. The three-inch-wide shaft of sunlight that shone down on the very edge of the rock, nearest the group became thick and golden, almost like the fluid in Sachiel's fountain. It splashed down on the black rock, and the star like light that gleamed within the stone shown several shades brighter.

The same sensation he had felt the night before, of power surging through his body, threatened to overwhelm him again. He focused on the caging sensation Carlel had helped him to find.

He had also just realized that the stone was covered in a thick layer of dust, which is why it had looked sanded.

"Chamuel." Sachiel wept into her brother's ear.

"Sachiel?" Came the other angels confused voice. It was a smooth deep tenor on the brink of baritone, but still with the hint of youth in it. It also had the hint of a middle eastern accent. He sounded as if he were equal parts desperately anguished and unfathomably relieved. Tears streamed down into his hair as he realized it was, indeed, his sister who had come for him this time.

"It can't be…" He moaned in a thick voice. And for a second his words were drowned in sobs. "I felt you turning when…" His wet eyes grew wide as everyone else stepped into the golden light.

"He found me…" Sachiel sobbed with a glance at Cole. "Somehow…he stopped it." Chamuel looked at Cole with tearful gratitude and disbelief in his eyes. He breathed heavily and took in the pronouncement slowly. His nod was more of a bow, and Cole awkwardly bowed back. Not knowing what else to do. Chamuel set his gaze on each of them as he realized who had, if unwittingly, finally come for him.

"Jophiel…Laphaliel, Carlel, Goramel. Thank you but…do not touch it!" His thick and slow voice sounded hysterical as Cole went to wipe away the dust to see what the stone looked like underneath. "In your state it would most likely kill you." He finished as quickly as he could. Cole pulled back his hand, disappointed but also curious.

"He's right you know." Came the taunting, high clear voice of the witch herself. It echoed around the chamber and sent waves of chills down to their bones. They all turned toward the depiction of the two stone angels. She was standing on the back of the male and leaned against the naginata. Both Sachiel and Chamuel let out angry hisses at where she stood.

"Do you know who made it? Why it is there? Why was your old, dearest friend holding back the river against it? Or have I washed away all of those memories?" Lilith asked in a domineering tone while pointing at the stone. She gave a little girlish laugh as she turned and wrapped a leg around the naginata. She spun around it gracefully and did a little pirouette to put her face next to the stone woman's. She looked like she was truly having fun.

"I was hoping you would get here a bit later…" She gave a pouty face. She heaved a sigh as she stood and ran a finger over the stone woman's head. "As it is…you can only see the first two pieces in my collection." The group quickly glanced at each other.

"Damn…she likes to talk." Brad whispered as she rounded the woman's statue.

"Oh, do you not know?" She asked innocently, when her words didn't have the effect she'd obviously wanted. They all simply stared, they had come here to save their would-be companions and take down the gate, not banter with a demon queen. She pointed a lazy hand at the statues, then at the black stone.

"These aren't statues…I mean, *now* they are." She gave a disgustingly satisfied smile. "Courtesy of my husband, he knows what I like. And he is *obsessed* with making things out of stone." She rolled her eyes and gave an embarrassed little smile. As if she had just admitted she only accepted chocolate with her roses.

"Open the gate when I shoot." Paul said almost inaudibly. Chamuel gave him a slow look. Lilith didn't miss it.

"Oh? Coming up with a plan?" She said and let out another soft laugh. More chills. "You must know by now there is no way to reverse the gate. Another of my husband's workings. Feel free to hop in if you like." She moved out of the light. The sound of something sliding across the ground hit their ears along with her voice.

"But be a little more patient though. I did want to show off my work. This one might be a bit too…contemporary for you." Her girlish voice seemed to be moving away from them.

Then, a woman's body hit the side of the prone angel statue. She draped sideways over the back of the statue and looked lifeless. Her blond hair was matted with blood and her bright blue eyes stared without seeing. There were several cries of anger and anguish. Coupled with Lilith's laughter as she moved further down into the darkness.

"Wait!" Cole hissed, throwing out his arms to block his companions, as his ankle burned with fresh pain. He was reminded of how the snake in Sachiel's mind had lured him in the first time. The whole group was about to spring forward toward the woman's seemingly lifeless body. But they stopped at his word and motion.

"You still have one of those exploding arrows?" Cole asked, barely moving his lips. Paul nodded; rage visible in his glowing eyes.

"Whatever she wants to show us, she's going to make us wait and try to pick off anyone who falls into her traps. She wanted us to follow, let's at least be prepared, let's shine a little light on this psycho witch's life." Cole looked at Paul as Lilith's laughter retreated further. They realized this was a much larger cavern than they thought. The sounds of her laughter taking long seconds to bounce off walls that had widened considerably. Paul looked at the shaft of light Lilith was moving toward, and back toward the angle he would have to hit.

"There are several more creatures with us." Carlel said, raising an electrified hand pointing twice to the left and once to the right.

"How many is several to you? Because some people say five, others say three." Cole said as he pulled the necklace out of his pocket and the arrow from his belt. Carlel gave him a flat look.

"I'm not the thunder goddess," Cole shrugged," It matters for me."

Paul lined up his shot, ignoring them. Lilith was saying something but none of them were listening.

"Three. What lies beyond their bodies?" Carlel asked Tema flatly, flicking her head back toward Cole and Ann. That shut Cole up. He looked back at the statues; he could feel Ann do the same beside him.

He'd never been quick to anger. But this was too much for him to take without pulsating with fury. The scene now took on a new light as he realized that filthy, rancid, horrid thing had been dancing on *his* back. Running her disgusting finger across *Ann's* hair. Laughing in their faces as she did it.

He felt his anger rise to the point of madness, fast. What Lilith had prepared next for them pushed him past the point of madness. To utter revulsion and incomprehension. Until then, he hadn't truly understood that beings like these existed on the same plain as the ones standing around him. If it hadn't been for them, he would have broken then and there. Unable to ever stop staring and hating until his next life came to greet him.

"We've never gone past the stone." Tema said as Paul pulled back his bow string. Which was more like a bow rope, to anyone else.

"Imagine the worst and make it worse." Ann said in a hoarse voice. Paul whispered a spell and let the arrow fly. Cole felt his arm move by itself to sit over the entombed angels face. Chamuel only had a second to observe the dove with a look of shock.

"Are you ignoring me?" Came Lilith's voice from further into the cavern. There was a gust of wind, a second's pause and an explosion. A six-foot-wide area of rock and dirt fell to the cave floor with a clattering, tumbling smash. From around 55 meters up, a massive shaft of light shined down on Lilith's work.

Briefly, on the edges of the light, there were two figures visible near the grey statues. But they receded back into the darkness too quickly to be discerned.

At the same time Chamuel focused with the same hard expression he'd had when they'd come in. Only this time his golden eyes were open. Runes appeared in bright red light around the rim of his left iris. From those runes sprung what looked like a hologram of a complex seal floating a foot over his face. It was a perfect circle set with six others, each bordered by three more concentric circles. Each were packed with moving angelic runes. And several different elemental symbols that danced around their circles while spinning. Cole took that as his cue, he dropped the necklace, and it disappeared after crossing the seal's threshold.

Sachiel turned and vanished into the jewel on Tema's wrist. Lilith had been too preoccupied with walking further into the cave to see this. The whole party moved forward several yards. Brad with the machine gun pointed toward where the figures had disappeared. They had to smash up against the walls to stay concealed as eyes adjusted to the light.

Lilith turned back to them and took in the sunlight with an evil smile. She was standing about a football field further into the cavern. Just beyond the statues the walls widened so much they were shrouded in deep darkness. Twenty feet closer from where Lilith stood, the cave floor dropped away to some unseen depth. A one-foot-wide stone path ran out from the middle and level with the rest of the floor. It led to a sort of throne. The seat of which fit the catacomb style that had lined the entry way. It seemed fitting that this creature made her seat from a pile of human remains.

"Why, thank you, now my work can be seen…what do you think?" Lilith said waiving her arms around in presentation. She gave them a sinister smile as they approached, and their eyes roved around the trench.

Beside and below the throne. In a space fifty-feet-deep and farther out than they could see. Were heaps and heaps of more bones…there were thousands of them and more. It was a collage of death, and Lilith was its proud artist. Judging by the rust-stained bones she added to it often. They were all horrified, nauseated and beyond fury as they approached the ledge.

What sent the three still purely mortal beings to their knees. Was that most of the bones piled in a massive heap were very small. Much too small to have made it even to toddler age. They were past tears, past anger or terror at the sight. Their brains almost couldn't register what they were seeing. Horror and revulsion clawed at their hearts and minds. This was more than a disgusting act of a depraved psychopath. One that couldn't even comprehend that that's what she was, thought she was beyond it, a pure and bonified *monster*. And they hadn't just been forced to be witness to it in this moment. Though they couldn't recall, these bones represented Lilith's bid to rid the world of they, themselves. This was *their* history.

Cole lost most of the food Paul had given them. It left bile in his mouth and worsened the already intense stench. Ann tried to calm him with a hand to his shoulder, but she had tears running down her cheeks. Brad lowered his head as if in prayer, pain etched in his rigid body. Lilith took in their horror like a thunderous ovation. She looked absolutely delighted.

"Sha dim monster." Carlel whispered. Agony and fury in her voice.

Paul knocked an arrow and pointed near where they had seen the figures in the shadows. His bright blue eyes gleaming. Tema did the same but pointed in the opposite direction. They were paying more attention to the task at hand.

"Can you figure out which ones are yours?" Lilith said with wide, interested eyes. Like a child learning about how old sea turtles get.

Electric lines of energy ran down the length of Carlel's arms. She grabbed Cole by the scruff of his shirt and lifted him to his feet. An act which pulled Ann along with him. She in turn, pulled Brad up, her new strength made it look easy. Lilith backed several paces to the foot of her bone throne with another evil smile. What had not easily been seen before, as it was mostly covered and integrated into the seat itself, was what looked like a live body, only asleep.

Cole knew the face, they all did, it was Sachiel's body. Inlaid into the bones that made up the demon queen's throne. Lilith sat on her throne of slain and tattered enemies. Only now searching for the missing Sachiel and realizing she wasn't there. She didn't seem to mind much. She leaned back and placed a hand on the angel's head, getting comfortable.

"I wouldn't want to deprive them of their fun." Lilith said motioning around the cavern. "It has been a long time since they've sampled such *illustrious* guests." She said it sarcastically. There were the low sounds of laughter around them.

Whoever had been in the shadows had moved closer. The pair nearest Paul slinked into the edges of light between the group and the statues. They were each about Paul's height. With pitted black eyes but mostly human looking, and they wore common police uniforms. The scene by which these creatures had convinced their would-be companions to trust them played out in Cole's mind. It was something he could at least grasp onto and be angry about. His numb body began to feel again as their mouths split open in too wide, Jacko lantern grins, with slavering black shark's teeth.

"You remember what we said?" Carlel said to him as she prepared to meet the creatures. "We *stand* together." Ann dropped her backpack and Cole followed suit. As he did so he nodded toward the pit.

"All things considered; it was pretty cheesy." Cole said clearing his throat.

"You made it up." Carlel said in a flat undertone.

"*Damn it.*" Cole said as Carlel turned from a beautiful looking girl, into a blindingly bright, human shaped mass of pure electricity.

The sound of it ripped through the air as the shark men roared in defiance. Brad, grim faced, lifted into the air and disappeared into the darkness. Ann unsheathed her bastard sword and Cole got into a ready stance; his arrow held like a fencer. He realized how outmatched he was when Paul fired his first arrow.

The two police dressed demons vanished in a flash of black and blue to avoid the shot and start the fight. Carlel became a vivid blue-white streak. The sound of her lightning cracks and charges blaring in the enclosed space. Paul's shot had missed. Apparently, the legend stood until true demons were involved. The sound of Brad's gunfire almost sent Cole to his knees, and he realized the big southern man had gone to back up Tema. She was keeping her cop busy by rapid firing arrows faster than Cole could keep up with. He figured her magic must be a multiplier like Paul's but slightly different. As her arrows didn't seem to run out or lessen as she fired.

Paul was trying to find the right moment to strike as Carlel somehow kept both her opponents away from them. Cole and Ann were both doing the same, but as Paul was taking seemingly random shots of disappearing arrows, Cole realized they were going to have to have a wide opening to be of any help.

That opening came around three minutes into the thunderous crackling and thumping shots. When Paul fired off a shot that finally brought one of the demons onto the humanly visible plain. The cop dressed demon tumbled into a faceplanting stop. With one arrow in his calf and several other shafts poking out of his shoulder, hip and stomach. Black, rotted blood seeped from each of the shafts as the creature let out a hideous growl of pain and protest.

Cole almost felt pity for the monster as its frustration showed at being slowed down. Then he thought about the blond woman. And whoever they had been breaking to pieces on that phone call. Cole would not show him any mercy.. He slashed downward and sent a five-foot-long scythe of blue green energy that he had been charging up and focusing. It angled downward toward the demon's position and cut a two-inch wide and three-inch-deep gash in the ground where it struck. The monster rolled back from the strike and came up closer to the statues of the defeated Jophiel and Laphaliel .

"Careful where you strike, little fool." The demon sounded as if an alligator could talk and had learned sarcasm.

He ripped the arrow from his calf without a hint of pain and pointed it toward the woman draped over Cole's statue body. He tried to say something about Cole accidentally killing his own. But was cut off by rapid, .50 caliber gunfire. Paul had set down the bow and had his pistol pointed at a brightly shining area off to the left.

Carlel had the other demon locked up and held in place. Paul put five bullets into its chest before Ann moved in. The creature was thrashing and howling in pain and rage, black blood spilled from its chest wounds and an arrow through its thigh. Carlel had it on one knee, with one arm twisted and an electric foot to its back, to keep it down.

Carlel moved out of the way just in time as Ann moved in with lightning speed. She relieved the creature of its head in one quick slash. This one didn't turn into smoke as it rolled away.

Cole tried to stop the demon by the statues, but his slash missed again. The creature roared and moved at the same time. As her back was to it, Ann couldn't turn fast enough. She was hit as if by a professional linebacker. The demon's teeth sank into her shoulder as they both went flying over the edge of the pit. Cole felt his heart pounding through his chest as Carlel flashed in after them. The sound of Ann's panicked scream was the only thing Cole could hear as they crashed into the massive pile of bones. A shower of remains hit the edge of the pit as Cole sprinted and leapt in after them.

As he flew through the air, he wondered what in all of creation he could even do to help. And the only good thing to come of Lilith's artwork was that it was stacked high enough, so he didn't die or break upon landing. Ann had managed to roll and kick out, to get the creature off of her. But her shoulder was a mass of shredded flesh and blood. Cole hit the pile of bones in a panic and slipped and rolled his way toward her. Not letting the difficulty stop him. Carlel had the demon occupied for now, but it had been spurred to new heights after seeing its partner get ousted.

Carlel's pained screams came through the flashes of electric movement and sound. Along with angry and enraged roars from the demon. Bones were blasting off in different directions as the two titans clashed. Cole reached Ann; she was kneeling on a pile of bones in shock. Her eyes were wide, face twisted in pain as she tried to stop the bleeding with her opposite hand. Cole rapidly pulled off his shirt and pressed it against the backside of her shoulder. She was bleeding too much, if he didn't get her help soon, she would pass out from blood loss.

A smashing noise reached them along with a grating, triumphant demon's roar and blinging light.

Carlel had been pinned against the wall, she was kicking at the demon's body, but her strength wasn't that of a physical kind, and her body wasn't what it used to be. And she seemed to be running out of gas. The creature moved its head in, it's too wide mouth aiming for Carlel's throat. Cole moved without thinking. His slash produced a line of energy like a long whip that wrapped around the creature's neck.

He wouldn't have been able to slow the creature down if it hadn't been for Ann. She grabbed his hand that held the arrow with her bloody, crushing one and heaved with him. They both growled as they fell backward, thanks to Ann's strength. The creature choked out an angry scream as it fell backward with them. At the same time Carlel charged every ounce of her electricity into one hand as she was pulled along, still in the demon's grip. She planted the hand firmly against the beast's chest with a scream and let loose. It burned a three-inch-wide hole through its body and all screams stopped while black smoke billowed from the creatures wound.

She rushed over to the others as Cole immediately began trying to wrap his bloody shirt into a makeshift bandage around Ann's shoulder. He looked at her in a panic and she knelt to give Ann a serious look. Ann squinted at her through her pain and there seemed to be some understanding going on between them. Ann pulled the shirt off of her shoulder and nodded.

"I cannot heal it like Sachiel would." Carlel said in a rush.

"Just do it." Ann said and she stuffed Cole's shirt into her mouth. Carlel outstretched a hand to her shoulder and electric energy coalesced around the bleeding gashes the demon's teeth had left behind.

Ann's scream of pain was almost drowned in the shirt and the sound of the charge. Cole had no time to grieve his inadequacy. He had been unable to prevent or help with the situation in any significant way. Ann looked on the verge of passing out so Cole pulled her in and held her up. Carlel wrapped her arms around them and at the sound of an electric charge. They were flying in the direction of Lilith's throne. They hit the narrow stone pathway and Cole prepared to see the witch queen face to face.

But she had stood and moved back toward the other side of the cave. The battle still going on had moved toward the entrance. Tema lay on the ground near the edge of the path. She looked alive but unable to continue the fight. Cole set Ann on the bone throne as Carlel leapt full over Lilith to rejoin the fight. She didn't seem to mind as she just watched looking mildly amused as she leisurely moved toward the entrance.

Ann had lost consciousness in the jump and Cole laid her as comfortably as he could, considering. He hesitated for a moment, looking at her steaming shoulder. The bleeding had all stopped but it had been too much at once. He had a moment of splitting thought, torn between trying to help and staying with Ann. He knew she would have told him to go if she was able to. He could imagine the look on her face as she thought he might be pitying her.

He stopped to make sure Tema was still breathing before sprinting back toward the entrance. The others were still at it. But unable to get close, they had only been able to keep the demon dodging, too quickly to catch. Carlel was about to change that.

Brad was using the walls to hold himself steady for his shots. And Paul had taken Tema's quiver and was imitating her rapid shot form. While using the rocks he'd brought down from the ceiling for cover. Lilith didn't make any move other than to smile at him as Cole passed.

"Better hurry teacher! It's almost my turn. Prepare yourself." She crooned after him.

Indeed, it looked as though the cop dressed demon the group was fighting had slowed as it tried to doge the many shots being thrown at it. Cole watched two more arrows sink into its shoulder as it paused to try and meet Carlel's charge. And there were already at least five sticking out in all directions. He felt a savage pleasure at the sight as he ran to take a position next to Chamuel. The angel was growling and shaking his head around, trying to free himself to help. His lank white hair flailing around in his anger. Brad was positioned high up on the wall behind him and was taking pot shots with his handgun.

"Hey, how much longer is she going to take?" Cole asked to the struggling angel. He stopped flailing and concentrated.

"It should not be long." He smiled viciously and made Cole wonder what was happening inside him that made him look so terrifying. Cole checked Lilith's progress; she was about halfway toward them.

"Well, we don't have much time, and we need her." He was thinking of the unconscious team members. At Lilith's only half interested look, he understood that she was much stronger than her teammates. So, she wasn't expecting to have much fun.

To confirm they were out of time, Carlel caught and held the demon in place. Paul filled it with arrows so that it looked like a pin cushion. It struggled against Carlel's hold for a few shots. But as several went through vital areas the beast went limp and Carlel let it drop to the ground. It was followed by a slow clap from Lilith's direction.

"Wow." She said unimpressed. She moved the last stretch of space instantly in a streak of black smoke. She kicked the body of her compatriot and it hit the wall with a sickening crunch. Carlel moved out of the way so that she was on Cole's right. He felt a bit of comfort at her presence. But it wouldn't last.

"It only cost you two members to take out the help." As Lilith said it, her business suit melted and turned into a skintight, paper-thin material.

It resembled a mat black version of the black stone. But the stars glimmered many shades less brightly. Lilith spun around slowly as if to showcase the new fit. Rather than looking angry or determined, she only looked mildly excited. For a long second it seemed no one wanted to make a move.

Then Paul took an exploratory shot at her with his desert eagle. She lifted a forearm and sparks flew where the bullet hit it.

She didn't even flinch at the force. The demigod rolled and took up a new position in case she responded. Carlel sent a bolt of electricity as he did so. Lilith used the same forearm to absorb the lighting, the stars on her suit shining a bit brighter.

She concentrated and rolled her shoulders gracefully. She pushed Carlel's power back at her with the other hand in a fist size ball of electric energy. Carlel dodged the strike and it hit the wall behind her, taking a foot deep chunk out of it. Cole had a moment of frustration. She could absorb their energy? This wasn't fair at all.

Then the two went at it for real. Lilith stayed in the same spot as Carlel flashed in and out, in blindingly fast attacks. Lilith merely pivoted, ducked and twisted, dodging or pulling Carlel around to throw her at the walls. She looked concentrated but not struggling as they fought. At one particularly hard throw, Carlel hit the entranceway wall with a grunt of pain.

Cole sent a scythe of blue-green energy at the stationary demon. At the same time, Brad took two quick shots, as did Paul. Lilith, in one smooth, lightning-fast movement twisted, so that Cole and Brad's shots hit nothing but the magic absorbing material. She glowed a shade brighter as her hands shot out and snatched Paul's arrows out of the air. In concert with her spinning movement, she threw the arrows. With such force they made thumping sounds against the pressure of the air.

Cole heard Brad scream, before crumpling to the ground with another bone crunching clamor. Paul took an arrow to his firing shoulder and gasped out a pained shout. Lilith looked maddeningly triumphant as Cole felt his stomach drop. Carlel was on a knee, blood dripping down her forehead and looking completely gassed. Lilith turned to him with savage pleasure on her face as he realized he was the only one left.

"The teacher...last to fall this time. And where did the healer go? She couldn't even face me after her last failure." She laughed and this time there was a sinister and hateful tone to it.

He didn't know if it was because she was in a heightened state, or if his adrenaline had made him forget about it until now. But as she laughed his ankle flared with such pain, it sent him to a knee as well. He clutched at it and Lilith looked at him with a hint of interest. She hadn't even known the bite had happened or that it had been affecting him until now.

"It seems her memories of me have even crippled her allies." She said laughing again and lifting a hand. The pain in Cole's ankle skyrocketed and shot up his leg.

The pain continued to intensify as Lilith's eyes widened and flashed in pleasure. He dropped the arrow and scrabbled at his ankle with both hands trying to push the pain back into the area Sachiel had encased it. She approached him slowly as he growled in frustration and helplessness. He gritted his teeth and forced himself to pick the arrow back up in a trembling hand. He slashed at her, she absorbed it. He locked eyes with her, his breathing heavy and pained. She gave him an evil grin as she lifted a hand only feet away from his face. As his own blue green energy coalesced in her palm she said, in a low and superior tone.

"I just want you to know, I've said this every time I kill you. We have your brother. He still thinks you will come to save him." Cole didn't have a brother as far as he knew. But he glared into the demon's black eyes all the same. Putting as much of his disgust and hate into it as he could. She continued delightedly, "You could not save your friends, and your brother will die by our hands. I want the echoes of your many failures to stretch across the ages of your soul, Angel." She spat the last word with savage venom.

"What have any of us done to deserve this?" Cole asked shaking his head in disbelief. Lilith cocked her head and looked as though he'd asked a stupid question.

"Done?" She asked. She let out an involuntary little laugh.

"Nothing." She whispered with a little half smile. The blue-green energy flared, she slowly prepared to send it back into his face, relishing his inability to respond.

Cole shook his head again as he stared back into her triumphant face. He didn't have anything to say to such a creature. It would be the same as trying to pet a wild dog with rabies and a thorn in its paw. Fruitless, and more likely than not, he would just get bitten. If he had the power to do something about it, he would have. But as it stood, all he could do was stare back his defiance at her existence.

There was a massive flash of golden light at the other end of the cavern.

And Lilith was replaced by a being that looked only like Sachiel in the fact that he somewhat recognized her brightly glowing facial features. She was geared in her dragon scale armor and gleamed from every inch in blinding golden light. Seven-foot, bright gold white wings extended from her back and flared in anger. Even her hair had gone a shade of luminescent gold. The black Ulfbhert sword shined brightly at her hip. She radiated and pulsed with waves of healing energy. Cole felt his body pull in that energy like a parched desert receiving rain. Accepting it as warmth, as hope spread through him like fire.

Lilith smashed into the entrance wall with such force, it cracked and splintered up to twelve feet around her. The cave itself rattled and several pieces of stone fell from Paul's blasted hole in the ceiling. Rather than dying or passing out or showing any signs of damage. Lilith hit the ground like a cat and scuttled freakishly fast to put the black stone between her and the new enemy. In the time it took her to do so, Sachiel pointed a mailed hand at Cole's ankle. He had pulled up his pant leg to see black veins seeping outside of the golden circle. The pain, along with the veins receded and the circle tattoo became darker and stronger in its soothing power.

"The others." Cole breathed deep in relief. "Help the others."

Sachiel nodded as Lilith let out a harsh laugh.

"As if I would let you." She said. Black smoke coalesced in both of her hands as she finally prepared to start fighting with her own power. "I beat you at your best. You think you scare me now?"

There was a deep, rumbling laughter from the end of the cave Sachiel had just come from. It seemed to rumble even the walls of the cave. Indeed, more bits of it fell to the ground at the sound. Lilith's fury turned to confusion as she turned toward the laugh. Walking toward them with supreme confidence in his step was a man around middle height between Cole and Paul. He was strikingly handsome with dark eyes and dark hair and beard salted with white shades. He wore a midnight black tailored suit with crimson tie and undershirt. His steps clacked in the deep way expensive dress shoes always did. Even the wave of sound that came from his shoes seemed to emanate confidence as he approached.

"You…but how?" Lilith hissed disbelievingly as she watched him approach. The man breathed in deeply and seemed to suck in all the air in the cave. The stench of death was washed away as cool morning air came whistling in from the holes in the ceiling.

He exhaled with a loud grumbling sigh. Cole had the same feeling of countless souls screaming from some unknown place, as he'd had with Lilith. The man observed his surroundings more carefully as he made his way over. In a deep rumbling voice, the sound more dragon than human he addressed Paul, struggling to pull the arrow from his shoulder that Lilith had thrown with such force. Only the feathers poked out from the front.

"Dear nephew." Without waiting for permission. He bent down and pulled the arrow through the back of Paul's shoulder blade in one swift movement. Paul hissed in pain but nodded to the man, a hint of apprehension in his eyes.

"Uncle." He tried to sound as if he were merely greeting the man. Rather than profusely bleeding from a wound caused embarrassingly by his own weapon. The new entity lit a fingertip with red gold fire and poked at the open wounds. The sound of cooking meat flashed twice as he cauterized Paul's shoulder. Paul was in obvious pain as he hissed and ground his teeth at each action. Cole watched the interaction with a mixture of excitement and confusion. He had a good idea who this was and agreed with the angels' choice.

"Thank you." Paul choked, through a strained breath. The man nodded and looked pleased by the thanks.

"Seraphim witch." Lilith spat at Sachiel. She seemed angry now. This new presence wasn't as much of a push over as she thought everyone else was.

"That's rich…coming from you." Cole said as he got his breathing back in control.

"Silence, I've killed you a thousand times, and will again." Lilith hissed at him. The force of her words made Cole want to run and hide in a corner forever. But he held her gaze. The new man watched this interaction, half amused. Then he turned his attention to Lilith.

"How long has it been *woman*? Since you and your sha dim daemons turned on us and cast me into that prison?" Lilith held herself up, her anger giving way to something along the lines of…embarrassment?

"If you had only accepted my offer…" She said defending herself. She seemed to get hold of herself, and her confidence and anger came back to her. "You accepted everything else." She said taking on the air of someone who'd made a point that gave them a leg up. Paul gave his uncle a look, and the being rolled his eyes.

"*The one time*…your aunt says hi, by the way. Don't look at me like that." The new-comer contended with his long-lost nephew. Paul gave him a 'wow' sort of look.

"Your father took half the world into his bed. My other brother, the other half. I was not that bad. She is the *first* woman."

Paul put up his bloody hands and shook his head slightly. The God, as Cole was thinking, shrugged and threw the arrow away. "No matter." He said. Red gold fire slowly leaked into being around his hands and forearms. He gave Lilith a come-hither look.

"Time to rectify my mistake." He rumbled. Astoundingly, this, above all else, seemed to have hurt Lilith more than anything so far.

Interesting, Cole noted for future reference. *So we attack her pride.*

"Mistake?" She took on a haughty stance, her eyes flashing in anger. "The only mistake you made was not joining us." She said arrogantly, as if speaking to an idiot. "I'm better than your darling *Sephy* will ever be." She finished, her confidence returning in full measure.

The God sunk his chin and his eyes grew darker, his face grim. Then he gave the demon queen a half smile and answered flatly.

"Not in a million lives."

The battle recommenced in Lilith's scream of anger. Faster than any of the mortals, and faster than even Paul could follow.

Like the bones had been exploding when Carlel had been fighting the underling, there were now chunks of the cave stone that were blasting and chipping off the walls and ground as the two came together. This time in flashes of black smoke and red gold fire. As impressive as it was, Cole could feel that the two were still holding back in the enclosed space.

The noise of their clashes was deafening and the area around the hole Paul made in the ceiling started crumbling away quickly now. Flashes of heat and icy cold were washing over him as Cole put his arms over his head. Bits of the flying stone had already scratched and cut areas of his bare skin and he yelled to Sachiel.

"They need your help!" He screamed pointing toward Tema and Ann. Paul had started to run over to where his sister lay. Sachiel took note with a nod from where she was kneeling over Carlel. The black sword drawn as she placed a hand on the other angel's head.

Cole ducked and ran over to where Brad had fallen. He was conscious but his left leg stuck out at a funny angle. His opposite hip had half an arrow sticking out of it. He was grimacing through the pain but still had his gun out and ready for any moment he could get a bead on the demon.

Sachiel reached him at almost the same moment. She hadn't said anything since her reappearance and didn't now. She merely turned Brad over, pulled the arrow through with a resounding scream from him. And lit him up in golden light. Cole watched in amazement as Brad's leg cracked and popped its way back into place. Brad lay face down breathing heavily through gritted teeth for a moment, as he realigned himself mentally.

There was a massive electric charge and cracking noise as Carlel got back into the fight. Electric lines splintered throughout the cave and mixed in with the blast waves of smoke and fire. Each of the combatants becoming visible for milliseconds as they caught each other's movements. Sachiel turned and gave one massive pump of her wings to take her over to Tema's position.

Somehow Lilith was still able to take note of this movement, and rather than having everyone back in action. She decided to send the golden angel out of the fight. Cole, due to her speed, only half recognized the demon stop a few feet in front of him before she took off from behind Sachiel's position. Cole was hit by a mass of cold wind from the side she'd come from then at the force of her take off.

Bits of stone clipped and cut through his skin as she flew through the air.

He screamed in warning, but it was too late. She hit Sachiel hard enough to send the black sword tumbling toward the ground. Sachiel let out a cry of pain and was sent straight through the top of the cavern over the mass grave. Stone flying outward and falling as she crashed through the roof. Made all the more solid by how much power she'd taken in. Chamuel let out a scream of frustration and anger, shaking violently in his stone prison.

Cole felt his heart sink and his frustration rise. He knew just how Chamuel felt. She'd hit Sachiel from behind, yet again, and he could do nothing about it. Lilith was still just too powerful. Her suit absorbed their energy, and she didn't seem to be slowing down even fighting two angels and possibly an ancient god. Not to mention she'd taken out two others with ease. It was as if he were in his own prison, made of ineffectiveness.

Brad pushed himself to all fours groaning and cursing, he shook his head and got to his feet, grim determination still on his face. He gave Cole a pat on the arm and with a nod, he moved past to take up a shooting position. And just like that, with the small gesture, Cole realized it didn't matter. Even as he leaked blood from a dozen small cuts and couldn't figure out a way to help. He was still able to think, still able to try.

He scanned the cave. The sword had landed almost straight up and down, sinking several inches into the stone below. Cole thought it must have something to do with the power emanating from the gate and Sachiel's solidifying power. That the sword had become as real on this plain as it had been in Sachiel's mind. He couldn't help but feel as though the sword was important. After the angel's reaction to it, and the affect Sachiel's memories made real seemed to have. It was made with the power and memories of three arch angels. Hell, one of the arch angels had become the devil himself. There must be something to it.

He sprinted forward to take the sword back. Blasts of heat and cold were now being added to by lines of stinging electricity that traced over his skin and left red burn marks. Bits of ceiling stone fell away from the two large holes now in it. Chips of the stone were still flying and every few seconds, Cole felt another chip take a piece of him with it. The battle had taken so many pieces of the ceiling, wall and floor, the ground was almost fully covered in it. It was no longer a flat even surface but pitted and covered in shale, gravel and large, falling stones. More and more sunlight came flowing in as the fight went on.

He hadn't touched the sword since he'd passed out after making it. He grabbed the wire hilt and felt the power of it pulse into him in a flash of hot rage. The affect was so that he tore it from the stone floor with almost no effort. He turned back to try and find a place safe from falling or flying stone.

Brad had taken up position behind the black stone and was failing to find a place in which to fire. Cole, now a bloody mess, went to stand next to Chemuel's head as there were no falling stones or blasts near this area. Even the higher beings seemed to be avoiding it. When he turned back to the fight, he was astonished at what he saw.

Sachiel had made it back into the cavern and was kneeling over Tema. Paul was next to them with a worried look on his face. A slow flash of golden light gave Cole the comfort of knowing she would be alright. Ann was coming to with all the noise, her eyes fluttering in the sunlight. Somehow, the falling stone had crashed down near, but not on top of her. Her shoulder was no longer steaming but covered in a mass of deep, jagged bloody grooves and black singe marks.

With the sword in his hand Cole could see these things clearly and closely as if they were right in front of him. But more amazing than that, he could follow the battle going on in front of him, as if it were in regular motion.

The fiery god, Cole was fairly certain, was Hades himself. Leave it to Sachiel to make such a good pick for help. Hades circled the fight from up and to his right while Carlel flashed forward and backward, swinging and kicking out bolts at Lilith from several feet away. Lilith still moved so quickly and gracefully that most of the strikes missed by an inch while the others were absorbed and sent back. Carlel twisted and turned to avoid her own power.

All participants looked breathless and sweaty as they had been exerting themselves at peak performance in such a small space. Hades moved in for a physical strike and Lilith flashed too fast for

Cole to see even now. She appeared underneath the hole Paul had made with his arrow. Cole missed his window as she moved away, dodging Hade's blast of red-gold fire. She bounced off the wall and up the roof on all fours to come down on Carlel's position. Carlel flashed to her left and out of the way.

Ann was back on her feet, Cole was relieved beyond measure to see her sprinting toward their statues. He had half a second to wonder what she was doing. Then she pulled the blonde woman onto her shoulder, and grabbed a previously unseen man by the scruff of his hooded sweatshirt. She proceeded to drag the captives over to their position. Cole sprinted over to cover her movement. But none of the higher beings seemed to mind it at all. If they'd been hit it would've been by accident. Sachiel had now reentered the fight and Lilith was hard pressed to keep up with all of them. So Cole *thought*, as her face twisted in fury at the angel's joining.

But it seemed that was what the demon had been waiting for to go all out. She now started attacking more than she was dodging. Sending each member of the advancing party flying this way and that, with veins of black smoke. But as she attacked more, she left herself more open to attacks. After being sent into the stone wall, the lord of the underworld saw his opportunity, while Lilith spent an extra millisecond to attack Carlel.

As Ann set the two captives near Brad, Lilith was sent hurdling into the entrance wall again. She scuttled forward to get away from the charging Carlel. Without thinking, Cole took advantage of the moment; he slung his arrow wand at the demon. The blue green whip caught Lilith around the throat as she stood up. Her evil eyes turned toward him in an instant. Fury raged as she grabbed the whip with one hand and yanked him toward her. The connection between him and the new weapon wasn't just touchy feely. It pulled him along with it, instead of being torn from his grasp.

As he went flying through the air, he realized what a bad idea it had been to use the whip. And as Lilith sent a side kick into his chest plate, and he felt, and *heard*, at least five ribs crack in response. The sword hadn't given him any bodily strength or protection against her. But as she kicked out he swung the sword and cut through the mat black armor into the demon queen's calf. As he was sent flying back the way that he had come she screamed in surprised rage. With a jolt of fear, he realized he was going to land directly on the black stone, and that he was shirtless. With no barrier between him and whatever power Chamuel had been afraid of him touching with a mere finger.

Even more embarrassing than hitting the stone center, back whiplashing backward and slamming his head on the flat surface of the stone; even more embarrassing than the quack of pain that escaped his lips and the scream of utter terror and pain that escaped them afterward, as his body touched the stone and he was hit full in the face by the stream of magical light pouring from above; was that he was perfectly positioned to land directly on the imprisoned angel's face, in a sitting position.

He didn't have any time to think about this as his entire being took in and was filled to the brim with the bright golden light. The scream coming from his lips, the pain and fear of the moment, and everything happening around him, faded into white gold light.

Ch. 14

He came-to in rows of booklined dark wood shelves. As he observed his surroundings, he realized he didn't know or recognize any of the languages the books were written in. Though some of them slightly resembled the angelic script he had been seeing lately. The carpet underneath his feet looked old and worn down to almost smooth, flatness. He tentatively moved down the row, keeping himself on guard as he had no clue where he was.

As he neared the end of the row, he heard bustling feet and thick boiling fluids, the tinkling of stirring in a glass container, swiftly followed by the poking and beeping of unseen buttons reached him as he came out on the third level of a massive library.

The center of the circular building was an open area filled with a single long laboratory table, complete with an active chemical making and processing unit. That was blinking and beeping as some new thing was being made. Coiled, twisted and bowled glass lined the table. Some parts were being heated with burners, others being added to by drip systems, and still others being cooled by what looked like dry ice from underneath. He stood perpendicular and at the center of the table. So that the other person in the room, on the opposite side, wasn't fully in view.

Cole saw the top of an old, wild grey haired someone. He hurried back and forth between the instruments. He was twisting burner nobs, adding vials to drip systems, and draining fluids that dripped to the ground in a frenzy, with the old man grumbling angrily.

There was a staircase to his right that led down to the floor level, so he decided to take it. As he was passing the second level the old man seemed to notice his presence, though he couldn't have gotten a good look from under the level of the glassware. In a tired and distinguished old voice tinged with a German sounding accent the man exclaimed.

"Jophiel! You are alone? I thought I felt…well never mind. Good. Come, come, be quick about it, I could use your help." Cole felt a jolt of surprise but took the steps two at a time. Sensing the old man's urgency, though he didn't know why. As he approached the table, he saw the old man's hand poking through the glassware. It pointed toward one of the burners underneath a thick blue bubbling fluid to his right.

"Half turn to the left in three, two, one..." Cole hurried to do as he was told. The fire under the burner lessened. The bubbles in the quickly boiling fluid increased in size and turned the bubbling into slopping.

Then the old man's pointing hand appeared several feet further down and to his left. Cole came to a halt in front of a thick bowl with a pestle set next to it. It looked as if the red powder in the bowl had been hastily crushed down and there were still chunks of whatever substance, left in it. As Cole took the meaning and crushed the last of the substance to powder. The old man rushed to the other end of the table.

There was a loud beeping noise, as whatever the old man had been making finished. Cole heard him open the mixing equipment and grab several vials from inside. As he crushed down the red powder, he heard the old man adding the fluids to the mixture.

"Ok!" The old man yelled down to him. "Add the powder to the right in three, two, one…!" Cole looked up and to the right to see a dark red substance flowing down through a tightly coiled glass. It fed into a line that ran over to the boiling substance he had just cooled. He dumped the powder into the drip and saw a stir stick underneath, stained in the same red color. He stirred as he heard the old man making changes on the other side.

"Good, good! Burner back up." Cole did so. And the old man rushed back down to the end of the table with all the dry ice looking substance.

"Come, come, come, come, come." He spouted as he ran, Cole followed his movement. "Pull all coolants! Quickly now, quickly." Cole heard sliding and falling as the old man pulled off all the dry ice and let it fall to the floor. Cole followed suit, the colder than ice substance stung as he pulled it off all the areas that held the slowly flowing fluids.

The heated fluid from the other side of the table moved over to the area they were pulling from and mixed with the cooled fluids. Some of the cooled fluids, in a mixture of colors ranging from yellow- green to pinkish-blue. Moved more quickly over to the area Cole had just been working in. As they did so the mixtures coalesced and became a deep brown-gold color. As they both reached the end of the table, pulling the last of the coolants and standing straight, Cole got his first look at the man.

He wore an old looking, grey tweed suit, that was drenched in sweat. His old and lined face was red with exertion, but he looked pleased, as the fluids all mixed together in proper order. He brushed himself off, sending puffs of different colored powders through the air.

As he did so, he gave Cole a satisfied side look, expecting to receive a reciprocal look. But Cole had no idea what they had just been doing and stared at the man blankly. The old man, at seeing Cole for the first time, did a comical double take. He reached out to put a finger to Cole's chin and lifted. Then turned it left and right.

"No no no no no." Said the man as he inspected Cole up and down. He poked and prodded and lifted his arms and inspected his hair. Cole was so stunned by this action he just let it happen. When the old man was finished, he stepped back with a flabbergasted look on his face. Cole raised an eyebrow at him.

"What did you do to yourself?"

Cole raised both eyebrows and shrugged. "Since...when?" Cole asked confused.

The old man looked stricken at the question. He stepped closer to Cole and put a warm hand to his forehead. Cole watched as the old man's face went from confused, to dark as his eyes scanned Cole's, roving from side to side as if he were reading rapidly. When he stepped back, it looked as though he'd aged even further. His back bent and he looked on the verge of passing out. He put his fist to his chin with an angry look and paced several times while talking to himself.

"That damnable child. No patience, no love for any beauty or ideas but his own." The old man said in frustration while gesticulating with his free hand. "Now I know why your brothers came to see me. I should have paid attention...I was not worried about you." He added to Cole, then realized Cole wouldn't know what he was talking about. He waved a hand at the look Cole gave him.

"It…won't matter to you now." He stopped moving and seemed to concentrate hard on an unseen problem.

"I was…kind of in the middle of something." Cole said cautiously. He thought he knew with whom he was speaking and didn't want to give offense. The old man shrank and looked apologetic.

"Yes, yes. My son's creative process is a bit…unrefined. Though I do not work closely with mortals, maybe he is right…" The old man looked deep in thought, then looked horrified at his own words.

"…*Your son*? Didn't he tell us all to be nice to each other?" Cole said under his breath. He wanted to scream and rage at the pronouncement but held himself back.

The old man looked confused and seemed to think about his words. For a second as his eyes moved back and forth as if reading again, only this time, he seemed to be observing things in the air around them.

"Ah. I see." He said and shook his head ruefully. "In your time, he has convinced everyone there was only the one favored child." Cole looked at the old man. His ability to be surprised was getting kicked in the face lately so he just waited. "There are brothers. The one you have been dealing with...has gone over to the other side in many ways."

"So, you're not talking about...you know, Jesus?" Cole mumbled.

"Yershua? I am. And I'm not. He hasn't been to your world yet." Cole gave him a confused look. "You must see the genius in it, even if it hurts. Lucifer imitated part of what his brother is. What you are. The compassionate, healing and self-sacrificing portion. He called to the whole world to accept and love each other, for peace. And said all their evils would be forgiven, even as his agents closed in for war and control. It encouraged all those who believe in his brother's words to show themselves as his enemy. It made them easy to turn; the demons use acts that can be perceived as evil against a soul to produce guilt, self-resentment, hatred, jealousy and the like to give up their own freedom and submit to being ruled. In truth, I don't hold anything against a soul if their goals align with our side, freedom, and peace. A soul can forgive itself and work toward its own and others freedom regardless of any action they've taken. Joining a team isn't the same as servitude." The old man pondered his own words as Cole stared at him, taking in what he was saying with disbelief and anger.

"Perhaps, he really was trying…king of the middle ground?" The old man mumbled hopefully to himself.

"Then…where is the good one? Jesus or Yershua? Where do we fit into this?" Cole cut him off.

"Doing the work closer to home. Where he is most useful. He cannot be everywhere if not for you. You are one of his generals, as *was* his brother, Lucifer..." The old man didn't seem to understand the gravity of what he was saying to Cole's short-lived brain. He was attempting to take this in as the old man trailed off into thought at the last part. Then tried to defend himself. "I did not teach him to be this way. We sent him with you and the others to *learn,* not to…I thought he would keep his word, and if he didn't, you would be able to hold him back." The old man didn't continue speaking.

Cole was getting used to thinking about the greater implications of what he had been taking in the last month. At least, he was trying to fit his and his companion's existence into the timeline. He thought about the suffering of Sachiel, Carlel, the world itself, Lilith and her mountain of bones, lifetimes and generations decimated because one side thought their ideas were better. Dice and his report of missing friends and entire peoples being wiped out, the old man's information, trying to explain what had been happening. He seemed to see it as just one small piece of a much larger picture. But it wasn't small to Cole, not small to his friends or his people. It had quite literally ripped them apart, piece by piece.

"I know you probably have a different viewpoint. But, what's been happening, everything Lucifer has done…" Cole's voice rose, "How can he think he's just…making art or something?"

"No, no, not art…We are making beings of power, a place they can exist. A universe filled with the greatest beings, and world's capable of holding them, sights, and provender beyond imagination."

The old man seemed to be in a very good daydream for a moment before he continued, slightly melancholy. "He is just too jealous to do it the right way. He can only accept existence if he has a part in it, control over it. If I can just..." He had the manner of pleading and Cole took it to mean he wouldn't be punished for speaking his mind.

"Jealous?" Cole asked angrily. "It's gone beyond that. He's been hunting and killing everyone, including me...everyone you sent him to *learn* from. He destroyed entire races and destinies while you've been...what? Working on other projects?" The old man gave him a pleading look. He pointed to the glassware with hope in his eyes.

"What we've just made...they will help to repair what has been done. It took longer than expected but..." The old man seemed to know these words wouldn't have any affect on Cole's human perspective.

"He's gone too far." Cole said angrily. "It's one thing to come to a disagreement and even blows...this is pure evil." Cole said quietly. The old man withered again but nodded in acknowledgement.

"Your brothers said the same…" He said under his breath.

"I don't know who, where or even what you mean by 'my brothers' because of his…creative process. This is going to mean war. When we've all come back together…I don't even like fighting, I only ever do it if I have too." Cole shook his head and sighed out an unamused laugh.

"I guess he always gets what he wants." He recalled Sachiel's words about favor. He tried to get the old man to meet his gaze. "You know we're right…and I need your help." Cole said. The old man looked as though he were struggling terribly within his thoughts. Cole couldn't blame him; he'd just asked the man to help him beat his own son.

"Make it payment for helping you with your experiment." Cole said pointing to the glassware. He knew it was feeble, but it was what he had. The old man seemed to be arguing internally, as his face grew redder, and his eyes roved around. Finally, he seemed to come to some sort of conclusion. He heaved a sigh as he pointed toward one of the bookshelves with a halfhearted hand.

"Row 42." Was the man's only response. Cole moved over to the shelf the man had indicated. His steps stomping out his anger at the situation he found himself in. How much he'd rather be making mirrors or on a real vacation with Ann and Sachiel was immeasurable.

Though the light green bindings on the books were in angelic script, he understood what they meant. There were several dozen that looked interesting, but almost all of them looked too complicated for him to make work. He turned back to the old man with a confused expression.

"Don't look so surprised." The old man tried to say it with humor. But it was as lack-luster as his decision to help. "You wrote them…Understand, I will help, but the circumstances are complicated."

Cole turned back to the shelf with an angry expression now. It wasn't enough for him to have had to learn he'd once been much smarter than he was now, or to learn he and his friends had been targeted and killed by psychotic, sociopathic demons, *multiple times*. Now he had to research his own writings for help. He searched the bindings and marveled that he had invented or co-founded them in the first place, that he had been on a level he couldn't even understand anymore. As he took several of the books from the shelf, he imagined the work it had taken, the moments of experimentation and discovery he could no longer recall.

When he came back to where the old man was standing, his arms laden with a heap of books. He remembered Brad's look of grim determination, after having been impaled and his leg broken and having witnessed their enemy's cruelty and psychosis. If Brad could still fight after that, so could he, after what he'd learned. They could only work with what they had and move forward. What had been done couldn't be undone and it wouldn't help to dwell on the past. The old man nodded to him as he checked the volumes he'd chosen to grab.

"How will I get to these when I go back?" Cole asked.

"Concentrate on which you want, I will pay attention long enough to send them to you." The old man said off handedly. Cole nodded but still didn't feel as though he'd been on the winning end of this deal.

"Could I do that for any of these?" He asked looking around the library. The old man looked at him warningly.

"Most of what is here would kill you if you tried to use them. You have been broken down so far, your power is…indistinct, disorganized at the moment. You chose well, but you may not be able to get even these to work." The man indicated the books in Cole's arms.

"Speaking of…I think I'm about to die of overcharging." Cole said sheepishly. In response, the old man poked at the third book in Cole's stack. Cole understood and nodded.

"You do not have the patience to study right now. So just focus on the words…I will do the rest." The old man said with a comforting smile. He seemed to think for a moment and spoke. "You know…you weren't made to fight. But your power was equal to that of your enemy, and considering the predicament you have been put in, if you chose to be one of our soldiers it could make a strong difference." He hurried over to a shelf nearby and grabbed another book as Cole felt slapped by his words again. He thought about it, he could never be a good soldier. That would take some serious consideration. But what choice did he really have? His friend's lives might depend on it.

The old man came back with another volume to add to the stack. The cover was a battered blue next to Cole's battered green. The old man set it on top of the stack. Cole inspected it and looked at the old man in surprise.

"One of Laphaliel's." The old man gave him a look. "You two have always worked very closely with each other. Tell her...tell them all, I apologize. I never thought, with most of you together it would end up in this state. Or that he'd gone so far beyond our reach. I should have paid more attention." The old man said sadly.

"You could tell them yourself." Cole suggested. The old man looked at him warningly again.

"My boy...I am split down a thousand times over just to speak with you here. Do you have any idea what you hold in your hands right now? It is the only reason you got here." He pointed back toward the glassware.

"Where is *here,* by the way?" Cole asked.

The old man shrugged. "When two beings of high power must meet from a distance. They are brought to a space that connects them. That they can both understand. It does not really need to *exist,* as you understand it. Or even be the same place to the beings meeting there." Cole looked lost. The old man pointed back to the project they'd just been working on again.

"You think toying with the functions and powers of the universe looks like a chemistry set?" He shook his head with a smile, then remembered to say, "Ah, speaking of power transfer, your world…she is starving. I know your plan, but she will take back everything she needs without needing to reverse or destroy the gate. Though…that *will* need to happen, to spare Chamuel the temptation and pain it could cause." Cole thought about this as his vision started to fade, he shook his head to try and get it back into focus.

"Wait, then…what do I do?" Cole asked. Then the most poignant question that should have been his first, came rushing out before he could no longer ask. "How do we end it?" He shouted, as the room faded. The old man looked relieved at the question. And

Cole heard the answer as if he were at the opposite end of a long tunnel.

"The residual power of original creation must go somewhere! This conflict is derived from who gets what. The real fight will come when all power is distributed. As you have seen, because they are at a disadvantage, they will do anything to claim what power they can." Cole felt as if he had heard these words before. Something in the recesses of his ancient soul resonated with old man's explanation.

"So." Coles faded voice came out as loud as a whisper. "We have to put it somewhere it will do the best for…for." He understood what his place had been before this life. And why he had lost so miserably. His expression went flat, and he merely nodded. The old man smiled as the library faded into golden light.

Ch. 15

From Ann's perspective it looked as though Cole had hit the stone, hard. Definitely hard enough to break bones at the sound he'd made. He'd probably cracked his skull when he smashed it onto the top of the blocks surface. She'd set the prisoners, their would be companions down, satisfied they were safer here. Only to have her stomach drop and her heart twist with dread as she watched Cole try to get back into the fight. She thought she might have a full-on heart attack when he was thrown back out of the fight with a bone crushing reality check.

His scream tore through the cavern as the light from above came down full over his blood-streaked face. His body transformed akin to the transformation that Carlel had gone through. But instead of electric energy, the bright blue-green-gold wings and thin streaks of energy that coalesced around him looked like whisps of ethereal, trailing sparks of energy dancing and roving all around him. As she moved forward to rip him away from the stone, her heart racing, he vanished. In an instant, he came falling from above, bellowing a war cry that shook the cave like an earthquake. She skidded to stop and leapt back away from the stone.

Cole came-to, falling from the cave ceiling, still screaming in pain. He could feel power cascading, roiling and exploding inside and around his body. He knew if he didn't get rid of it soon, it would kill him. He noticed that he still held the sword in one hand, and the arrow in the other. He slammed them together and forced them to join into one, using more power for the one act, than he'd ever used in his life. It formed the only thing that would be able to handle what he knew he had to do, though he hadn't known it would work before he did it. As he pushed every ounce of power he could into the new weapon, it raged and gleamed with golden-blue and crimson streaming fire.

Cole came down on the black stone still screaming. He threw as much force and weight as he could into stabbing the blade through the surface. With the sound of metal screeching and tearing, as sparks cascaded up into his face and all around him, Cole was able to push the flaming blade to within an inch of Chamuel's stomach. Blood streamed around his ears and from his many cuts, dripping onto the dusty black stone. Cole took one deep breath and smiled despite the pain, at the angel's stunned expression.

The prisoner looked back and forth between Cole's eyes and the blade in rapid succession. Cole gave a mighty twist and scream. Ignoring the pain that all his injuries were pushing into his brain, he poured every ounce of the power surging through him into the Ulfbhert, and the crack it had created in the prison. A twelve-foot pillar of gold, blue and crimson flame flared and raged into existence around him. And with the sound of an entire mountain being split down the center. The black stone, along with the sword, shattered to pieces. Cole was tossed toward the entrance wall, as that side of the stone fell away first.

With the breaking, came an explosion and wave of force. It threw Cole in the direction he was falling. He hit the wall ten feet up and hard enough to dislocate his shoulder, he landed next to where Ann and Brad were shielding the other prisoners. His body was a mass of pain and confusion, but he kept his eyes on Chamuel to see what would happen. He wasn't disappointed.

The angel slipped out of his encasement and rolled onto his hands and knees amongst the shattered black stone. And what the old man had said about the world taking back what was hers, came to life.

Chamuel had no time to revel at his freedom. As the spell drawing power into his body, locked in the stone, was finally broken. The golden stream of light from above connected to a point directly behind the angel through the broken prison. With a great heaving sensation, the ground beneath them rumbled and trembled. The earth itself was drawing in the light, and subsequently, the angel himself, where a lot of the stored power was being held. Three great cracks splintered out from Chamuel's position, and he lit as if he were made of the golden light. The power being pulled from him filled the three large cracks as the angel screamed and the cave floor lit in golden fire.

It wasn't a natural scream, and Cole could only designate it as such because it was audible for the first half second and Chamuel's mouth was open. But it soon turned into a sound and force that went past audibility and drowned out everything else, turning into soundless pressure. Brad and Ann threw themselves up against the wall and covered their ears as the earth around them shook and quaked. The ceiling of the cavern crumbled and gave way in total silence as sunlight poured in, casting the previously fighting giants into morning light.

Even they, were driven to the ground, covering their ears while trying to dodge and roll away from the falling stone as the earth shook. Breathing in its first full breath of pure creation energy in thousands of years. Sachiel made her way over to where Cole lay, blurring this way and that, silently. He was bleeding and broken in many places and was close to passing out when she reached him. As the quaking came to a stop and Chamuel rose from the ground. Cole's injuries were healed in another flash of golden light and a lot of intense itching and pops of pain. Most of his injuries were healed and disappeared, but several left light scars he would continue to carry.

The new angel was a few inches taller than Cole and built like a professional sprinter. Stark, striated muscle covered him from chin to foot. Golden white dragon scale armor came into being around his naked body as he lifted his arms and tilted his head back in joyous freedom. He spread his fourteen-foot wingspan wide and held out a hand toward his fallen stone friends. The naginata flew to meet his outstretched left hand and he pointed it toward Lilith. Anger etched into his face and golden fire in his eyes. She was rising from twenty yards ahead of him and under a large flat stone, as the naginata started to fly. The eight-foot stone she was under flipped over like it was made of Styrofoam. A look of surprised excitement was in Lilith's eyes as she stared at the newly freed angel.

"So be it." She said determinately. And with a hissing crackling, roar, she transformed. The beast she melted into looked like a mix between a long, muscular bodied cheetah, with a viper's pitted head, and long spiral horns that came to a sharp and straight point two feet from her forehead. If she were to be weighed, it would have been somewhere in the region of two thousand pounds. She was massive.

That didn't bother Chamuel in the slightest. The blade of his spear glowed sliver gold. And with the sound of a concussive wave and the splintering of stone. Lilith was pressed flat against the cave floor, legs sprawled in all directions. The sound of her hissing roar came through the constant wave as if from far away and warped. Chamuel turned his head slightly.

"Sachiel!" He called; all the slowness he'd displayed earlier was gone. "To the doorway, I do not know how long I can hold her." Sachiel nodded and searched the cave.

Shooting out from under a pile of rubble came Tema's outstretched arm, the jewel shined brightly on her wrist. Sachiel turned to a golden blur and vanished into the stone. Chamuel's expression became more focused and pained. Lilith was starting to move, slowly inching her feet back under her, but it was taking all the power she had to do so. As she finally got her feet underneath her, her transformation faded, and she rose slowly in her human form again.

In the meantime, Cole and the others had gathered and were running toward where Paul was digging Tema out from under the fallen rock. Hades was near the wall beside the statues. He looked tattered but mindful, watching for the moment Chamuel's power broke to recommence his fight. Tema was also busy waiting, still, with her arm outstretched. All were waiting to see what happened next. It was something all of them should have expected, but didn't.

Lilith rose, Chamuel's power faded and the wristband on Tema's wrist flared brightly. As Lilith prepared to pounce on the archangel, many forms started to appear in the hall around her, one after another. They stood in the open spaces, crouched on the fallen rocks and some even hovered in the air above. They were male and female alike and most held weapons ready. They all had eyes locked on the demon queen.

Some looked like ancient deities in their stature and dress. While others just looked like normal people, dressed in clothing that would have fit any style of the day for the last several thousand years. Lilith spun this way and that, catching only glimpses of the grim and angry faces around her. It was only then that she finally broke and looked truly terrified. She growled in frustration as the group prepared to descend on her.

From directly behind her, as if a split in spacetime itself had torn its way into the cave, sprang into being, a five-foot rip of utter blackness. From that blackness came the upper half of a man's body, a gleeful look across his youthful and handsome face. Before anyone could react, he grabbed Lilith by the arm and yanked her back through the slit with a surprised expression on her face. The rip promptly and noiselessly zipped itself back up. It was so anticlimactic and sudden that everyone in the hall wanted to scream their frustration. There was utter, stunned silence for a moment. Then one of the godlike beings spoke in a deep voice.

"Are you telling me Hades was the only one who got to fight that smug witch?" Laughter erupted from most of the beings in the cavern, even those exhausted from battle

"Mountain goddess, was it sweet." Came Hades' dragon voice from near where the other had spoken. He sat, leaning back on a pile of fallen stone, looking tired but with a satisfied expression. More laughter met his statement. Cole looked around the gathered crowd. There had to be at least fifty beings at levels he could only guess at, all around the room. The one nearest him looked like a burly thirteenth century knight in hunting leathers. He laughed along with the others, and it seemed like it had been a long time for all of them.

The laughter was cut short by a loud slow clapping from the area of Lilith's bone throne. Which had been reduced to just a pile of bones; Sachiel's body crumpled amidst the wreckage. Standing next to the pile of bones, another rip in the air next to him, was the young man.

He wore a midnight blue blazer, slacks, and velvet black undershirt, with a black leather belt and dress shoes. He was built like a young boxer and was handsome beyond what had been discernable as he'd poked in and out of existence previously. Even though there were an array of massively powerful and talented beings in the room; so much so that the air seemed to quiver, and the sunlight seemed brighter; not even one made to move toward him. He finished his slow clap and looked around at all of them with the air of knowing they wouldn't dare to try.

"Wow." He said. He found Cole off to the side and locked white-blue eyes with him. Where the whites of his eyes should be there was only darkness. Cole involuntarily locked in place as colder than ice ran down his spine and he puckered up.

"The teacher? Really?" He said and shook his head. He went back to looking around the room. "I mean, I thought it could have been any one of you throughout the years but…the pacifist? I guess I should have expected it." He looked back at Cole. His striking features marred by the cruelty in his glowing eyes.

"Do you know how close you cut it?" The young man was enjoying himself as much as Lilith had been. He waved a hand and said jokingly. "No of course you don't. You allowed Lilith to kill you…three thousand times? I'm surprised you know left from right." Then he looked mildly impressed. And threw up his hands in acknowledgement.

"A *manmade* doorway? Breaking *my* handcrafted stone with a memory of me made real? A weapon of power reinforced with angelic and demigod power? Your own mortal blood as sacrifice?" The young man shook his head in surprised disbelief. "That's dark for you. I like it." He let the words hang in the air as he continued to stare at Cole.

"Uh…thanks?" Cole didn't know how to feel about this. The man looked satisfied for a brief second then he turned toward Lilith's broken throne.

"Oh!" He turned back around as if he had just remembered something. His satisfaction had turned into superiority. "But…I do feel like I *must* tell you. My greatest tool is almost ready." He indicated the destroyed prison that Chamuel had recently occupied.

"You did destroy my best timing mechanism, and I commend you for that." He gave Cole a mocking bow. Knowing full well Cole had no idea what it had been for or how he'd destroyed it. "Buut, I'll just guess from here, yeah? Say…two months? Give or take a week or so." He scrunched his face and shrugged. He wagged a hand as if he weren't talking about destroying entire worlds.

"If any of you would like to take this opportunity to join us, step forward. Just ask the archangels how *powerful* they feel now." The young man's smirk and pronouncement were met with unmoving silence.

Without any hint of caring, he turned back to the throne and scooped up Sachiel's body, bones of those who had called him 'friend', fell away as he did so. Cole made to move toward him but the leather clad knight next to him, held up a gloved hand and shook his head. The fear plain to see in his eyes. The man-thing turned back to face them; Sachiel's suspended body draped over his arms. The anger that emanated from everyone in the hall was like a palpable heat wave, he gave them a mock surprised look.

"For her? Really? Took me less than twenty minutes…" He lifted Sachiel's body a bit, then shook his head and shrugged again as he said the last part under his breath. "I'm only taking her because Lilith doesn't have her throne if *this* isn't a part of it. But, if it affords you all the motivation to come see us…" He side stepped toward the black slit in the air. A look of maddening superiority on his face.

"You know where we'll be." And with that he stepped through the split and vanished. Again, there was silence for a long moment before the same godlike being from before grumbled,

"He turned out to be a real asshole."

Ch. 16

Chamuel took charge of the large group that had appeared in the no longer cavern. Shouting for everyone to move outside. Most moved out through the roof in order to correlate and plan their next move. Some leapt, others climbed the fallen stone, some flapped and still others hovered their way out. The mortal looking beings were forced to run over to, and up the staircase. Everyone seemed to want to leave the cavern as quickly as possible.

Many of them yelled thanks over in Cole's direction as they moved out. He had a head spinning moment, receiving gratitude from beings he hadn't imagined existed a month prior to this excursion. It was only bearable because they kept calling him different names, and none of them the one he went by. They must have recognized the title he'd been given. But it served to keep his head from getting too big in the short process.

After a minute of this, he had collapsed against the wall with Ann next to him. She leaned her head on his shoulder. He had spent a few seconds fussing over her newly scarred shoulder before she brushed him off it. They sat for a few seconds in stunned silence, appreciating each other's company.

Brad had gone to check on the prisoners they had originally come for. After most of the commotion had died down Cole looked back to the area to see Chamuel speaking to Sachiel. He was indicating their possible comrades and shaking his head. Sachiel's golden glow had died down a bit after healing everyone and she looked able to speak again. They were arguing about something. He could hear random raised syllables but had to know what was going on. Cole took Ann's hand gently and heaved them back up to their feet to see what the problem was.

"We do not know how they will behave when woken. They could still be in shock; they could react violently." Chamuel was saying as they approached.

"Can you not handle them in their current state? They need to be brought into our confidence, and likely, they will be the ones to lead in the coming conflict *if* we can reawaken their power." Sachiel retorted.

"I may or may not be able to handle them. They may wake and destroy the world we have all suffered millennia to try to protect."

"Woh." Said Cole tiredly. The two angels turned toward them.

"Who are 'they'?" Ann asked.

Their two would be companions were leaning against the wall in sitting positions. The one Cole recognized as the blonde woman he had seen at the airport in London. The other was a youth no more than sixteen, more than likely of Indian descent. It looked as though Sachiel had healed their physical wounds, but neither were waking. Brad knelt next to them, listening to the angel's debate.

"I do not like to give her any credit. But it was fortunate the sha dim drugged them before bringing them to this place." Chamuel said.

"I can reverse that." Sachiel said, while inching toward them.

"Absolutely not." Chamuel said warningly.

"They've been goin on like this for a couple minutes." Brad said with a half-smile. He looked satisfied that the captives were at least alive, and their physical wounds had been healed.

Carlel and the sibling demigods had been conversing with several of the newcomers. But now came over when they saw Cole and Ann approaching.

"The fruits of our labor." Tema said with satisfaction, as they came nearer. Carlel's eyes grew wide as she came from behind Paul to get a good look at the unconscious pair.

"…are many and sweet." Brad added, with an unbelieving shake of his head. "But somethings wrong with 'em., Big guy doesn't wanna wake 'em up." He finished with a nod toward Chamuel. Paul gave them a wondering look but it was Carlel's reaction that surprised Cole and Ann.

She approached the unconscious pair slowly and cautiously. "I should think not." She said. None but Sachiel and Chamuel understood when she lifted each of their left eyelids. "But…I thought they had just been chased out of Hycalion somehow. I have never even heard of one of them dying." She said in an awed voice.

"None of us have. As far as we know, it has never happened." Chamuel said, as if restating the obvious. "They could have no power at all…or they could vaporize us off-handedly without control over themselves." He said toward Sachiel.

"Ok, no more suspense. Who are these guys?" Cole asked, looking between the angels. Sachiel answered, and her hope in the phrase was plain to hear.

"They are knights." Cole was letting that sink in when Ann patted Sachiel on the arm.

"Aw, that means they did come to help." She said appreciatively. Sachiel nodded happily.

"As heartening as that may be…they were defeated." Chamuel said under his breath.

"Which means we do not know the enemies' capabilities anymore." Carlel said with concern on her face.

"You gunna let that stop you?" Brad asked with a sly smile. All of them looked between each other and knew the other's answers without needing to say anything.

"So then…where did they go? How do we get there?" Ann asked. Cole felt a swelling of pride for her. He wondered if their previous lives had helped prepare them for the last month. Or, if Ann was always just this awesome. But he had to bring them back to their current reality.

"They could have surprise attacked the knights, like they did us." Cole said remembering what the old man had said about how powerful he'd been. "They won't have that on their side this time but, wherever they are, we can't leave *our* world without help for what's about to happen. The changes could already have started." Ann squeezed his hand gently and gave him an approving look as everyone, but the angel siblings, nodded.

"He has taken position where he could absorb most of the flow of light coming to your world." Chamuel answered Ann's question first. He waved a hand through the air, adding, "The stream that you have seen, is merely residual energy he can't take for himself. The mechanism of which, is his base of operation, and his vessel to move his armies. I have been staring at it for longer than I care to remember. If we do not go there, your world will be destroyed either way. We will have to split our forces, or find a way to help your world without physically being here."

"Where is this base?" Cole asked, nodding.

"Just beyond all matter in your solar system." Chamuel answered.

"Past the Kuiper belt? It took us over thirty years to get anything that far. Are we going to make it in time?" Cole asked. Chamuel answered.

"We have all whom we need to construct a vessel that will take us there in less than a minute. All it needs is...the engine." He looked at Cole with expectant eyes.

"Could you manage it now?" Sachiel asked warily. "It seemed as though you had changed during the confrontation. But you are back to your normal state now." She sounded disappointed; Cole felt her disappointment keenly.

"No, I didn't go through any personal hell or anything but..." He gave Carlel a look and turned to a middle space, thinking about what he had experienced. He wondered if the old man would keep his word.

He concentrated hard, bringing his thoughts back to the pile of books he had hoped to receive. He held out a hand and focused on the one he wanted. Almost immediately. Dancing swirls of green-blue energy tinged with gold, warped into a rectangular shape for several seconds before it appeared. His dusty old green book. The title on the front translated to something like *Transformation and Transference*. The angels all gave each other wide eyed looks.

"Does this mean you spoke to-" Sachiel started.

"He said he's sorry." Cole said with a bit of contempt in his voice. He flipped open the book and without trying, as if there was a breeze blowing through the underground pit, it turned to the page he needed. The pages were filled with circular symbols, each lined with script, and notes of his thoughts here and there. "We weren't the only ones dealing with aftermath or collateral damage. He thought we'd be alright if we were all together." Cole finished, not watching any of their reactions.

"Unfortunately, that is what ended up being the very problem that led us here." Chamuel said, as Cole studied his own ancient manuscript.

"What of the others?" Sachiel insisted. Cole glanced up at her.

"By any chance would the others be referred to as my brothers?" The angels gave each other excited looks again.

"Yes!" Sachiel said excitedly.

"Did he happen to say which brothers?" Chamuel asked quickly. Cole looked up from the pages to give the angel a questioning look.

"How many brothers do I have, exactly?" He remembered Lilith's words and added another thing to the list of things he would have to do. As soon as he could, it would take top priority. The angels all answered together as they tried to explain.

"You gather many, throughout many lifetimes. When you become an angel, you'll remember all of them." Sachiel stated.

"If they rise, they will remember you. It is one of our greatest moments to have an old sibling rejoin our family." Carlel said.

"And your line has been particularly potent so far." Chamuel said.

"I expect you would have already reascended if not for this…intervention." Sachiel said glumly.

"You're winding me up again." Cole said finally and flatly, he was feeling increasingly anxious at the amount of work piling up around his ears.

"You have three brothers among the best and brightest of us." Chamuel said with a smile. "Zadkiel, Uriel and Korofen." Even just saying their names seemed to give the angels strength and pride. Cole recognized one of the names that had been listed as missing by Dice's report. Zadkiel, that must have been the brother Lilith had spoken of. Sachiel's look when they had heard the report made more sense now.

I'm on my way, Zadkiel. As soon as I can. Cole cast his thoughts through the broken roof into the blue morning sky. He could only hope there was something in the strangeness of the cosmos that could make the message heard. Ann gave him a wondering look as he thought it. He also recognized the name Uriel, another of the great beings of heavenly legend...his brother. But the third he had never heard of. The weight of what they were saying was slow to sink in as he didn't truly understand what it meant to have a brother. Let alone *brothers*.

"They sound like pretty serious guys." Ann said, taking in more than just the words.

"Two archangels and a retired knight. Three including him, and he was second only to The Metatron, who was a strange case." Chamuel confirmed and nodded to Cole. Cole looked between the angels with a slow nod. Whether or not he wanted to be a soldier, they needed him now. And now that the secrecy was gone, they all stood straighter and stronger than they had only a minute before as they looked at him. Whether he liked it or not, Cole wasn't who these beings saw or needed. Jophiel, a being he had only ever read sparse legends of, was who he'd have to try to become.

"So, Uriel and Korofen should be together at least." Sachiel said. "But without Jophiel or Lucifer's power, it would still be difficult to get here. And that is if they did not run into any opposition." The statement sunk a few things into Cole's mind that started to make sense of the larger picture.

"Or…if they went looking for opposition themselves, they're pissed." Cole dragged out the last word as he flipped back and forth between two pages.

Maybe it was because he really had been as good as these beings seemed to think he was. That he couldn't accept the losses and reach through his terrible memories to his power. Or maybe it was something entirely different. If he hadn't been through all he had in his short life, one of the notes he was drawn to, might have sent him over the edge, yet again. It roughly translated to;

We have received communication from the center. Under the circumstances, the strongholds are unassailable, as they are perfectly protected against known power. The work being done here is paramount, but we can trust Sachiel and Chamuel to continue

without us. Lucifer and I have concluded; to break the sieges

Yershua has spent so much on, it must be one of us. I have already

elected to volunteer. Cole was floored by what he was seeing come

to light. The old man must have a sick sense of humor, that this was

the first thing he thought to show him. He read on. *I still do not know*

if I can trust the morning son as Sachiel does, even now. He is

capable of the greatest good, yet the greatest evil I have seen. If only

his work were not so instrumental, no…I should be more like her in

this matter. If only we could win him fully over to our cause. He

seems to serve whichever side suits him on any given day, and his

motives are still unclear at this-

"What did they say?" Carlel asked. Cole had to take a long

and deep breath to steady himself to continue the conversation.

"They showed up and said what I told him." Cole said as the

answer he was looking for came to him like a jolt of electricity.

He gave Carlel a suspicious look before he laughed morbidly

to himself; he couldn't help it. It didn't matter if he couldn't muster

up the power he'd once had. Or that he couldn't remember what these godlike beings, or even his old self had planned. What was done was done, he couldn't change that. But there were several actions he could take to give them the best chance to get it all back. No matter how unlikely it was, or if he could pull it off. Because now he knew he'd had a part in its doing. Or at least, it was the idea that had come to his old friend, now enemy. And they'd all been forced to walk that path. Someday, when he'd studied his notes and got more details, he would apologize to Sachiel for her taking all the blame.

The others were looking at him quizzically as he slowly stepped around a pile of rubble. Still chuckling and putting pieces together in his mind. He observed the splinters of the black stone. The surfaces that weren't covered in dust looked like endless pits stuffed with tiny stars that were still visible in the morning light. The star light transitioned between shades of blue-green, red-gold and purple-silver.

"Now you are doing the winding." Sachiel said, joining in his chuckle involuntarily. Cole turned back to them with a half-smile and pointed toward the pile of shining remains.

"We're going to need all of that." He said shaking his head and smiling sadly. The angels quickly glanced between each other. But Ann's eyes widened as she saw what he was forming in his mind.

"Oh!" She exclaimed. "It made him that mad?"

"Just think about it." Cole answered her in his thoughts. She processed it with a slow nod.

"But...what did your brothers say?" Chamuel asked, seemingly worried at Cole's mental stability.

"Oh, them?" Cole said nonchalantly. He looked back at the stone and gave them a long pause as he put together a plan. He put his hands on his hips and felt the butt of the berretta he'd brought along. He'd never even thought of using it. Another testament to his pacifism.

"There's a new war, and we're going to be busy."

Bonus moment from one year later:

Cole stared up into the starless black sky, trying to avert his eyes from the ring of light that looked like the sun in the middle of an eclipse. The landscape around him was in eternal evening light, which could have been a good thing for hiding if his enemy wasn't made to see better this way. This world made him feel heavy, as if gravity had been turned up several notches. Even in the cool air he'd started to sweat as his heart raced, but that could be due to being so close, with no hope of back up, unless he succeeded.

Mixed with the sounds of otherworldly birds and animals he wouldn't be able to put a shape to, if he didn't see them. Some sounded close enough to toads, eagles, howler monkeys, and a cacophony of smaller creatures. But from what he'd seen so far, they would look different than anything he was used to. Sachiel's voice emanated from the black, starry sleeve he wore over his left arm. At least he had figured out how to use the black stone for communication, he thought ruefully as he looked at the broken pieces of the gem he usually wore on his wrist.

"You are sure Laphaliel is safe?" Sachiel asked in a panicked voice. Cole had only narrowly escaped, due to Ann's quick thinking, again.

He could have had the team explode out into a full-fledged fight, but he didn't know how that would turn out and they hadn't found what they'd come for yet. Who could have guessed the reconnaissance team; he and Ann, had been followed? Ann hadn't caught wind of any complex thoughts, and they had spent three days without anyone ambushing their gate. Someone must have caught wind of what the gems falling from the sky meant.

Cole and Ann really needed to find a better way to travel than Ann chucking bracelets as far as she could and popping out randomly. Especially since they weren't even on the level of middling demons yet, even with the upgrades. It hadn't been too hard of a task to find the main vessel, but they should have expected the enemy to be passing information. If it weren't for his new power, he wouldn't have made it out of there alive. He cursed himself again that he had only been able to make it work for himself.

"Objectively." Cole said angrily. Ann had quickly convinced the demon king into showing her his hunting prowess to win her over. All while signaling for Cole to make a break for it. The massive king's dully glowing red eyes had gleamed at the prospect of taking an angel. Something a low-level demon couldn't help but try to take advantage of. But she had only bought them a short time with her promises.

He wasn't about to let that happen even if he had to storm the campsite alone. Ann still needed help moving in and out of the gems and their extra gem was currently in demon possession. She wouldn't be able to escape unless she fought her way out. In any case, she would buy him as much time as she could, no matter what she had to do with so much on the line. If Uriel hadn't finally found them when he did, the whole team would be nothing but newborns or naked souls right now. But he had put so much on their shoulders that the team were taking heavy risks. Cole was hard pressed to keep coming up with new weapons and ideas to get everyone as up to speed as he could. And only God knew if the hunting party had called in some real heavy hitters.

"What do you mean by that?" Sachiel asked infuriatingly.

"Meaning, for now...probably. You know how persuasive Ann can be." Cole said, still angry. "Hold on, stay on standby, I could have something here."

He had just seen the flash of a light green-brown tail as it entered into the dark river down below, from the opposite side. From his vantage point. Huddled behind a protruding lump on a two-story high root of the most massive species of tree he'd ever seen. He zeroed in on the reptilian cat-like creature he had found by the water's edge, in its retreat. Fortunately, it had been willing to help him with the promise of food it didn't have to hunt. Cole had promised it fish like it had never tasted before. And indeed, he did have two slabs of fresh salmon, courtesy of his new power. That was stinking next to him, as he waited impatiently for the creature to return.

He only wished he could have found a spirit, but there was no hope of that, this close to the main vessel. He would have to play on the living creature's desires, rather than simply purifying and asking it for help. With a solid creature, it wasn't too hard to accomplish if you knew what they wanted. He watched the creature, peeking from its hiding place as it glided through the water toward him.

He wasn't on the largest root of the tree he hid in, just the one closest to the deep waters that ran through the forest of mile high trees around him. He stood tentatively, checking the area in case the creature had been followed. He picked up one of the slabs of fish as the creature exited the water and nimbly found its way up to where Cole waited. The creature was the size and general shape of a regular house cat, only scaled with a longer snout and flat tail, made for swimming. Before Cole got to questions, he presented the salmon to the creature. It snatched the food from his hands and slung it back. Gulping the raw meat down voraciously and turning to the other piece without saying a thing.

"We'll get to that. Now you know I'm good to my word, I need to know if you have the information I need." Cole said kneeling in front of the creature's quarry. It gave him a brief look but seemed to be looking through him as it answered in a weird, cat scratchy voice. He'd decided to call it a catigator, all things considered.

"There is talk of what you seek. The little ones see much, as only we bother to catch them." It leaned over to look at the slab of salmon, its body leaned forward unconsciously to be closer to what it wanted. Gaining a body put one's spirit under such strain, Cole thought. It amazed him how much work one could put into a spirit. Only to have it enter its own vessel and forget everything it had learned for lifetimes while it got used to bodily desires. He was in no position to judge though, even he struggled with them, and he had lived thousands of lives. On the plus side, while the body stayed in control and its soul wasn't fully formed, neither its lightness or darkness played much of a roll.

"I don't need rumors; I need a location. Can you show me?" Cole said repositioning himself between the catigator and the fish. The creature deliberated for a moment, seeming to try and find a way to get what he wanted without taking so much risk. Cole felt his anxiety and frustration mounting as every second felt like an objective eternity.

"I can take you close enough to show you. If…" It leaned around him again. Cole grabbed the slab of fish and handed it over impatiently. He watched the creature become satisfied as it gulped the last bit of fish down. He would have felt excited if Ann had been by his side. As it was, he just felt anxious and rushed. He wouldn't have a plan and he would be alone for the first bit. He looked up to the black sky and gave a silent request.

To the creature, he said, "Take me there." The catigator's head fell back down to face him. The creature looked him up and down, knowing he didn't have any more of what it wanted. He could almost hear it wondering if it was worth taking him after already being paid.

"There's more where that came from, if you get me where I need to go." Cole said. It could be true, he thought, if he ever happened across the creature's path again. He would give it a truck load of fish for showing him the way.

"Follow." The creature said shortly and turned toward the river. It bounded forward and leapt from the edge of the giant root. With one more quick check of their surroundings, Cole dove into the dark water after the catigator. It was lukewarm and thick, but he could see his new acquaintance waiting for him as he got his bearings.

He could make gateways to anywhere he wanted now, regardless of distance. One of the fruits of his studying his own manuscripts. He had studied the work he and his old friend had been doing together when he'd been taken down. The only problem with it was his miniscule human mind. It was why he was the only living, breathing being that could pass through them. He had to be able to encompass whatever was going through his gate when he enacted the spell. And all the complexities that made up another living creature still escaped him. The only reason Sachiel's worked like they did was because *she* could.

It was still very useful in many ways though, he thought proudly, as he made a ring with his thumb and forefinger. He put his mouth through the tiny blue green seal that appeared there, as he grabbed the catigator's outstretched leg. When he did something like this, he tried to place the other side of the gate somewhere it wouldn't be seen. He shuddered to think what someone would do if they saw a bodiless mouth, hovering and breathing heavily in some random place. His world had gone through enough, without that kind of nonsense. Right now, he was breathing the clear earth air right on the other side of his bedroom door. He hoped the initial spurt of water hadn't gotten on any of his books.

He kicked as flipper like as he could as the catigator pulled him along with minor difficulty. It could either breath under water or could hold its breath for a long time. They spent a while traveling through the warm river water at a good pace, pushed along by the flow the current. The dully glowing stars on his arm cast a pool of light around them. Cole had to stifle screams as creatures he didn't know, came in and out of view at the edges of the light. He guessed they were big enough not to be hunted for a short period of time as the catigator hadn't seemed afraid of jumping right in. But animals couldn't always be trusted to be thinking of their predators all the time. He supposed he could have taken anything that came their way if it were just an animal, but demons took many forms.

He needn't have worried as the catigator pulled them along without anything coming too near. The globe of unfamiliar light keeping water creatures at bay. They went far beyond the place Cole had seen the animal come from in the water. Covering a distance, he could only hope was taking them closer to where he needed to go. They came out of the water as the current seemed to be getting swifter. The catigator pulled them over to the side of the river he'd seen it on previously, and onto the muddy bank between giant tree roots.

Cole marveled that his sleeveless white suit and cowl were dry and clean of mud as he followed the catigator. He had elected to change up the suit from the long sleeve ones the girls wore. And they weren't just for show, it seemed. The little creature hurried along the outskirts of the tree they had just come out next to. It took them a full minute to get around the giant tree, even at a run. Leaping over and around the smallest protrusions of roots. The sound of falling water took up most of the noise in the area. The swifter moving current became clear as they came out at the edge of a cliff, on the other side of the tree, to a waterfall.

The waterfall fell what looked like several miles, turning into nothing but a thick rain as it reached the ground below and settled into a large, dark lake at the cliffs base. The wide valley that stretched out in front of them was barren of the trees that made the forest they stood in. The main feature of which, was what he and Ann had been spying out. Though they had come in several miles to the right, where the valley wall slowly sloped instead of falling away. They had been caught when they drew back to plan their next step.

In the middle of the valley was a giant structure made of the same starry black substance over Cole's arm. It was a five-story high block whose edges fanned out from the base into a perfect flat square at the rooftop. Cole knew that if he could see the whole structure, what he was looking at was an upside-down pyramid, mostly underground. Where their enemy had crash landed and sprung from to take over this poor world. The enemy horded thousands of years' worth of magical energy here, to make their soldiers and new recruits as near invincible as they could. Giving their side rechargeable amulets and gear with massive stores of power they usually wouldn't have in them.

The enemy couldn't make malleable objects out of the real stuff though; Cole had learned that while fighting Lilith. What they used was a toned-down version of what he and his team had been able to make. But it had taken twelve of Cole's friends, all connected, to change the spell work his old friend had put into it. And if it weren't for Carlel's skills, they never would have found what needed to be changed.

The toned-down stuff was still good enough to absorb most energy attacks if the wearer was at all competent, but it couldn't hold the power for long like the real stuff, and it didn't stop the demons from being freakishly strong, Ann level strong in most cases, and gigantic. Cole had learned that, when the kings party had held them down and crushed the stone they wore on their wrists. Laphaliel's manuscript had provided what they needed to keep their arms from being crushed along with them.

"I've seen the ship." Cole said to the catigator as it presented the structure by looking back and forth between them. "I need to know where to get *inside*."

"The second underground level, according to the little ones." The catigator said while looking him up and down, hopeful Cole would produce another payment. Cole felt a rush of true excitement now. That made sense to what he'd seen on Lucifer's ship.

His excitement was muted as tiny little figures emerged from the forest edge, around where he and Ann had been spying originally. Cole focused in on the spot as the stars on his arm glowed a shade brighter while he used its power. As if high powered binoculars had been placed in front of his eyes, he saw the scene clearly.

Ann stood out in her white cloak amongst the group of twenty black clad hunters, the smallest of which was nine feet tall. They were all humanoid in nature, if humans wore mat black, starry, plate armor, and had glowing red eyes, and horns of all different shapes and sizes.

Ann was now in chains and being dragged behind the giant king's large grey horse-like creature. It was also clad in plate armor of the same kind. Cole felt his heart thump as if it were trying to escape his chest. He cast out his thoughts toward Ann; her upgrades were pretty awesome too. She made it look as if she were just examining the landscape as her head slowly turned to where he stood at the edge of the waterfall.

Oh, hey babe. Looks like you made a friend. Her thoughts came into his mind calmly. Their eyes locked from miles apart, her right one was swollen and bruised. She gave him a slight smile as the closest hunter yelled something inaudible at her. She looked at the demon king's back after a slight roll of her eyes. Cole couldn't imagine how she had stayed so calm through all of this. He had been jumping out of his skin and about to go full crazy since they had parted.

Are you ok? What happened?! Cole shouted into her mind, his fury at her swollen eye spiking.

Let's just say the king wasn't too pleased when I showed him my moves. Ann sounded as if she were laughing in her thoughts. *Did you find what we were looking for?*

What the hell does that mean!? Cole shouted maniacally. He felt like the catigator after his fish.

Just imagine the scene between Jabba and Oola...Pretend I'm a really good dancer. It was nothing like Squidward on the talent show stage, I swear. Ann continued to laugh in her thoughts. Cole calmed enough to join her, imagining Ann doing a bad imitation of Napoleon Dynamite. *You know where to go now, yes?*

Yes. Cole responded, trying to get himself under control.

Then you better hurry, it won't take us too long to get there. Ann responded seriously.

I'm on it. Cole said as he pulled his vision back to normal. The catigator was watching him with a look of animal innocence.

I have faith in you. Came Ann's fading voice as the catigator said. "You smell as if you've found a mate." The creature nodded and looked around the base of the giant structure as if looking for said mate. "Strange, you came to this place for that, but now I understand your desperation."

"What? Ewe-no." Cole spluttered out in defiance of the creature's words, but it didn't listen.

"I must warn you." It said as Cole failed to convince it. "Everything that lives there will be eager to kill you. But if that is how your species works…may I have payment *before* you go?" Cole took a deep breath as he massaged his eyes. It still left a strained feeling in them when he used that power.

"Are you still listening?" He asked out loud. She wouldn't have heard his conversation with Ann but would know he was close to where they needed to be.

"I am here." Came Sachiel's amused voice from his black sleeve. With a pang of embarrassment, he could hear multiple snickers behind her. He ignored them.

"Be ready by the lion gate. It's going to be fast and you're coming out into a fight." Cole said as he focused in on the structure and measured where he would have to put the other gate.

"That's a funny way to say it." Came Brad's voice. "You sure you want us there? I don't wanna come out into anything weird." There were several more laughs from around him. Cole rolled his eyes. The catigator had leapt back and hidden behind the nearest protrusion of root. It was now poking its head out and looking at him with warier eyes. Cole backed away to step onto the root carefully while he continued to focus exactly where he needed to go. Having never gone there he needed to do a lot of guess work.

"They're taking Ann to the ship; I can see them from here." He tried to explain as he outstretched his black and starry hand to the ground below him, drawing on the massive stores of energy within. A three-foot wide, shining, blue-green seal traced into being there. He wouldn't be able to communicate back to them as he performed the spell, but they knew what was happening, and he didn't have the time to banter.

"That makes more sense, but it aint any less funny." Brad said as more laughs rolled around him.

"Shut.up." Cole said to no one. He dove straight down into the gate. He left the catigator alone, looking around for any sign of his short-lived companion.

"What a strange creature." It said as it turned back toward the river and bounded away.

Made in the USA
Middletown, DE
12 September 2022

10274934R00276